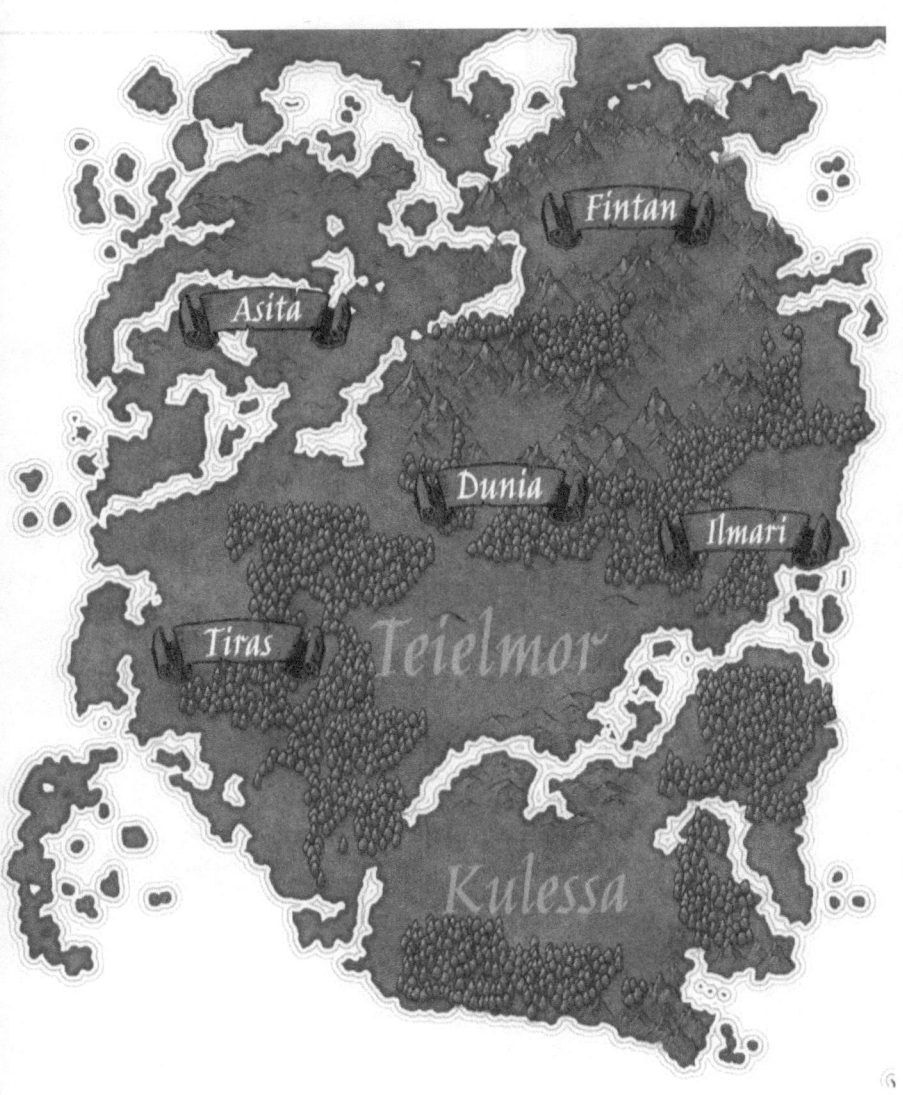

Author's Note

Thank you for getting to page—uh—five. Before you proceed forward, I do want you to know this shit is fucked up. Like real messed up. If you picked this book up thinking "wow, I can't wait to dive into this amazing author who can transport me into a new fantasy world I'd love to be a part of" you'd be right. Only this fantasy world is seriously messed up. Like, it's on my own top ten list of fantasy worlds I'd never want to be in. Mostly cause we're human and humans suck in my books.

ANYWAY... I've started doing larger trigger warnings, so people aren't freaking out halfway through or skipping over parts that trigger them (cough, cough, Shanna). Soooo, here they are...

TRIGGER WARNING: This book contains scenes of violence, death, mentions of rape, nudity, sexual assault, weapons, drinking, crude language, severe mental trauma, PTSD, stalking, starvation, war, physical abuse, military conflict, childhood trauma, sex, and gore.

If this was a checklist for you, nice (winking badly here). Otherwise, just proceed with caution and don't review my book with just the trigger warnings, unless you rate it five stars, then I don't give a flying fuck.

I hope you love my book!

ECHO

HER DARK WATERS CHRONICLES

BOOK 2

This book is dedicated to:
The grey hair that popped up as soon as I had my son. He's
not a terrible kid, my hair just thinks I'm old now.

Prologue

Awakening with a start, Idoh sat upright in bed. His hair clung
to his skin, slick with sweat, the bed sheets constricting
around his legs as he kicked them off. He had a dream. One
that did not make sense, yet he believed it to be a sign from
the gods. He had dreamt of a girl. A Selkie woman who had
disappeared years ago. It was a strange dream, one that
seemed to span the length of months, yet he was positive he
had only been asleep for three hours.

His aunt, the Queen, believed in prophetic
dreaming. She claimed she had once dreamt of his arrival
before he had been sent to Ilmari to live with them. He had
called it a load of crap, nonsense that came from Tiras lore,
however, something about this dream felt...real.

Idoh produced a flame from his finger, igniting a lamp by his bedside. His room lit with the yellow glow, the clock confirming what he suspected, it was only a few hours past when he originally fell asleep.

He closed his eyes, rubbing his fingers against them. The smell of smoke hovered in the air, the stress of that dream having a physical effect. Idoh needed to get a hold of himself. The woman who was coming as an ambassador later that day was a human. She was not going to be a Selkie. She was not the missing Lady of Asita. She was simply a well-educated human there to discuss politics with fae.

The image of her bright smile was stuck behind his eyes, a pain within his chest throbbing with each thought of this dream woman. Arya was her name. In the dream he had said it over and over, calling out to her by it and gifting her the nickname *Little Flame*.

Idoh shook his head at the feelings that blossomed in his chest. She was not real, the lost Lady of Asita was likely dead, and the woman coming was a human. A disgusting, war hungry, human.

Picking himself off the bed, Idoh proceeded to dress. It was no use waiting around to proceed to fall further into this mental insanity a dream had caused. Perhaps it was time for him to take courting more seriously. If he found himself a partner, produced some heirs, he would be able to shake off the feeling of his need to find this woman.

Idoh left his room, almost immediately running into Leif. His shaggy hair was a mess, under eyes darkened from lack of sleep, finger gripping his chin as if he had been deep in thought before Idoh interrupted.

"Sorry," Idoh muttered, not willing to divulge himself to Leif's antics so early in the morning. Not with that woman's image behind his eyes.

"Idoh, wait," Leif said. It was a different tone than he was used to from the carefree man. His cousin never sounded so serious. Like he was an heir to a province.

Idoh stopped, not looking at Leif as he suspected what he was going to ask. Dread filled him as he realized his aunt may be right.

"I know this is going to sound unusual," Leif started, "but did you have any strange dreams last night?"

Idoh hesitated before he answered, his fist clenching so the nails dug into his palm. "I did."

"About a—the woman—the human ambassador?" Leif was stuttering, something unusual for his normally charismatic self.

"Arya," Idoh confirmed, partly wanting to say her name aloud. To hear it said in the emptiness of the corridor like he was calling to her. Like she was already in the castle, waiting to be beckoned by him.

"Arya," Leif agreed.

So, he had the dream too.

"Have you told anyone else?" Idoh asked.

Leif shook his head. "No, I just awoke from it."

The gods were planning something. Idoh could feel the wheels of destiny turning, everything that had happened in that dream a warning. Idoh refused to let Arya get as hurt as she did in those months of unknowing. If this was a sneak peek into their future, Idoh needed to stop every attack that bastard Phobus had done to her. Perhaps kill the man as soon as he stepped off the carriage.

Idoh turned to Leif, the cousins meeting each other's eyes and sensing the same determination from one another. Maybe it was Leif's influence, but the need to protect burned within Idoh's core, calling to him as if it was his sole purpose in this life.

"Ah fuck," Zephyr said from behind Idoh.

The three looked between each other, all knowing the same thing, but Leif confirmed it. "You had the dream too?"

Zephyr nodded. "Arya is coming today."

The sound echoed through the halls hollowly, like a warning to those spirits who still wandered there. An order to the afterlife to prepare to protect Arya from beyond the grave.

"What do we do?" Leif finally asked, breaking the eerie silence they subjected themselves to.

"Nothing," Zephyr replied firmly, "Arya will likely not know what is happening and that we know what she is. We don't want to scare her, but we are not going to let Phobus touch a single hair on her head."

Idoh nodded gruffly, taking the order like the trained soldier he was. Arya was going to be safe under his watch. If it meant no sleep, so be it, she was more important.

"She's the one we needed, isn't she?" Leif asked, another question they already knew the answer to.

"Yes, and she won't know it until later. Neither one of you are allowed to disclose the secrets of the Nox," Zephyr demanded.

Idoh clenched his jaw. He didn't want to withhold information from her, not when everything she did was without thinking of herself. She needed to know how to protect herself, then she would be able to do what was needed. Help them in the way she was destined to. And the darkness that surrounded the name, Evelyn.

"I need a drink," Leif rubbed down his face.

Zephyr hummed his agreement, waving his hand for them to follow. They entered his room, watching as Zephyr opened his drawer to pull out a bottle of purple ambrosia, sparkling to prove it was the good stuff. Three small copper cups were lined up, the liquid poured halfway into them. The boys grabbed their relative cups, bounced them on the wood before shooting the toxin back.

The sting was washed out by the heated feeling that only came from Idoh's element, ambrosia magnifying the feeling of his magic. It was why the drink was so expensive to anyone outside royalty, the power went straight to an average person's head. Only those with a sane mind and will to live could enjoy a shot like that.

Zephyr groaned, wincing from the shock of the drink, his hair tussled by the small breeze he summoned. "Let's talk. We need to figure out what to do about Arya."

With the plan in place, Zephyr, Idoh, and Leif waited on the steps of Castle Lofta for Arya to arrive. It had been an exact replica of the dream he had, waiting the same amount of time, having the same dull conversation with Mies. Idoh had been colder to the man than what was normal for him, unable to forgive what he had forced onto Arya. He was a slug in Idoh's eyes and it would take a lot for him to make up for his shortcomings.

A carriage finally pulled into the drive, white horses stepping exactly as they had in his dream. Idoh surveyed the humans operating the coach, a potbellied man with a wooden pipe in his mouth and a young, scrawny human hanging off the side by the luggage.

He watched everything while forcing himself to be calm, taking in measured breaths, the wait killing him. He needed to see her again. Idoh's instincts begging him to protect her. She was so close, yet still so far.

Stopping, the carriage door was opened by the potbellied driver. A tailored suit appeared before the man stepped out himself, neither Arya nor Phobus. Someone else entirely.

Idoh went cold.

"Sir Ettum Ostrim of Kulessa. Assigned human advisor," The man announced.

Idoh watched as Zephyr put on a fake pleasant smile, his eyes also scanning within the carriage to see if there were any other stragglers inside. Unfortunately, it was only this man.

"I'm sorry, we were given notice that the one taking the position of ambassador was going to be female," Zephyr explained.

"Ah, yes, my colleague had decided it was best for her to stay in Kulessa and do more womanly duties," the man bragged, smirking at the sentence.

Winslet rolled her eyes, crossing her arms with disdain for the man already. If Winslet already disliked him, Idoh knew it was going to be a long few months of trade deals. Winslet liked everyone.

But it also meant something else entirely. Arya was not in Teielmor. Arya, if she was alive, was still in Kulessa. Doing "womanly duties" according to this buffoon of a man. One they would get rid of soon enough.

"Come inside, Sir Ettum and tell us of your life in Kulessa, we're dying to hear how you came to be an ambassador," Zephyr said with faked enthusiasm.

The man obliged, walking in beside Zephyr while the rest of them fell behind. Leif and Idoh locked eyes for a moment, reminding themselves of the true reason Arya had been allowed into Teielmor again. She was tasked with poisoning the king.

"We need your help," Leif was the first to speak up in the darkened room, a sinister smile beaming through the blackness.

"Seems our little angel didn't find her way back."

The voice sent shivers down Idoh's back, something not many people could accomplish. There was a melodic tapping of fingers as he thought. Idoh briefly glanced at the white wolf that sat obediently by his side, then to the shimmering raven perched on the back of his desk chair. A chair that almost looked too much like a throne.

"Don't make me beg, Emeric, you know you want her just as safe as we do," Leif said.

Emeric's white smile dimmed, his teeth grating as he knew Leif was right. Of everyone, Emeric needed Arya the most.

"I'll do it for a price," he snickered, yellow eyes bouncing from Leif to Idoh.

"What price?" Idoh asked. He never liked the deals made with Emeric. Not in the slightest. In each life they lived together, there was always a twist that led to death.

"Zephyr is not allowed to have her," Emeric said with a sickly glee.

Idoh's chest tightened at the deal they were about to strike. It did not sit well with him, they were going against the one person who kept them together in this life, yet at the same time, Zephyr was the reason Leif and Idoh were asking for Emeric's assistance in the first place. Something Mies and Winslet had begged of them when Arya first went missing.

"Deal," Leif growled. There was something of hatred beneath his voice, a darkness that allowed him to be considered a member of the Nox that Idoh forgot about until moments like this.

Idoh nodded his confirmation, unable to speak true words.

"Wonderful, as far as the imposter goes, the one who came in her place, consider him taken care of. A symbol of my gratitude for trusting me with such an *important* matter."

Idoh clenched his teeth, feeling Leif's eyes on him. Idoh did not look to his cousin, focusing on the danger that was before him. The only one who had not died life after life.

"You may leave."

A gust of wind pushed the two out of the room, door slamming in their faces.

"Did we do the right thing?" Lief asked in a half defeated voice.

Idoh didn't respond, walking from the door and down the halls to the training room. He had to let out his anger somehow.

Part One: Godly Influence

1

While used to the chill that accompanied the dungeons of Kulessa, Arya had not experienced a cold like this in some time. The isolation of the cell she was trapped in blocked everything but the breeze from the iron barred window. In the summer it was pleasant, the stone throwing off the cold like her own personal pool, in the winter, however, it was torture.

Her body shivered in the corner of the room, ripped and ragged cloth falling off her thinned frame and hair matted to her head. She did not look like the diplomat that Arya would have been after the seven years of training, but like any other prisoner in the dungeons. If anything, she was weaker.

There wasn't a real reason as to why Roderick had decided to forsake the efforts of training Arya for Teielmor. She was much more patient and took the lessons better since it was her second time learning. In fact, she had been praised for her acceleration in the materials the same day when she had been thrown into the cell she currently sat in. All hope of getting to Teielmor stopped that day, survival becoming her main priority.

The faint squeaking of a rat caught her attention.

Arya looked up, managing to tense her movements to the point where the creature would have no awareness of her presence in the room. A creature of chaos was in control where Arya once had been, and with that new creature came a new understanding of what her magic could actually do.

Narrowing her eyes, Arya focused on the mammal. It scurried about, sniffing at the crumbled rocks of the floor and the wood that made up the door. It was searching for the scraps of crumbs that Arya knew were not there. Any remnants of food was devoured by her. The food that did not stay down was to be forced back down as she could not risk the waste of nutrients.

She continued to feel out the water rushing through the rat's body. While separated from her skin and not having been near the ocean, Arya had been determined to figure out what power she still had left. Only then did she realize her dream self had withheld a tremendous power behind pathetic weakness. One that could've saved her many times over.

Arya shot out her hand, the rat screaming as she controlled the movements in its body. It walked stiffly across the room toward her, attempting to pull away but unable to stop the progression of its legs.

Halting the defenseless animal in front of her, Arya watched its eyes move erratically. There was some familiarity in the motion, her own once looking the same under the control of Phobus and Roderick. Now, she was the one in control. The one who would ruin the life of this disgusting being.

Reaching out her hand, Arya petted the rat's head, caressing it sweetly. She smiled at it, gripping it by the torso as it rose up when she commanded it.

"You're such a good, sweet creature aren't you?" She asked in her thick Selkie accent. It rolled with her words, the air filling with the smell of salt and sand. "Shame we had to meet like this."

Without another warning, Arya bit into the rat's neck sending it squeaking in protest. Blood dripped down Arya's chin as she drank the liquid, pulling with her teeth so the flesh came off in her mouth. Life in the rat's eyes died with the pooling blood, Arya chewing what she ripped from its corpse.

That's when the door unlocked.

It shocked her, the sound foreign in the cold place. Arya hunched with the corpse of the rat held between her hands, blood dripping down her chin and onto the stained and torn strip of fabric that served as her clothing. More blood pooled just below, between her feet where she crouched. It was a disturbing look, especially to the new occupants who entered.

Two guards had come through the door first, both clad in silver armor, the type they only wore when Roderick was showing off his power and wealth. Nothing that was actually helpful to his protection, or theirs for that matter.

When seeing Arya they stilled. She was sure their faces would have shown the complete disgust of the scene before them, but honestly, at that moment, she could care less. In fact, while looking at the new occupants, Arya took another hungry bite into her prey. Who knew when she would eat next. Fuck, they were most likely going to take this meal from her as well. What terrible timing.

As if reading her thoughts, the two advanced on her. She tried to run, stars spotted her vision, causing her to stumble. It was an idiotic move on her part, even for being as feral as she was in that cell. Where was she expecting to run to? The other side of the cell? Stupid girl.

It was not hard for the guard to throw iron cuffs onto Arya's wrists due to her disabled state. The burn ignited her sense of self preservation, the fight inside dying with the pain.

She could barely see where the guards led her, focusing on keeping her legs beneath her body. They practically dragged her up the spiraling stairs, her knees and bare tops of her feet becoming bloody from the action. Through her shuffled walk, Arya listened to them talk.

"What does this visitor want with the fae prisoner anyway?" One of the men asked.

The other shrugged. "Fuck if I know or care. Shit, Roderick may just be selling her off to another man again."

Arya grit her teeth at the thought. Roderick had slowed down on his distribution of her body, but never stopped completely. If this was another man she was supposed to whore herself out to she would rather die.

"Now, now, let's not get too rash there, Arya." The voice hummed cheerfully.

"You're one to fucking talk," she replied aloud, not caring if the guards heard her or not.

Her bloody footprints were left behind her in the walk through the castle. Golden floors painted with streaks red.

They turned her into the main ballroom, a place that she had only been to when she was first brought to Kulessa. Flashes of Meriah gripping her hand next to her went through her mind. It had been spring during that time, but with both of them nude and on display of the King, it was colder than the chilliest of nights. Colder than her isolated cold cell in the dungeons.

The ghost of her past disappeared as Arya was faced with the acts going on around her. Cages of women lined the room with noble men queued behind each door. Cries of sorrow and pleasure mixed in a disgusting display of lust. The women were nude, covered in sweat and oil. Some were chained inside their cages, the iron necklace burning their skin.

They were fae.

All these women were fae.

Arya glanced around seeing how many there were. More than she could count at a look. All were posed to accept the next man that was ready to take them, some experiencing multiple at once. Was this to be Arya's life now? Did isolation break her enough where she deserved to be fucked by the noble humans?

A large throne sat in the middle of the room on a dais of three stairs. Roderick sat with his large belly extended, a woman with her hands and feet chained knelt between his legs, head bobbing up and down. From the markings that trailed over the woman's exposed skin, Arya knew she was fae. Dullahan to be exact. A being so powerful yet was trapped under the rule of a vicious and power hungry king. Reduced from the being of destruction to that of an everyday victim of humanity.

Roderick did not seem entertained by the deed, instead talking with the man who sat beside him as if it was natural for a woman of fae origin to be latched to his erect cock. Then again, maybe it was.

Through all the displays around Arya, the man next to Roderick was the most interesting. He was hooded, his gloved hand placed calmly onto the seat. While she could not tell what the man looked like, his clothing and shoes were fine, signifying this was a man of wealth. It must have been why the guards were wearing their silver.

The guards threw Arya forward causing her to fall to her knees before them. The sting of her knees told her she most likely drew blood from the incident. Habit making her look at her palms to verify the hypothesis. She was correct. A small bead of blood dotted the heel of her hand, red mixing with the pale vision of skin kept from the sun.

"Is this the one you heard about?" Roderick asked the mystery man with a breathy shudder.

The cloaked man leaned forward, Arya seeing the bottom of his pale face through the shadow. He smiled, the gesture sending her heart into a flurry. He rose from his chair, kneeling so that he was close enough to touch her. Arya couldn't move, paralyzed by the idea of the man being so close. What an idiotic thing, yet there she was, on her hands and knees, letting this random person get close to her.

His hand cupped her chin, thumb brushing over the drying blood from the rat on her face. Without hesitation he drew back his hand, licking the blood from his thumb. Arya's mouth dropped open as he hummed, head bouncing to the side...like he was considering the taste.

"Why is a beauty like her locked up?" The man asked. His voice rolled over the noise in the room like he covered it with a blanket. The moans and screams silenced, his voice the only noise Arya could hear. Dark and thunderous.

"I was under orders from Evelyn to keep her guarded until the right time," Roderick said casually.

Who the fuck was Evelyn?

"Understandable, our sister is one for her secrets," the cloaked man chuckled as if locking away a woman was not the worst thing that could be done. Then again, this was the same place where Arya's sister, Meriah's corpse was used after her head was severed from her body. Nothing was off limits.

"It's good you'll be taking her," Roderick said with a pleased sigh, petting the head of the Dullahan woman in his lap. "Means those idiot fae are at least four steps behind us in our plans."

The cloaked man turned from Arya so fast she could barely catch his movements. His hand wrapped around Roderick's throat, his index finger sporting a sharpened silver claw that dug into the skin above Roderick's artery. Everything went quiet and the people stilled as they watched the dark man lean forward and whisper into Roderick's ear. It was the first time Arya had seen the man pale, his golden skin dimming and eyes widening. Whatever the cloaked man had told Roderick made him remember his place. One where this mysterious being was over him. More powerful without needing the luxuries that came with the title of king.

"Take her," Roderick said, his voice wobbling with each word.

Beneath the shadow of the hood the man smiled. "Good seeing you, brother."

Roderick didn't respond, shoving his hand down on the woman's head that latched to his dick. She gagged, chains clanging against his legs as she struggled against him. Arya watched in horror as Roderick stood, spinning the woman so she was pinned by the throne and shoved his cock further into her throat. Tears welled up in her eyes, nails clawing down Roderick's thighs.

The cloaked man offered a hand to Arya, who reluctantly took it, unsure what was worse. Being trapped in that room with Roderick or going with this man that even the king was scared of. Perhaps the latter, but at that moment, all

Arya could see was the horror of the forced actions that woman was going through and knew it would be her if she didn't leave. All she'd ever be was a malnourished whore to Roderick. Forgotten in a cell in the cold.

Arya walked the best she could with the man, her limp and instability evident to everyone around them.

"Do you normally eat rats for meals?" The man asked, catching Arya by surprise.

She looked up to the hooded figure. "You would eat rats too if trapped without any other food for long enough."

There was a low rumble that could have been a laugh coming from the man. Arya took it as a good sign before he said, "there are worse things in the world than rats, let us hope you never have to find out like I did."

Arya nodded, unsure what he meant. Her life could not get much worse than it already had, could it?

"*Do not trust him, child,*" the voice warned, "*we do not associate with those in the Lux.*"

Arya kept the warning in mind. No person who associated with Roderick or this Evelyn person could be trusted.

Humans can't be trusted. They will turn on her the moment she needs their help. Every human she encountered was a no good, worthless, power-hungry traitor.

Fae can't be trusted. While she didn't know if they had the same dream, Leif, Idoh, Zephyr, Winslet, Mies, her parents, brother, *any* fae of influence had not come for her. They rather assumed her dead than go into human territory to rescue her.

31

Most importantly, Arya couldn't trust herself. Hope kept creeping back into her self consciousness and that was not allowed to happen. Not if she was determined to keep living.

Trust no one.

A book waited for Arya in the carriage that the mystery man led her to. It was a simple book, wrapped in the brown leather that was used in the old times. As Arya slid into her seat, he pulled out a thick blanket from a cubby beneath and fluffed it over her. The gesture was strange, kind almost, but she would not let herself become used to such niceties when there was still no saying on how this man planned to use her.

"My name is Ivan," he said as he sat folding his hands in his lap.

Arya stilled. She looked over the man in front of her unsure of how to respond. Positive he was a human she was not trusting of him, but still, he took her away from Roderick.

"I assume you know who I am," she replied.

He nodded, his body leaning forward with the motion. "Yes, I had been sent to retrieve you."

"By who?"

"That will be revealed in time, for now, we have a long journey ahead of us. It is best we ride in silence as you never know who is listening."

He was suspicious. Ivan knew more than Arya did and one way or another she was going to find out what was going on. For now, however, she was going to listen and play the part of the sweet innocent Selkie. Malnourished, beaten, raped, and pitiful. That was her game plan and Ivan will be her pawn. No one can hold back from saving a sweet darling Selkie.

The carriage began to travel down the road when Ivan said, "Oh, you'll be wanting this."

He pulled a box from his cloak with one hand. It was easily the size of a small hat box. When Arya opened it her body came alive and a rush of magic filled her. Hesitantly, she touched the object inside, wary it was a trick. Her fingers came in contact with the fresh skin of her seal coat. Without another minute's wait, she grabbed onto the coat, holding it to her chest. Just having it in her hands filled her with so much happiness and relief that Arya couldn't help but cry.

Tears spilled down her cheeks and she sniffed the leather. It still smelled like the salt of the sea. It smelled like home.

"Where did you get this?" Arya asked, her eyes glancing up to the hidden figure before her.

She felt his smile as he said, "I have my ways dear."

Not willing to risk her skin, Arya kept quiet, curling into the coach as it bounced along the uneven road away from the castle she'd called prison for many years. Now, she was off to a new place with new people and new challenges. Ivan was dangerous, but something about him made Arya calm with her caution. He was a different kind of danger that she was somehow familiar with.

Opening the book that Ivan had left for her, Arya began to read. "*Mythology of the Dark Seas?*"

"I'm told the serpent tales are the best in that book," Ivan commented.

Arya bit her lip, nodding before turning to the first page. A swirling picture of waves between the scaled tail of a sea dragon was drawn within, men on ships showing their silent screams as the monster attacked. On the middle of the serpent's head was a symbol, one that seemed awfully familiar for never having read the book before. Ignoring it, Arya continued, diving into the one thing she had missed most while in isolation. Fantasy.

2

Arya had awoken in some strange place, not remembering falling asleep in the carriage. The room was massive and she was dressed in fine Selkie silk. It was formal wear, like she had seen her mother dress in for weddings and funerals. Gems were encrusted onto the gown, her hair let down, curled, and for the first time since she could remember, Arya was not hungry.

She stood from the bed she sprawled upon, going down candle lit corridors. They corralled her into the darkness of the other halls too terrifying for her to stay in. She opened a door, one carved with flowers and painted purple petals. Golden trim accentuated the grey color, and with the candle light around her, it almost looked welcoming.

As she pushed open the door, taking several steps inside, more candles ignited. They lined the walls of the room, some hovering in the air as if by magic. In the middle stood the cloaked figure. This time, however, he was not obscured as much. His cloak was gone, replaced by a simple black cape with a violet lining. The mask of a demonic horned creature covered his face, hair hidden beneath the hood.

As she entered, he turned to face her. His slim body was dressed in noble fae attire. Ivan held out his hand to her, the candles flickering as he did so. Without hesitation, not even a second thought, she approached, a smile on her face. As their hands connected, warmth flooded her body engulfing everything in pure safety and warmth.

"Arya," Ivan's voice called out to her but he sounded far away. "Arya, wake up."

Arya gasped, clutching her skin to her chest and pulling back into the carriage seat. The light outside had dimmed, the last streaks of sun dancing through the purple sky. Ivan crouched before her, his fingers pushing back her hair from her face. That same warmth filled Arya, something so familiar about it she was tempted to see who was beneath the hood.

Arya reached up, attempting to push back the hood when her wrist was encompassed by his hand. "Not yet, my sweet flower."

"Who are you?" She asked.

There was a low rumble of a laugh in his chest that sent a swirl of memory to her. What that memory was she couldn't remember but she did know the smell of lilacs and sage.

The dream made Arya nervous. The happiness she had with Ivan in his formal clothing was enticing. She didn't even know this man's face let alone what his intentions with her were. If he was associated with Evelyn, Roderick, or simply any humans, he was the enemy. His accent was enough to persuade her. A dream was simply that, a dream.

Arya looked past Ivan, brushing off his hand as she realized the carriage had stopped. They were outside an odd-looking house—no not a house, an inn.

The carriage had been parked already, the horses standing in stalls to the side. A warm golden glow emitted from the frosted windows that looked almost welcoming.

"An inn?" Arya asked, not forgetting the last time she had been at an inn. It was not real, but still the memory of Phobus murdering the poor servant girl on their way to Ilmari was enough to scar her for life. Would this man torture and abuse the help in this household as well? What were his perversions?

"The horses needed to rest. The journey to my manor is a long one and I was not willing to kill the creatures just to get us there faster," he said.

Arya nodded. Dreaming had made her forget the danger she was still in. She needed to figure out a way to escape and get back to Ilmari where her friends waited. Surely, even if she was just a Selkie in trouble, they'd take her in.

"Come, I ordered a bath for you and new clothes so you don't have to continue to wear those rags."

She blinked slowly, trying to process his words. "Why are you being nice to me? I am your prisoner."

There was a pause before Ivan replied, "Because no matter if you are my prisoner or here on your own free will, you will be treated with kindness and shown mercy."

"If you're planning on getting my hopes up just to crush them, don't bother. I'm already without hope. I won't run, I won't fight. I'm just here." Arya explained in a hard tone that lacked any emotion.

There was an audible sigh from Ivan as his head dipped. He retracted his hand, moving out of the carriage. "Even if you don't plan to trust me or have hope, I will still treat you with respect. Roderick did some awful things to you, Arya, but I am not him and you will come to realize that."

"You still work for him," she spit as she exited the carriage.

Ivan scoffed, shaking his head. "You're mistaken, Roderick works for me. When I learned of your kidnapping, years too late, might I add, I came to get you."

Arya matched his scoff, rolling her eyes. "Oh yes, a few years too late. You do see the state of me, right?" She motioned to her frail figure and rotted clothes.

Ivan did not respond, Arya simply impressed she had enough will power to fight back. It had been some time since she was able to talk back to a human. The sass from her fae side came to help.

Refraining from responding to Arya, Ivan walked into the main entry leaving her alone. She was astonished by the act. He knew she could run if she wanted to. She had said that she wouldn't, but there was the opportunity. The horses were right there to steal, the open road marked on a very clear path with signs pointing in the direction of Teielmor. She could leave right that moment if she wanted to. Escape finally. Get back to the fae lands with her skin and safety promised.

Turning, Arya walked in after Ivan. Running was not her any longer. She was too broken to run. Too hopeless to reach Teielmor without ruining herself and finding another way to get caught by humans.

Inside the inn was just as warm as it looked. A fire burned in a hearth, crackling with life. Wooden walls were decorated with pelts of animals and taxidermy heads. Behind the counter was a plump woman with her hair held back behind a yellow cloth. Her rosy cheeks were high, the smile on her face accentuating them more.

"Hello dear, are you ready for your bath?" she asked.

Arya nodded, not trusting the woman enough to use her voice.

"Follow me."

The woman led Arya down the hallway covered in candles in various heights. Wax dripped from their resting spot creating lines to signal the candle's past.

Turning a corner, the woman entered a room that had smoke lazily creeping around their heads. No, not smoke, mist.

A tub was placed in the middle of a large room filled to the brim with bubbling water. It sat over a well stocked fire, flames licking around the sides. Salts, soaps, and rocks lined the side of the tub, the various options open for Arya's choosing.

"The master left a box with your new clothes on that chair over there," the woman said, "and there's towels in the basket beside it when you're finished."

"Thank you," Arya said.

The woman chuckled, placing her fingertips to her lips. "Oh, of course, my lady."

Arya's brows furrowed at the title, turning with an open mouth as she watched the woman shuffle out and close the door. Perhaps it was just a polite thing. She did call Ivan her master. Then again, it reminded Arya that she didn't know Ivan's intentions or his past. For all she could guess the mystery man owned the bathhouse-inn they were at.

Shaking her head to rid away the thoughts, Arya began to strip the loose fabric from her body. She then dipped her toe into the water, realizing how perfect the temperature was. Hot, but not scalding. It took no time before Arya was submerged from the chin down, her knees barely lifting over the surface.

Water fell over the edge of the tub as she entered, not putting out the fire but creating more steam in the room to hide her in. Arya closed her eyes, letting the feeling of the water consume her. The only thing that would make that feeling better was her skin.

She shot up, realizing she had left it in the carriage for anyone to take. Panic began to take over when a voice said, "Don't worry, it's safe."

Arya turned, seeing a girl kicking her feet as she sat in the chair her new clothes once occupied. The girl was older than a child, but her short stature made her look like one. Her skin was dark like the night sky, cheeks dotted with freckles as if representing stars. Her hair was a silvery-white, haloing her head with her intense curls. Keeping with the childish look, the girl wore a large tulle accentuated dress. It was cropped at her calves, not like the fashion of the humans, but that of Tiras women.

"What?" Arya asked.

"Your coat," the girl said with a cheery smile, "it's safe, you don't have to worry. I was told to keep track of your belongings, *especially* your coat. Gotta keep my Selkie lady safe."

"Who are you?" Arya asked, lowering herself into the water so this girl did not see anything she didn't want her to see.

The girl bounced off the seat, shoes clicking across the tiled floor to Arya. "My name is Estelle. I am here to help and assist you in whatever you need. Master Ivan had instructed me to make you feel comfortable."

Estelle was doing the opposite of that. Standing above Arya who was exposed in a bathtub of water. She was nude, and while normally Selkies did not have an issue with their bodies being seen as hers was, Arya was not raised in Teielmor this past decade. She was shown time and time again exactly what her naked body made humans do.

Shifting uneasily, Estelle took a few steps back and grabbed a brush off the counter. "Do you mind if I help with your hair? It might make you feel better."

Arya hesitated before nodding. That was one thing she was already despising. Manage her knotted and matted hair.

Estelle bounced forward, pulling a stool to the head of the tub and began to pull at Arya's tangled mess. She was soft with her strokes, taking it from the bottom and working her way through each knot and clump that she came across. It was relaxing, reminding Arya of when her mother used to do the same thing to her as a child.

Estelle hummed as she worked, Arya closing her eyes and focusing once again on the water. It was what she really wanted more than anything. To swim again. A nagging thought in the back of her head told her not to trust the girl playing with her matted hair though. Something about the way she was all too keen to be close to her.

"I know you're nervous about being here," Estelle continued, "but give it time. Master Ivan is not a cruel man by any means. He does what is best for us, and now you as well.."

"Us?" Arya asked.

Estelle nodded. "It's me, Rook, and Embry that you'll interact with the most."

"Why is that?"

"Because you are an important part of the plan, my lady. Ivan knows, you'll know eventually, and everything will fall into place."

Arya furrowed her brows. None of that made sense. "What will I know?"

"I cannot tell you that. It's something you'll have to find out for yourself," Estelle said sadly.

Arya shook her head, frustrated with the lack of knowledge being provided to her. When would she know all she needed to? Who the fuck was Ivan and why did he send Estelle?

Shrinking down into the water Arya resigned to knowing nothing. It wasn't as if she had known anything more. It was another human captor who allowed her more freedom than Roderick did. She was being cared for again, and had this woman to help her. She was along for the ride at that point.

"Hey, Estelle," Arya began, sitting up once more to ask the woman about their new destination. However, when Arya looked around there wasn't a single trace of the girl anywhere. It was as if she disappeared into thin air. "Goodbye to you too."

Sinking deeper into the water, Arya closed her eyes imagining herself back into that dream. Imagining a dance with her masked rescuer that would become her new keeper. Imagining a life where she did not have to suffer by the hands of Roderick any longer.

A life where Arya was just a pet Selkie... for now.

3

The dress that Arya was given was simple. It was not sexual in any means, but plain with elegant features. It was a baby blue color, allowing her eyes to dance with life that she wasn't sure was real. Her hair, which was combed out thanks to Estelle, curled as it dried.

Walking into the hall, Arya found another person waiting outside the door. This time a man.

He was tall, towering over her with white hair tied back in a black ribbon at the base of his neck. Icy blue eyes looked at Arya as she exited, the once scowl on his lips twitching upwards as if he was happy to see her.

"That gown looks lovely on you," he greeted.

Arya's eyes narrowed slightly at the comment, her foot stepping back inside the room in case the man decided to advance on her.

"My name is Embry," he said with a delicate bow, "I'm sure Estelle has mentioned me."

Arya nodded, feeling some comfort in knowing that the sweet girl that Estelle seemed to be would warn Arya of this man. It was not that Embry was threatening by any means, his frame thin and the glasses that hung on a string around his neck signified he was more a scholar than a fighter. Still, a man is a man no matter how harmless they appear at first.

"She did mention you," Arya replied.

Embry nodded, his smile growing. There was a twinge of guilt inside Arya as he looked upon her. It was like she was supposed to know him from somewhere but she could not recall why she felt that way. She'd never met this man before. Never heard of his name, shit, he wasn't even in her dream.

"I know it's a lot," Embry said, "but just trust us it'll all make sense soon."

"Trust is not something that I easily give." Arya laughed. The motion surprised her, not laughing, even in a sarcastic sense in months.

"After all you've been through, I can understand why."

"You don't know half of what I've gone through," Arya hissed, the aggression coming full force out of her. How dare this man assume he knows anything of what she suffered? A human man who never once set foot in the dungeons or watched his family and race be tortured.

Embry nodded, his smile dimming. "Then tell me."

"So you can use those ideas against me?" Arya laughed cynically. "I'll pass."

"No, so I can better understand how to treat and help you."

The genuine concern that floated through the sentence shocked Arya. This human wanted to help her? Why? She was fae, his enemy, the one his master kept captive for this Evelyn person. Why would he want to help her in any manner? It was a trick, it had to be.

"Not all of us are bad, Arya," Embry said with some hesitation. "I know you are struggling, I am just offering an ear without any judgement."

The anger within her receded to be replaced by that gut curling guilt again. She owed this man nothing, so why did she feel like she did? That her anger toward him was unwarranted.

"You can't undo what they did to me."

Embry nodded, shoving his hands in his pockets aggressively. "No, that I cannot."

"Talking does not mean I forgive them or *humans* for what happened to me."

He sucked on his teeth, nodding his head to the side as if he agreed with her. As if he was *on her side.* "We can hate them together."

"Are you fae?" Arya blurted, the connections coming to her instantaneously.

Embry smiled once again, his icy eyes locking with hers. "Ivan was right, you are smarter than I gave you credit for."

Arya's heart quickened as she took a few steps forward. Once again she looked him over, trying to find any clue on what province he was from. Instead, she asked, "how did you end up in Kulessa?"

Embry's brows rose. "Ivan took me here to keep me safe."

Safe in Kulessa? There was no such thing. She'd seen first hand what humans do to fae when they get the opportunity.

"Teielmor was not safe for someone like me, so Ivan offered me a trade to come here. To help him with his work, I accepted." He paused. "Ivan is not a bad man, in fact, I'm sure you'll come to grow fond of him like the rest of us have."

"The rest of us? You mean there's more fae?"

Nodding, Arya took his arm, deciding she would risk it. She would try to trust him. He was fae, he wouldn't hurt her right? Her mind went back to Phobus's true identity in her dream, the fact that he was half fae yet still hated everything she was. The man who took glee in beating her until she vomited blood and could barely walk.

Embry did not seem like he was anywhere near the level of Phobus, but he was a different person. Someone who could be better at disguising his true emotions.

Against her better judgement, Arya accepted his arm, hanging on it as he slowly led her down the candle lit halls. If it had been in a different time, it would have been considered romantic. Yet, there were more troubling things going through Arya's head at that moment.

"Tell me what happened when you were in Kulessa. Remember, I am not going to use this information against you." Embry emphasized. It didn't make Arya feel any better.

She let out a sigh, fighting against her internal voice to keep quiet about the abuse she experienced. "They killed my sister," Arya struggled to say. While in the dream she had time to heal and admit to Leif what had happened in the ritual space, Arya was just taken from Roderick. She spent more time in Kulessa this time around. Experienced more torture.

"Your sister?" Embry asked.

Arya nodded. "When I first arrived in Kulessa it was by mistake. My sister Meriah and I had gone swimming in Tiras, a current washed Meriah out to sea and I'd gone after her. A storm forced us to Kulessa, and humans took our skins. Roderick then received us and we were forced into sex work."

Embry's smile was gone, his focus straight ahead. His jaw was tense as he listened to Arya, nodding for her to continue.

"One day Meriah had stolen my skin and she had asked me to run to get help. I didn't get very far before guards caught me and brought me back. They were about to kill me before Meriah volunteered herself instead." Arya swallowed, the emotions missing from her story. "They made me watch as they cut off her head and then took turns fucking her corpse."

"Fucking hell," Embry breathed. "What happened after?"

Arya decided to forgo telling him about her dream of Teielmor and the voices not wanting to sound even more crazy than she already did. Instead, she began to tell him about the torture and abuse she received.

Arya went into detail about what she had learned in the five years she had gone through ambassador training and how Phobus had taught her with his cane and kicking. She explained how she was starved and body mutilated by multiple different humans, the experiences not registering as her own. It was like she was telling someone else's story. Like it was someone else's life.

She told him how they rejected her as the ambassador, exchanging her for a human who never arrived in Kulessa. How each ambassador was sent back for insulting the fae and one killed for attempting an assassination of the King before the ambassador program between Kulessa and Teielmor was stopped and war threatened.

She told him about the solitude, about her eating rats to survive and how, after a while, it didn't seem so bad. She described the cold nights and how she believed she had been forgotten about when it came to basic needs. Food, blankets, water, all were forgone when it came to Arya. Like they had planned for her to perish in that cell. Then she told him about Ivan coming to get her.

"Now I'm here."

Arya realized they had been making circles in the halls, all connecting in a circle around the inn before coming back to the main entry again.

Embry was quiet, his hand secured tightly over Arya's which rested on his arm. "I'm not sure what to say."

Arya shrugged. "You told me to tell you."

Embry nodded, his brows furrowing. "I expected the beatings and definitely neglect when I saw how skinny and frail you looked, but the sexual assault and torture..." he trailed off rubbing his jaw with his hand.

There was no emotion within Arya. It was just facts she gave Embry. Situations she lived through but felt like she didn't. It was numb. Her body rejected the idea she was hurt by those experiences, her mind refusing to acknowledge the pain and suffering she did come to know all too well.

"It's life, shit happens," Arya said plainly.

Embry turned to look at her, raising his brows as he puffed out a laugh. "Shit happens? Fuck Arya, that term is used for people who stub their toe or forget their coin pouch, not someone who was tortured for years and sexually assaulted on top of that."

Again, Arya shrugged. "I survived and now I'm another person's prisoner. My life is just something that happens now."

Embry sighed, running his hand through his white locks. He stopped in front of a door, pushing it open. Inside, a fire burned in a quaint little stone hearth, a rug and two chairs sitting before it. Behind the chairs was a large bed that reminded Arya of how tired she actually was. No matter what she experienced or the type of sleep she was used to, nothing compared to a nice bed and warm fire. Fuck, when was the last time she had just warmth to assist her to sleep?

Somewhere to rest that was not filthy or rock hard. Shit, when was the last time she had a *real* blanket?

She stepped inside, Embry cautiously tailing her. Something in the room, while enticing, felt off. Felt wrong.

"Arya..." Embry warned but before he could continue a figure sipped from a tea cup in one of the chairs by the fire.

Their nails were long and dyed blood red. The creature was pure white, skin silky smooth without blemish until it got to the ribbed silver horns. They protruded from where a normal humanoid's eyes would have been. Instead, this creature had one cloudy grey eye in the middle of their face, a deer-like nose connecting to their mouth.

The tea cup it held was not filled with the brown or green liquid Arya was used to seeing in the human world, but a sickly thick liquid that was darker than the night sky. A void almost. It coated the lips of the creature, a thin reptilian tongue licking at the edges.

While the creature was terrifying there was something about it that Arya was not scared of. She knew this being, whether it had been in this life or the last. It didn't mean to hurt her. Not that she thought of anyway.

"It has been a while since I have sat in front of a fire, Arya," the creature said. Its clawed hands set down the cup, folding nicely in its lap. "It is nice, don't you think? Just the simple presence of fire and air? A delicate balance that two elements combine to create. Beautiful."

Embry was white, his face pale and mouth slightly open when seeing this creature talk. But Arya had known this being. Had heard its voice in her head time and time again. In fact, she had read about it in her books as a child. This was the deity of the humans. Siion.

"What are you doing here?" Arya asked.

Siion looked back to Arya, ignoring the trembling figure of Embry behind her. "Are you not happy to see me?"

Arya shook her head without care. "You are the human deity. You don't have interest in me."

Siion chuckled, the sound like two logs being thrown together. "That is where you are wrong. Humans are a declining race and I am being forgotten. Evelyn is making sure of that."

There was that name again.

"Who is Evelyn?" Arya asked.

Siion snorted. "Your enemy. My enemy. Our common threat. She plans to make the humans more powerful, threatening the way of life for fae and humans alike. She was the reason for your torture, the reason you are here instead of married off in some loveless marriage with some fae noble." Siion kicked their hooved feet up to emphasize their hatred. "Evelyn needs to be stopped. The Lux need to be stopped."

Evelyn. The Lux. Nothing Siion said made sense. Then again, nothing really made sense to Arya recently.

"And you expect me to solve your problems?" Arya asked.

Siion scoffed, rolling their eye. "As the descendant of all five provinces you should want to preserve your fae ancestry."

Arya pursed her lips, crossing her arms. "Sounds like you are just trying to make your issue mine." She raised her chin in a challenge. "You can't stop her can you?"

Siion growled, two rows of serrated white teeth poking through. "I expected you to be more polite."

"Shame you came to me after your people tortured me."

"Humans are not evil, they're just stupid," Siion muttered.

Arya rolled her eyes. "Tell me, Siion, what is it you want from me?"

Siion locked eyes with Arya gifting her a black outlined grin. "I want you to marry Ivan."

"You want me to marry a human? Do exactly what you want to *stop* happening?" Arya puffed an exasperated laugh. "If you think I will willingly do this, you're insane. A god lost in their old ways."

Siion chuckled, cocking their head to the side as they watched Arya. The amusement on their deer lips was disturbing to say the least. "Don't worry child, of all *humans,* he is the most compatible with you."

The way they emphasized humans sent a chill down Arya's spine. It was like Siion was planning something she wasn't privy to know yet. Then again, gods are going to do what gods do. Manipulate their worshipers.

Arya looked back to Embry who was still frozen in fear of the deity, her eyes rolling in response.

"What's in it for me?" Arya asked as she crossed her arms.

Where Siion's brows would've been shot up, the first set of wrinkles creasing their skin. "What do you want?"

"Freedom," Arya blurted without thinking. It was a shocking revelation to her. The thing she wanted most still was the freedom to escape and never have to worry about being caught again. "I want to be able to enjoy my life."

Siion's uncomfortable smile returned to their face as they nodded their head. "I suppose that is fair, though you will have to stay married to Ivan for at least ten years. Once those ten years are up you will have the freedom to explore the world as your heart desires."

Rising from the chair in front of the hearth, Siion bent over in the room, standing at least three times as tall as Arya. It extended one of its blood red claws out for her to shake on the deal. Arya stared at the extended hand of this deity, one far more powerful than she could ever imagine. How marrying Ivan will help them with their Evelyn problem Arya didn't know, but what the end result would be was her freedom.

"Arya, wait!" Embry finally said but it was too late.

Arya's hand connected with the god's a swirling power engulfing the two of them. Golden stars erupted from their hands, and a burning sensation began on her forearm. While painful Arya was not about to cower in front of the god of humans. She stared right into Siion's eye, determined not to break. The god smiled menacingly, gripping her hand tighter. Then, without warning the pain stopped and Arya stood alone with her hand extended to the air.

"What did you do?" Embry breathed.

Arya bit her lips together, staring into the void where Siion once stood. "I'm not sure."

4

Embry had practically dragged Arya down the halls of the inn, throwing her into a room. While thin, Embry was hiding muscle beneath his clothing as the effort used was not much. The man was barely breathing hard.

He slammed the door shut behind them, Arya rubbing the wrist he had dragged her by.

"Arya is your betrothed," Embry hissed to the figure at the desk. It was Ivan, his dark hood still obscuring his face as he looked at papers. The news didn't seem to be a surprise to him causing Arya to wonder if he had also struck a deal with Siion.

"So you got a visit from a deity as well then?" Ivan asked without emotion. "Which one?"

"Siion," Arya responded.

That drew his attention, the hood propping up in her direction. "Siion?"

Arya nodded. "This news doesn't seem like a shock to you, who visited you?"

That dark chuckle filled the room, Ivan leaning back in his chair. "What makes you think you are privy to my conversations with gods?"

Arya's brows rose at the comment, her confusion and rolling questions coming to a halt. Sass was the only thing left. "Oh, perhaps the fact that I am to be your wife and the *gods* were the ones to decide. I'd just like to know which god will be pissed if things don't work out."

"They'll work out," Ivan said amused.

"You sound awfully confident," Arya pressed, "Keeping information from your *wife* doesn't sound like the start of a good relationship."

"My wife is a traumatized Selkie in the lands of humans and she believes I will just willingly admit my secrets to her? Perhaps you are crazier than you let on to be." Ivan chuckled, kicking his feet onto the desk in front of him.

"How dare you," Arya growled, rolling up her sleeve and balling her fist. Embry stopped her advance, gripping onto her shoulder and pulling her to his chest.

"You promised me you'd be different this time," he said.

This time? So there had been other women. Wonderful.

Ivan groaned, throwing his feet off the desk and folding his gloved hands in front of him. "Raena came to me."

"Raena?" Arya snorted, that was the last god she expected to show up in front of Ivan. Raena was all about love, the deity that reigned over Tiras and the Gean-Cánach.

"She must see potential in me," Ivan teased dryly.

Arya rolled her eyes. "So what, she told you to marry me in exchange for...?"

"Nothing," he said.

"Nothing?" Arya laughed angrily.

Ivan shrugged. "While you may find this hard to believe, I do in fact like you, no matter how hard to handle you become."

"Oh yes, me hard to handle, forgive me *kidnapper* for willingly accompanying you to your manor so you can do what you will with me."

Ivan laughed, a sound that was more familiar than Arya liked. "What I'm going to do with you is marry you, then allow you to live without worry in my little manor for as long as you want."

Arya narrowed her eyes at him. "Don't tease me."

"I'm not. As much as you'd like to believe I am, I'm not a bad guy, Arya Abano."

The name struck her like a dagger to the heart. It had been such a long time since someone had called her by her true name and not Hemore. She had almost forgotten how it had sounded coming from another's mouth. How raw and emotion filled it made her.

"When's the wedding?" She mumbled, the shock of her name still rolling through her head.

"Estelle," Ivan announced loudly. Out of nowhere the little pixie girl appeared behind him, tilting her head to the side like she was expecting an order. "Get things together for a wedding between Arya and I."

Estelle's eyes brightened looking between the two of them. "A human or fae wedding?"

It was a good question. With human weddings there was not a magical component to them as there was with fae. It was simply for show and legally binding with submitted paperwork. There was no loyalty or forced devotion between the couple which is why human married women seemed much less enthusiastic about their partners. It was all about safety from what Arya understood. Safety and status.

Perhaps this would be a good thing. With Arya marrying Ivan it would make her above Roderick in rank. Whatever was above a king, she wasn't ever taught such thing. It means she could get her payback. One way or another Roderick would fall by her hand, and she would make sure it was a slow and painful process.

"Fae," Ivan said bringing Arya out of her head.

"Humans don't have the magic needed to produce a fae wedding," Embry said in a hissing tone. It was strange, the words coming out almost like a warning.

"Good thing we have Rook then."

"I'll get right on it," Estelle gleamed, twisting in her skirt and disappearing into darkness.

Rook, that was the other person that Estelle said would be at the manor with them.

"Is Rook fae too?" Arya asked, turning to Embry.

Embry smiled, a cocky grin that made her lose all sense and stare at it in wonder. It was so strange, when Embry smiled like that he almost looked like Kai. Same grin, same nose, same little blush of his ears.

"Rook *was* human," Embry confirmed.

Arya raised a brow, waiting for him to explain further. That was until Ivan interrupted. "Rook likes to explain her abilities to the new members, Embry. Remember your place."

Embry didn't lose his smile as he rolled his eyes. "Then how about we learn something else from you, Arya. Why did you make such a soft expression when I smiled?"

She was once again caught off guard. Was she really that easy to read? "You smiled like a man I knew in my past."

"A former lover?" Embry wiggled his brows.

Arya laughed, the first real laugh and smile she had expressed in gods knew how long. "No. You smiled like him was all, reminded me of a time when I could feel like myself again."

"I see," Embry said with a slowness that led Arya to believe he was thinking hard.

"Leave us," Ivan said sternly.

Embry didn't question the order, leaving out the door they entered moments before. It was strange, Arya wasn't nervous being alone with Ivan, though she did not trust him either. No matter if she felt nervous or not, she really liked Embry and him leaving was sad for her.

The room was silent save for the scratching of Ivan's pen across the final few papers on his desk. He didn't say anything before he slid the papers over to her tapping the end of the pen toward the bottom.

"Sign here."

Arya furrowed her brows, approaching the desk. Upon the table was a contract. Multiple small words were scrawled across the page. She picked up the document reading the first line.

Marriage agreement between the two parties shall follow all rules listed below.

"A marriage contract? Did you plan on this?" Arya puffed out tossing the paper on the desk.

Ivan snorted. "Of course I did. I was informed of the guardian's decision of the matter a week ago. I let Estelle know I needed a contract and thus, here it is. Don't worry, everything within it is tasteful."

"Tasteful?" Arya spit, "*If the two do not conceive an heir within the first year the contract is null*," she read with venom. "I was told I needed to last ten years before I was offered my side of the deal."

Ivan folded his hands in front of himself. "Your side of the deal?"

Arya cursed herself, biting down on her bottom lip. This is exactly what happened last time in her dream, one inch of safety and she tells everything to the first man to get her alone.

"What is this deal you made with Siion?" Ivan asked in a harder tone.

Arya sighed knowing it'd never last now. "Freedom. I asked for my freedom."

Ivan sat back in his chair, rubbing beneath the hood to where she assumed his chin was. "Siion told you that you needed to be married to me for ten years to secure that?" Arya nodded her response, cheeks heating with the pain of admitting such a thing. She was no better than a slave being tossed from one person to another.

Ivan nodded, sighing deeply. She watched as he took back the pen, digging through the other papers beneath a pile to pull another out. Quickly, Ivan signed the bottom, slapping it and the pen on the table over the marriage contract. "Sign it."

Arya looked over that page, letting out a breath. It was her freedom. All it took was her signature.

"This is my ownership papers," she said.

Ivan leaned back in his seat. "I am not owning you, Arya Abano. I came to take you from a tragic situation and help you, not dim your light. Sign that paper and not even Roderick can throw you back into that cage he kept you in."

"Dungeon," Arya corrected.

"What?"

"He kept me in the dungeon. Solitary to be exact."

Ivan's hands clenched into fists, his gloves tightening over his knuckles. "Fuck me."

Arya's brows furrowed at the accent his voice took. It wasn't human, it almost sounded fae.

Without a second thought she took the pen scrawling her name across the bottom of the page. The transfer of ownership from Ivan going to her. She had legal proof that she was now in charge of herself again. Had some sense of freedom in Kulessa.

Then, she signed the document below it. Arya was keenly aware of Ivan's breathing stopping for the few minutes it took her to sign, his eyes tracing over each brush of her finger down the pages where she read. It shocked her if she was being honest. The contract had nothing to do with her and everything to do with what his boundaries were.

The most important being that Arya was not allowed to see him without his hood before they conceived a child.

"Are you ugly?" She asked without thinking.

Ivan laughed, hood shaking. "No, I just like my privacy. I want you to know me for who I am, not what I look like."

Arya nodded. It seemed reasonable to her. She uncapped the pen, her name looping out over the page with less effort than it felt it should take. She didn't need to do this, her freedom was given to her by this man, the papers signed so she was her own person again. Yet Arya felt that the marriage was wanted by the gods. There was a reason Ivan was chosen by Siion for her. This was meant to happen. This was destined to happen.

Recapping the pen, Arya placed it on the table and slid the document toward Ivan.

"I refused to fuck you with the hood on."

Ivan snorted, nodding. "Don't worry, I have other ways to make it so you don't have to see me. You can imagine me as whoever you want, call out whatever name you want, and I will stop whenever you say to."

"You're big on consent for a human male," Arya commented.

Ivan stayed where he was not moving an inch. "Consent is important to me."

She decided to leave the topic there, stepping back from his desk. "When should I expect you in my chambers?"

"After we're married. Call me old fashioned or formal, but I like to do things the way it's always been done. Once you are my wife you will have everything my equal."

"Even money?"

Ivan laughed. "What are you going to do with money? You'll have everything you need."

"Books," Arya said.

"Books?" Ivan asked, sitting back into his chair.

Arya nodded. "I like to read, it's one of my favorite things to do and it helps me to forget."

Ivan leaned forward, stiff as if he was struggling against something internally. "I will have you know the place we are going is going to meet your standards, and if not, we will buy you out a bookstore."

Arya let herself chuckle, bringing her hand to her mouth. She tried to cover it with a cough but knew Ivan had seen it. Did it really matter? He was her betrothed anyway. "I'll hold you to it."

"Get some sleep Arya, we have a journey ahead of us tomorrow."

She nodded, turning toward the door. Arya placed her hand on the doorknob, head twisting so she could ever so slightly see Ivan's hooded form. "Goodnight, Ivan."

"Goodnight, Arya."

On her way out Arya caught herself smiling. She shook her head, riding herself of the feeling. It was indescribable, something she couldn't be feeling when forced into a marriage.

Arya followed the halls back to the room where she had the conversation with Siion, closing the door and leaning against it with a sigh. What has she gotten herself into?

5

Ivan wasn't joking when he had claimed they were in for a long journey. Arya had read the entire book he had given her, thoroughly enjoying the stories. They were ones she had never heard of before, enticing her to learn more about human mythology.

When they finally arrived at their destination, Arya was stunned. They pulled up through a garden that was parted by a gravel drive. Purples and blues were splattered in flowers around the entire view, dark greens rose up the side of the manor circling the singular tower. The stone was pristine, and the sky blue making the entire place seem out of a fairytale. Too good to be true.

The door was opened by a servant who wore a mask, Ivan leaving the carriage first. Once onto the ground, he turned, offering Arya his hand. She took it, exiting the carriage to what would be her new home.

"This doesn't look real," she admitted.

"It took a lot of work to make it livable."

Arya looked at Ivan, raising her brows. "You put work into this place."

He nodded, using their combined hands to lead her forward. "I bought it from a man who had it in his family for centuries. His wife had died, you see, never giving him any children, and he was too old to remarry, nor did he want to. He made me promise to make this home one that would last through the generations."

"That's why you have the child in the contract," Arya said.

"Exactly, a man who is that kind needed to have my word upheld." He confirmed.

Ivan brought Arya to the front doors, the wood old and worn but with the perfect amount of history imbedded into them. Unable to help herself, she touched the door with her freehand, a strange memory coming to her. It didn't feel like hers. Like she had been living through someone else's mind. There was warmth of the sun, her dress was far from the fashions of the world then. Arya opened the door, her fingers pressing over the carved indent of two letters in the wood. They had been lost with time, but the memory of them still lived there.

"Are you okay?" Ivan asked in a soft voice.

Arya nodded, her hand squeezing Ivan's subconsciously. She released him, swallowing as she passed through the doors and into the halls. It opened to a wide entry with a grand staircase that spiraled up to a second level. Echoes of children's laughter filled Arya's mind, calling out to her like it was her memory that had been lost to the location.

Music soon joined, the sound of joy and celebration came with it. Arya felt the pain and torment of wanting to remember such beautiful times. A ball of emotion welled in her throat but she didn't know what for. It was not her life that had happened here. This home was not hers, it was Ivan's and before him the elderly man who failed to fill it with his children. But she was still sad.

Leather brushed against her face, Arya looking up to see Ivan pulling back his tear soaked finger. Arya brushed her wrist against her eyes, eliminating the evidence of any additional sorrow. "I'm sorry."

"Why are you crying?" He asked.

Arya shook her head laughing at the absurdity of the situation. "I've never been here before, but it's like I can hear the parties and the children who had."

"Was there a lot of sorrow?" Ivan asked.

Arya shook her head, smiling against her will. "No, but I so wanted it to have been me who lived here."

"You do now," Ivan said hesitantly. "You'll come to find your life won't be as bad as you expect it to be. Not while I live."

She grimaced, nodding her thanks. For some reason, the ending threat of Ivan's death made her nervous. If there was something she should be scared of happening to them, she would like to know before it happened. To prepare herself and whatever future child they could conceive within the next year.

Ivan lead Arya down the halls, proving the manor was bigger than it appeared on the outside. Magic was in the air, hovering just within her reach, yet faint enough where humans would not notice it.

It confused Arya. Humans she had met were against magic, but then Ivan continued to prove to her that she was incorrect. It was strange to see, someone who seemed nice, yet she knew that could be a façade. A ploy to get her to trust him in order to gain her sympathy or, worse yet, her love.

All thoughts ceased to come to her mind as Ivan lead her through the plain double doors they stood in front of.

Blue and purple light danced over the room, the spines of books that disappeared into a strange collection of clouds, lit by them. Constellations were carved into the black floors, almost lighting up as she stepped over them. Their name was written in fae and common tongue along with a mixture of letters and numbers. Silver shelves housed more books than she could ever think to read in her lifetime. Tables with papers and pens laid upon them sat in the center of the room in multiple areas. Lamps on them lit at their entrance, as if beckoning Arya to take a seat at one.

The far wall was the cause of the purple and blue light. A picture was designed into the colored glass of the window. On one side sat a woman under a willow tree. Her dress was made of stars, focus pinned on the book she held in her lap. A large white and grey circle above her symbolized the rising moon, yet the dark purples of the sunset were still seen in the sky. One the other side was a man in a purple cloak. He leaned against a similar tree, looking out at the woman with a longing that tore at Arya's heart. His sky was filled with blue, the small specks of yellow coming over the horizon of beautiful waves. Between the two was a picture of a red book with golden trim.

"What's that book?" Arya asked.

Ivan tilted his head to the side, looking up at the window. For a brief second, Arya had caught a glimpse of the man beneath the shadows. One with a strong jaw and five-o'clock shadow.

"It's the Story of Dawn, you've never heard of it?" He responded.

Arya shook her head, directing her attention back to the red and gold book. "Is it here in the library?"

"No." His response was quick like Arya had insulted him by asking. "It is in another location, I would love to have it in my collection, but unfortunately, another has it."

She nodded. "What's so important about it?"

Ivan laughed, an angry sound. "It was stollen from me long ago. The man who has it now had also taken away something even more dear, the book the only thing that can remind me of it."

Arya furrowed her brows, not entirely sure what could be so important that a book is the only thing that would remind Ivan of it. She could not think of a single book that held a precious memory to her like that. "Is there a way to get it back?"

Ivan shook his head. "Not unless I plan to travel across the border to Kulessa, and that is not a risk I am willing to take."

Arya's heart pounded for a moment, the feeling balled in her throat. *I could get it for you'* she almost said. Then she remembered, she is his now. She had the deed to her life, sure, but without Ivan where would she go? There was no telling if the ambassadors would know anything about the dream she had. It was simply that, a dream. Her parents would throw her right back into royal living, and Arya was unsure if she could ever do something like that again. She was not the same girl they'd lost, that much was proven in the dream.

What of Leif? The voice purred in her head.

Arya thought back to the blond-haired boy she'd confessed to loving in her dream. The same one who was supposed to be married to her sister. The very man who allowed Arya to feel what she needed to in that make-believe world of her dream. Allowed her to scream and cry and yet still teased her like there was not a cloud over her head and the weight of the world on her shoulders. Leif Fenmore.

"Have you ever loved anyone before?" Arya asked Ivan staring up at the boy in the window. That boy loved the reading girl, doomed to never see her. Never meet her. Separated by panes of glass and a book.

"Once," Ivan said in a soft tone.

"Me too."

That drew his attention, and though she could not see his eyes she knew they were searching her for clues of the

71

person she adored. Her features would not expose such secrets. Not when that love was based off situations where she was not actually present. A fantasy world that would never come true. A false hope in a world where tragedy spoke louder than kindness ever had.

"Were they good to you?" Ivan asked.

Arya let herself grimace a smile. "So good it was almost not real."

The silence hung heavy in the room between them. It was suffocating, yet comfortable. Like a weighted coat Arya was willing to apply to herself. It kept out the cold, uneasiness of the topic. At least she had experienced love. No matter what form, love was important. It gave her a reason to keep going. It was her reason for survival.

"Let me show you to your room," Ivan said.

He turned out of the room, walking in a much quicker pace than he had entered with Arya in. She took one last look at the window, making a silent reminder of how it felt to have someone look at her like that. Then, without a second glance, she turned, her skirts twisting at her ankles as she followed Ivan down the hall.

Her room was not anything to wonder at like the library had been. It was a simple bed on a wooden frame with a slatted headboard. A blue and green rug sat beneath it, dresser and wardrobe mirroring each other along the wall. A singular window with a view of the plains outside was opposite the entry.

"I had more dresses put into your wardrobe and some basic necessities filled in your drawers," Ivan said.

Arya nodded, wringing her hands together. She looked over the room a few more times. She didn't know why, but she had expected more. Something spectacular. Extravagant. Not—this.

"Are you satisfied?" He asked.

Arya nodded though a ball of emotion welled in her throat. She dared not to speak, worried some of that emotion would leak out. Luckily, it didn't seem as though Ivan noticed. She listened as his footsteps left toward the entry. Each click sounding like a ticking of a clock, the seconds taking forever to pass as his step landed.

The rattling of his hand on the door nob was jarring. Her vision swirled with ferocity. He needed to go now or he would witness just how damaged Arya truly was.

"I will send Estelle to come grab you for supper once it is ready. Rest, it has been a long journey."

Arya struggled to nod, waiting for the click of the door and the sound of Ivan's boots turning into faded thumps before she took in a shaking breath. Her fists balled and expanded at her side, chest tightening with such force it felt as if she'd explode. Arya stumbled back, hitting the wall and sliding down to the floor. Her breathing was fast and erratic, the control on her emotions she held slipping like when submerging a hand full of sand into the tide. Tears came down her cheeks in hot streams as her hands came up to pull at her hair.

How was it she felt so trapped without being so?

73

Ivan wanted children from her, Siion promised her freedom after their marriage. The life she lived in her mind while imprisoned was *nothing* short of torturous, yet *here* she has her attack? This plain, ordinary room?

That's when the words escaped her lips through shuddering sobs. "I want to go home."

She took in a gasping breath, squeezing her eyes shut. "I want to go home. I want to go home. I want to go home."

This was not home. This was not safe. This was temporary, just like everything else in her life. Temporary and dangerous.

6

It was only Ivan and Arya in the too large dining room as they ate their dinner. The meal was more than Arya had eaten the entire time she'd been imprisoned. For some reason, however, it was not good.

She lifted her spoon from the creamy, teal soup she was offered, the smell of cabbage and horseradish coming out with the smoke in the most unappetizing manner. The meat she had been served was partially burned, the flesh dryer than the desert hills of Dunia. The potato seemed to be the only edible portion of the meal, and that was saying something as it was not cooked. It was a raw, whole potato.

"I-is your food normally like this?" Arya asked hesitantly.

"Inedible?" Ivan muttered.

75

She nodded. Without a word, Ivan stood, his chair scraping across the floor. It startled Arya, watching as the cloaked figure approached her. He held out his hand, an offer of some sort of adventure.

"Shall we go see what is going on in the kitchen?"

Arya's mouth opened and closed. "Are we allowed in there?"

Ivan snorted. "I am the Lord of this house, and you will soon be the Lady. You and I are able to go where we please."

With a small smile, Arya grabbed his hand, letting him lead her out of the dining room and through several halls. It reminded her of the sneaking around she had done at Castle Lofta, the secret trips to the water with all of her friends. A small thrill ran through her as they went down multiple flights of stairs. As they descended the smell got worse and the steps narrower.

Ivan pushed on a poorly manufactured door that was clearly part of the original structure. It opened without a sound, displaying Estelle dancing through the kitchen. She flung flour through the air, appearing in one area, only to disappear and grab an ingredient from another. Embry sat on a barrel drinking from a mug and reading a book, caring less about whatever Estelle was doing to the food she was attempting to make.

At one point, Arya watched as Estelle grabbed some foxglove that was hanging in the window to dry and placed it in the teal soup that was slowly turning a murky brown.

"Don't eat the soup," Arya whispered.

Ivan snorted. "Were you planning on it?"

Arya couldn't help but giggle, covering her mouth as she continued to observe the pixie-like girl. All was well until Arya noticed both Estelle and Embry look toward the door.

The fire flickered in the hearth, the room cooling and the hairs on Arya's arm raising.

From a side door that she could not see came a woman. Her hair was darker than night, eyes the color of newly drawn blood. Her porcelain skin reflected the glowing of the embers in the fire, seeming to display them upon her skin. She removed her hood, nails long and black. A sign of dark magic. Something Arya had only heard about in stories as a child. She didn't actually think it was real. Not until now.

"Is she here?" The woman asked in a voice that did not match her appearance. It was soft, curious, if not a bit like Estelle's.

Estelle rolled her eyes, continuing her dance of deadly soup. Her ignoring this newcomer did not strike the three as odd, but normal, Arya sensing their relationship was strained.

"She's here," Embry confirmed.

The woman nodded, wringing her hands together. A nervous gesture for someone who could control black magic. "Does she..." The words stopped as if disclosing a secret that only the three in the room shared.

"She looks like yours," Estelle puffed, "Every time she's a Selkie she looks like that."

Arya furrowed her brows at the statement. Every time she was a Selkie? As far as Arya knew she was always a

Selkie, from the moment she was born until she was kidnapped in Kulessa. Even when she prayed to the gods to be another type of fae she was still just a Selkie. Then there was the statement of '*she looks like yours*' what did that mean? Her what?

Before the group could say another word, Arya saw the door was pushed open by Ivan. Heads turned in their direction, shoulders of the woman slumping. Her red eyes looked over Arya filling with emotion that she could not determine. They took in each angle of her, slowly gazing at the loose fabric of her hollow stomach.

"Arya, may I introduce you to Rook, our resident witch," Ivan said in warning.

Rook breathed in her composure, chin tilting up much like Arya did within the walls of the Kulessan capital.

"A pleasure," Rook said with a harder infliction to her words than how she had spoken to Embry and Estelle moments before.

Arya pursed her lips, trying to read Rook better. It was the first time she had met anyone with dark magic, much less someone who was also a human and a user.

"How long have you been using dark magic?" Arya asked.

The question seemed to take Rook by surprise. "Most of my life."

Arya shook her head, placing her curled fist onto her chin. "You do know dark magic is bad for you, right?" Rook opened and closed her mouth but ultimately said nothing. "I am not one to talk about doing what you need to in order to survive, but black magic is a bit extreme."

"You don't know what happened to make me like this," Rook snapped, a growl laced in her voice. It surprised Arya, not for the sudden change in behavior, but for how much she sounded like Idoh.

"That's so strange," Arya commented, taking a step forward. Rook stepped back in response, the same way Idoh would when confronted with speaking with Phobus in her dream.

"What is?" Estelle asked with a menacing smile.

"You remind me of someone I once knew, someone I loved very much."

Rook shrunk once again, her lip quivering before she stormed out of the room. Arya blinked her surprise, looking to Embry for answers. He smiled weakly to her, walking in the same direction that Rook had gone.

"You did nothing wrong," he said, "she gets like that sometimes."

"Estelle, clean up this mess," Ivan ordered.

There was a disgruntled groan from Estelle as Ivan's hand pressed to Arya's lower back to lead her back up the stairs from which they came moments before. They did not speak the entire journey back to her room, the silence falling heavy in the air.

As they got to her door, Ivan stopped, though Arya felt as if he was avoiding her stare. "Did I do something wrong?"

Ivan shook his head. "Be sure to clean yourself up before bed and brush your hair."

Without a second for Arya to respond, Ivan was off, his cloak billowing around the halls as his feet made quick work of the stone path. She waited, watching Ivan until he turned a corner abruptly, disappearing from sight.

She sighed, feeling that crushing weight return to her chest once again. Perhaps she should just do as Ivan said and stay low. No matter how much magic floated around her, or how many fae were within these walls, Arya needed to continue to keep her head down.

"You are still a prisoner," Arya said to herself. "Just a different cell with different treatment."

Steam summoned her to the bathroom. There had not been bedside bathrooms in the castle that Arya knew of. She knew that the upper royals had clawfoot tubs brought into their rooms weekly, but nothing like this.

She stepped into the glowing aura of perfection, wondering how such a large room fit into the house. As she stepped, the tiles beneath her feet illuminated a dazzling yellow. A tree was off in the distance, glowing with pink blossoms. It overhung a small waterfall where the in ground tub was filled from. In reality, it was big enough for Arya to swim in, tiles turning into rock that was carved into stairs. It disappeared beneath the purple liquid, plants surrounding the sides like a secret oasis. It almost made her forget of where she was. What brought her to this place.

Arya began to strip her dress, letting the fabric fall to the ground in a heap around her feet. Nude and without a second thought, she proceeded forward, dipping her toes into the liquid provided to her. It was heaven, the water soaking into her body and releasing the tension in her muscles with each step forward. Her hands went above her head, removing the pins that had held back her hair for dinner, letting the curls loose around her shoulders.

At the end of it all, Arya sunk until her neck was completely submerged in purple. She felt the stress float off her and into this water. Every pain she experienced was cleansed while submerged, lapping of the pool like a giant, warm hug.

"Oh, fuck me," Arya purred as she waved her hands beneath the pool.

Utter and pure relaxation hit her. It was enticing. Lovely. Pure fucking bliss.

"You look like you're enjoying yourself," a voice said with a cheeky smile heard in her voice.

Arya shot up in the water, startled by the new presence. It was not like her to let her guard down so easily. To her shock, the woman who spoke was giant.

She sat on top of the waterfall, her feet splashing in the water as if it was their joint spa day. Her skin was a deep pink with purple dots sprinkling her cheeks. Loose flowing silks covered the more indecent parts of her body, yet still left enough skin to be seen in a seductive manner. Purple butterfly wings came from the side of her face, pulling back her lavender hair and brightening her white eyes.

Arya knew exactly who this being was, just as she had known Siion. "Raena."

The woman nodded approvingly. "So good to meet you outside of your head, Arya."

Arya thought back to all of the different voices that spoke to her while in the dream. Each having a different tone and thrill to their words. Were all of them gods? Would she be getting a visit from each?

"Don't fret, I know how much you like to think of the worst scenario," Raena said without much rush. "I come bearing gifts."

"Gifts?" Arya repeated. "What did I do to deserve such thing?"

Raena smiled, the wings on the side of her face flapping. "Can't a god spoil their star disciple without needing anything in return?" Arya narrowed her eyes at the goddess, crossing her arms. Raena sighed, rolling her eyes. She then lowered herself into the water, it only going up to her knees as she waded toward Arya. Arya stayed still as the goddess approached, not willing to let down her stoic demeanor for someone who could easily smite them. Something told Arya, however, that Raena needed her more than she'd like to admit.

"There is much for you to discover about yourself. Until you are able to, this may help you adjust." Raena pulled a simple golden hand mirror out of seemingly thin air. Arya took it, looking within. To her surprise there was only darkness on the other side. Her reflection missing through the glass.

"Is it some sort of trick?" She asked.

Raena chuckled. "My darling Sorrow, you cannot expect him to visit while you are nude in a bathing pool. I trained him much better than that."

Arya clenched her jaw. Who was this goddess attempting to give her meetings with?

"Why me?" Arya asked without thinking. "Why of all people in this world did you and Siion choose to honor me with your presence?"

Raena's antennae twitched like she was surprised by the question. "Because you are the gift of life and death, Arya. You determine that which the gods cannot touch. A mortal with the ability to remain immortal, yet never chooses to."

Arya closed her eyes, pinching the bridge of her nose. "What does that even mean?"

There was no response, Arya looking back up to where the goddess once stood. In her place was air. No proof the goddess of lust had ever been in the room to greet Arya. The only trace of her being the golden mirror in which she saw only darkness.

With the mood completely shifted from relaxed, Arya left the pool. Throwing on a simple chemise and night robe, she sat at her vanity, looking into the mirror. Nothing changed within it.

Arya threw herself against the back of the chair, crossing her arms. Why would a goddess of lust give her a broken mirror. It was completely insane for Arya to assume she would give her anything useful. Shit, all Siion wanted was for her to marry a human.

What would Ivan do if he found out about the goddess's recent visit to her? Would he confiscate her mirror? Even if it didn't work to show her what it was supposed to, Arya couldn't bear to leave without it. It was a connection to the spFyorrt world. To those who knew exactly what her purpose was because Arya didn't know anymore.

Her arms crossed in front of her, head leaning on them as she looked into the darkness provided to her. She listened to the sounds around her, the creaking of the old wood, wind hitting the window panes, all sounds of the world passing around her while she stared into nothing.

Then, the darkness changed.

A small light appeared. No—not a light, something more. Hair. Full lips. Green eyes. Golden skin.

Arya choked as she saw him. He smiled.

"Do you know how long it took me to find you?" He teased as if no time had passed between them.

Arya opened and closed her mouth, bringing the mirror closer. Her fingers brushed over his portrait, tears welling in her eyes. Could it really be him?

"Leif?"

"Hello, Arya dear."

7

"What are you doing here?" Arya whispered, bringing the mirror to the corner of the room to hide Leif from view of anyone who could walk in without notice. She was still in Kulessa, this could be dangerous.

Leif raised his brows. "Arya, I'm in a mirror, who are you hiding from?"

"I'm still in Kulessa, they can't see you or you could get hurt."

Leif snorted angrily. "Like an army of humans are going to come across the border because I'm talking to you? It's more likely you'll get hurt."

The brief images of Arya being held down and whipped crossed her mind. She pushed the memories away quickly before the next horrors happened upon her memories. There was a lot done, not a lot to protect her from.

"When can you come rescue me?" She asked in a shaking tone.

Leif sighed, rubbing down his face as if the question was slowly killing him. "I'm not allowed to. Zephyr is barring any trades from Kulessa since his father's attempted assassination. The borders are being patrolled heavily by the military on either side, even other fae are being searched before they're brought back over."

Arya didn't realize how intense things had gotten with the peace between Kulessa and Teielmor. With tensions this high, one incident could set off an entire war.

"Are you in Ilmari?" Arya asked, hoping her friends were all still together.

Leif shook his head. "I resigned from my ambassadorship months ago. Zephyr has changed since the dream—fuck."

Arya paled, her mouth going dry as she heard the first confirmation that others had the same dream she did. The same crazy situations, the same interactions created by the gods. All of it was done with the others.

"Who else had it?" She said in a whisper.

"Arya—."

"Who else Leif?" She yelled.

Leif looked down as he said, "Me, Idoh, Mies, and Zephyr."

Her teeth clenched together. Each of them knew and didn't come to help her? Zephyr had admitted his love to her in the dream, and he is the one blocking the border so there isn't a way for her to come back? Idoh promised to come get her if she was ever back in Kulessa. Where was he? What is stopping him? His duty to the crown? Was that where his true loyalties lied? And Mies... she did not have his mist now, but in that dream she was so important to him that he forced her into marriage. Was it too difficult without the mist to find her now? Was she just not worth it to him anymore? Written off as just another girl?

Taking a deep breath, Arya asked Leif the most important question she had been dying to know since the dream happened. "How is Winslet?"

Leif smiled. "If you're quiet, I'll show you."

Arya nodded, and watched as the darkened outline of Leif's body expanded around him to reveal the library in Tiras. The fire was roaring in the hearth, lighting the light purple walls in a burnt orange. Upon an armchair in the middle of the room sat Winslet. Her legs were curled in towards her chest, head resting peacefully on the winged backing. White hair danced down her shoulders and became hidden beneath the blue quilt she had over her body.

Arya sucked in a sob, covering her mouth so she did not wake the girl up.

Winslet was alive. Her friend was still alive and well. There was not a scratch on her. Her chest rose and fell, the smell of burnt flesh was not surrounding her, instead replaced by burnt wood.

"I made her come with me," Leif admitted after a while. "I wasn't going to live with the possibility of Winslet dying when I knew and could do something about it."

"Did the bombings happen?" Arya asked quietly.

Leif shook his head. "No, it was part of the reason Zephyr closed the border."

She nodded. At least he was doing good at protecting those around him. "What about Idoh and Mies?"

Leif shook his head. "I left before I heard what they were going to do. Idoh is probably by the border somewhere helping wrangle in the troops, Mies I did hear something about. Not sure if it is rumor or not though."

"What?" Arya asked, straightening herself from the wall.

"He's been disowned. Zephyr sent him home and is a well-known drunk throughout all Dunia. Starts fights, banned from certain pubs, family cut him off financially, so he works to drink."

Arya scoffed, unable to help her reaction. While she understood that he was in pain, she hated that was the route he chose to take. Arya had been through so much and she was able to withstand from drowning herself in alcohol.

"Where are you, Arya?" Leif asked.

She opened and closed her mouth. That was something she didn't bother to ask. In the capital she was able to figure out where she was on a map, now, she didn't know. "A manor of sorts, this man, Ivan took me from Roderick. I'm supposed to marry him Leif."

Leif's face darkened. "Is he forcing you to?"

She shook her head. "Not him, Siion."

He paused. "The human god?"

Arya nodded.

"Well fuck me." Arya watched as he pushed back the locks of blond from his face. "Just be cautious Arya, I'm not supposed to tell you this, but that man works for Evelyn. She's not someone to be messed with."

"Who is she? I keep hearing her name but never get told more than that."

"The less you know the better, especially when it comes to Evelyn," Leif responded.

Arya rolled her eyes, sighing loud enough so he could hear. "If I'm going to be stuck in Kulessa, you might as well tell me what to expect."

Leif stiffened, rubbing the back of his neck. Arya couldn't help but notice the muscles that rose to the challenge, surprising seeing as Leif was thinner before.

"There's a book," he said in a whisper, "The Book of Death, if you can find it, it'll explain more than I can."

Arya committed the book to memory, her goal for tomorrow to find that book. Hopefully Ivan had it in his library.

Leif looked behind himself, the darkness around his silhouette returning. "I have to go, but I will see you tomorrow night."

"Leif, wait," Arya called but it was too late. The darkness was back to the mirror, Leif's sweet face missing. Unable to help herself, Arya cried.

She clutched the mirror to her chest, gasping and crying loudly. She didn't care who heard, Arya was stuck there anyway. There was no way back to Teielmor, no way to get to Leif or the others, only this mirror so she could talk to him when she needed to. Every night. Her secret way to communicate with Leif. Her way to have a feeling of home again.

Crawling into bed, Arya clutched the mirror to her chest, curling into a ball. She imagined herself in that library with Winslet and Leif, snuggled with a book, listening to the fire crackle and Winslet's soft sighs. She imagined laying over Leif's lap as she allowed sleep to take her, his fingers dancing through her curls. She was warm in that desire, falling into the fantasy of safety once again within her mind.

Arya let sleep take her

8

The knowledge of Arya being trapped in Kulessa made the idea of her being a prisoner even more solidified in her mind. Even though it was much nicer than when she was owned by Roderick, she was a prisoner as long as she was on Kulessan soil. So, she decided to make the most of it. See how much she could learn while she still had free reign around the property.

It was with that new found energy that Arya had made the determined trip to the library, scanning over the books for one labeled: *The Story of Death.* It was her second wrap around the library when Arya felt a familiar tingle of magic around her.

"What are you looking for?" Rook asked.

Arya glanced back at the woman, her previously muddied dress replaced with a form fitted ruby top and black flexible pants. It almost was sparing attire.

"A book," Arya said.

Rook rolled her eyes. "Obviously, which one?"

Frustrated with the lack of her ability to find this missing book, she decided it couldn't be too much to ask Rook about it. "The Story of Death."

Rook rose her brows, lips curling up slightly. "Interesting choice, but you won't find it in the library. It's too special for that."

"What's special about it?" Arya asked.

Rook smirked. "If you want to read it, you have to follow the stairs down to the lowest level that this manor goes. You will see many doors with letters painted on them and dates. Go into the one marked *A* and the ending date left open. You'll find the book inside."

Arya furrowed her brows. "That was specific, why not go with me?"

Rook laughed. "If my mother found out I had gone down there with you she'd kill me."

Arya snorted, giving a soft smile. It sounded so sweet and innocent. Rook was still scared of her mother even as a grown woman. Arya really never had that relationship with her own mother. In fact, her parents were always so distant with her. She wouldn't do that to her child.

"Thank you for letting me know," Arya said.

Rook nodded, casually walking out of the library. "Oh, if I were you, I'd get a weapon, the rats down there are— large."

Arya nodded, though not scared of some big rats. She practically lived with them when in Roderick's care. Ate them too. Her mouth began to water thinking about it, causing Arya to cringe. How did she come to crave rats?

Taking in a deep breath, she walked to one of the armored statues outside the library doors and pulled out the polished metal sword. It was shaped like a snake, the balance of the weapon beautiful in her hand. Gripping the hilt, Arya began to follow the trail to the staircase that had brought her and Ivan to the kitchen the night before. It was a good first step to trying to discover the location of this book.

The stairs led her down to a lower floor, but something told Arya there was more to go. And so, after searching, behind a strange, narrow piece of wood, she found a tight corridor with water dripping down the sides and stairs carved into the stone.

It was dark within that passageway, Arya's eyes barely able to adjust to the minimal light. She was careful walking down the slick steps, but even with being careful, when there is not a clear sign that the rest of the steps down are missing, and she was expecting them to be there, well, that would lead anyone to fall.

The air whipped her hair and skirts around her body until she plummeted into the dark liquid that laid beneath. It rocked and rolled around her like she had been shoved in the middle of a stormy sea. It would've been fine if it hadn't been for the gods damned darkness. She couldn't see a thing.

Hoping for the best, Arya swam. Her arms ached at the new exercise, giving her even more of a reason to keep swimming. The pain in her arm increased, and Arya finally had enough. She willed all the magic she had into the water surrounding her. It stilled, lifting her gently over the thrashing waves and setting her down on shore. Of all the things for Arya to fight with, water is not one to fuss with. It was in her magic after all.

She huffed as she threw the remaining water off her body, wishing she was a master of multiple elements so she could have a fire to see *anything* with. That's when Arya felt a rustling by her gown. She squealed, jumping in the air a few times and moving from her spot. Then she remembered the sword she had when falling. Might need it now that she was practically blind and was facing the large rats Rook warned her about.

With a simple extension of her hand, Arya was gifted the sword from the water, loving the power that came from wielding magic again. It would be wonderful to be back to her full strength once she swam, but as far as she knew, she still had pattons of land before reaching the ocean.

Lugging the sword up to rest on her shoulder, Arya tapped the soil in front of her with her toe, making sure there wasn't another drop into nothingness. This time she was lucky, but she wouldn't be able to survive a bat of quicksand or pointy sticks.

Either way, this trip was going to take a lot longer than she originally assumed.

Arya couldn't see where the fuck she was going. There was no light, no sign of anything around her, just blackness.

What worried her the most was the noises. There was the shuffling of her feet over the dirt, sure. The crisp sound of her breaths and the way her joints cracked when she moved certain ways, but it was the other noises. There was hissing at one point. Strange coos and caws of different animals in the distance, yowls accompanying them soon after. Arya was not sure what sort of creatures lived in the complete darkness like this.

Then, she began to see.

It was small things, outlines and silhouettes of trees, but she saw them. She then began to see details of the grass and dirt patches she walked along. It didn't make sense, how could grass and trees live down in a place that was so dark?

A light grew brighter in the distance, a hole in a rock that had millions of tiny glistening crystals. All colors of the rainbow danced through those lights, much like the tree and stones of her bathroom. Arya grabbed hold of one of the loose crystals, prying it from the rock. It lit brightly in her hand, but after a second of hope filling her stomach, she watched the rock lose all light until it was just another stone.

"Fuck." Arya cursed to the empty world she'd become trapped in.

She looked back into the hole the light came from, wondering, if she moved her body just the right way, could she fit behind those gems and be protected from the outside? The idea was stupid, but nevertheless, she tried anyway.

The crystals caught on her dress, tearing some of the fabric and ripping at her skin as she proceeded through. She was grateful for the shoes on her feet as she could feel each little prick she stepped on. Bare feet would've been killer.

As she made it past all the sharp crystals, she found a small path. While difficult to cross into, it looked well worn, as if there was steady traffic coming in and out. Hopefully, that was a good sign.

She was grateful for the light the stones around her provided, so much so that she forgot the warnings that Rook had given her before she had left.

Her sword bounced on her shoulder as she walked, attempting to remember what Rook had said. A door with a large letter "A" on it. She had yet to see any doors, hoping she hadn't passed them in the darkness.

Behind her, a raspy clicking sounded. She spun, throwing her sword out toward the noise. The empty corridor greeted her. Clenching her jaw, Arya moved back in the direction she was originally walking. Her mind raced with what could be causing the noise, senses on high alert. Years of torture did not make her oblivious to danger, if anything, it increased her awareness of it.

More skittering announced the presence of something else in the tunnels with her, Arya quickening her pace. The doors were lost on her, the focus shifting to finding a way out of this one way hall of light.

Things began to shift in the tunnel, the crystals merging into one large one. The walls were jagged, but Arya could see her reflection upon them.

She was surprised at her appearance. Covered in blood. Arya searched herself to try and find the source of the liquid, unable to see any injuries she encountered. That led her to retracing her steps in the cave. The blood was once liquid, but as she examined herself she realized that it was dry. While normally she would've expected it to be a red color, the flakes she managed to peel off her skin were a russet brown. Like blood that had been found void of water.

Chattering from behind her made Arya come back to the situation at hand. She was still in the tunnels with whatever those creatures were. No way out except forward.

Deciding to try to create as much room between herself and whatever was following her, Arya jogged through the tunnel. There was only one significant change she noted as she ran. The light in the tunnel was dimming.

"You've got to be kidding me," Arya puffed, continuing forward. She just hoped her followers couldn't see in the dark either.

Then she hit a wall.

The crystal showed her another room. One where there were burning torches on the walls, and doors. Many doors with letters on the front. She felt around the crystal wall, attempting to see if she had come across a door in the tunnel. However, as much as she tried, Arya didn't see or feel anything to resemble any door she knew.

A figure walked into the halls. Arya had to squint to see any defining features, the crystal making it hard to determine if it was someone she knew, or a random passerby. What a person would be doing down in those tunnels she hadn't a clue, but to each their own.

Only Arya didn't have time to seek more details as a searing pain erupted from her ankle. She screamed out, dropping with her back against the glass. That's when she came face to face with that thing.

It was a horrid creature with wire hair that barely covered its wrinkled and nude body. The skeleton was malformed, arching and muscles were twisted into random knots throughout its back. There was no such thing as lips for this thing. Pointed and yellowed teeth were stuck into the burgundy and black gums of the creature, freshly coated with a layer of Arya's blood.

"Arya!" She heard Ivan yell through the barrier. He slammed his fist behind her, just as unable to get to her as she was to him. Trapped with this monster that now had a taste of her blood.

It licked its teeth with a grey ribbed tongue that Arya did not want to feel on her skin ever.

"Ivan, how to I get this thing away from me?" She yelled.

"Is it the rat?" He asked.

Arya snorted. "I'd never call this thing a rat, it's a monstrosity."

"You have to kill it, Ayra," he said, "It's the only way."

"Well fuck."

She was in no position to fight at that moment. She reached out and gripped the sword that had fallen to the ground beside her, pointing it at the creature in warning. It's glossed over eyes suggested that it could not see such warning, but at least it made Arya feel better. Curling her legs beneath her, she stood. It was not the most graceful ascension, but she was not there to look pretty, she just wanted to survive.

"Do not hesitate, strike it in it's head and get out of there!" Ivan ordered.

"And go back to the dark with the other creatures I can't see?" She protested.

"I swear on my life I will find you on the other side, you just have to trust me," he said.

She snorted, rolling her eyes. "Trust is short lived in my life."

Ivan didn't respond, his side of the crystal quiet. Taking a deep breath, Arya summoned every memory of Idoh's training she had. It wasn't a lot, most of it proved useless in Kulessa when every man she encountered in those dungeons were stronger and bigger than her.

Arya fixed her feet, angling herself so she was a smaller target for attack. The rat growled at her movement, shifting its hind legs like a cat preparing to pounce. The strange thing about this situation was not about the crystals, tunnel, or the fact that there was a whole functioning ecosystem beneath the manor where she lived, but that all Arya felt was anger.

Anger at this creature who was just trying to survive as she was in this hellscape. Unfortunately for this being, it was currently the target for those emotions.

Without a single slice of remorse, Arya did a quick swoop of her sword, the blade penetrating through the glossed over eye that once attempted to look at her. Pulling the sword out, the creature whined before slumping over. Arya cleaned the sword off on the body, flicking it in the air a few more times. With a new brewing determination and a building empowerment of anger, Arya limped her way out of the tunnel.

Ivan was not at the base of the tunnel as he had promised. What was there was a lit torch like the ones on the other side of the tunnel. It laid in a random spot a good toss away, lighting up the surrounding area. To Arya's horror, it was surrounded by more of those rat things.

They were multiple sizes and colors, but the one thing that was the same was their interest in the light. Like moths to a flame.

A hand wrapped around Arya's mouth, a small squeak of surprise coming from her before she tried pulling at the new foe.

"Keep quiet," Ivan whispered harshly. Arya stopped moving seeing a faint outline of shadows begin to consume them. Her heart pounded in her chest as she watched the light disappear and she was engulfed by the darkness.

Only, it wasn't dark.

The movements of things outside of the shadows lit up, pinging out to Arya in a florescent blue. She could see the outline of the rats, the strands of grass that moved around them, even small bugs that crawled below them. In this darkness, she could see.

"This is beautiful," she whispered.

Ivan shook his head. "This is a curse."

She didn't know what he meant, unable to ask as she was whisked over his shoulder without so much as a puff to signal it was difficult for him.

"Put me down," Arya hissed.

"Shut up or those things will attack us," Ivan grumbled.

"I don't care, put me down!"

Ivan threw her to the ground, his hand wrapping around her throat. It encompassed the entirety of it causing her to swallow. Why hadn't she noticed how large they were before? She saw the outline of his hood inching closer to her in the shadows, her eyes trying to find more beneath. She just wanted to see who this masked man was.

"Is that what you really want, Arya? To be the center of a mob attack?"

"Why do you care?" She spit.

Ivan growled, a sound Arya did not like. "Because you are mine."

"You gave me my ownership papers—."

"You think those pathetic papers would keep me from anything? You are to be my wife and you will listen."

Arya narrowed her eyes at him, her chin raising to defy any sort of bind he could try to put on her. "I am not your slave, your wife, sure, but never your slave."

She swore she could feel Ivan grin beneath his hood, though had no proof. "We'll see about that."

Arya cursed under her breath knowing she would not be the one to win this fight. Ivan began to move, the lines of his cloak flashing with each step he took. Arya followed, preferring to be with someone who knew where they were going. Even if he just lead her back to the manor, she was injured, tired, and emotionally exhausted. Not only that, but there were more questions than answers flowing through her mind.

Ivan stopped suddenly, turning to what seemed like nothing, only to reveal a mountain. Loose rocks fell around where Ivan dug, eventually removing a large rock with one hand and pulling out something from the hole. He shoved the object into Arya's chest causing her to stumble back as she clutched it. Ivan put back the rock as she examined it, finding it was a book.

"Next time you want something and cannot find it, ask."

"What is it?" Arya asked.

"The Story of Death."

9

Arya chased after Ivan once in the safety of the manor. She needed answers and more importantly, she needed company. The switch in her personality scared her more than she would like to admit. That person who slaughtered the rat was not her.

"I want to know what that place was!" Arya called to Ivan. She had lifted her skirts at this point, running through the halls the best she could with a wounded ankle. It did not look like he cared, in fact, it seemed he was mad she had gone down there in the first place.

"Hell, the Underworld," he replied gruffly.

Arya raised her brows, curious as to who this man really was. Sure, he saved her from the rat creatures, but he still bought her from Roderick, who, very obviously, liked this man. Roderick didn't like just anyone, it was only the perverse and dark of men he enjoyed the company of. Arya knew for certain, it wasn't just once that Roderick had let those same friends of his use her to their desires. The only rule was "don't kill the bitch". She got shivers just thinking of it, her pace slowing as she remembered the torture.

It was noticeable enough to where Ivan slowed, looking over his shoulder. "Is there a problem?"

Arya bit her lip before responding, "I need to know your intentions with me."

Ivan turned completely to her, the two standing only a foot apart yet it felt closer. In fact, Arya was getting dizzy, her vision swirling in the corners. She wouldn't falter though, not until she knew something of her soon-to-be husband.

"My intentions?" Ivan snorted, rolling his eyes at the statement. It felt like Arya was not worth his time to entertain. Fuck him for making her feel that way. "I intend to make you my wife and to have an heir. Was that not clear in the contract?"

"But why me?" She asked.

It was obvious to her that he was keeping something for himself, but she needed to know what. If anything, Arya just needed to understand why it was her that he had decided to take. Why not another human noble.

"Because," he said.

Arya waited for more of a response but he didn't offer anything.

"Because?" She scoffed. "Because is your only answer? What are you, a child? Can you not think of a better excuse than *because?*"

Why that single word irritated her was beyond comprehension. Were they not both adults? Were they not able to understand that this arrangement was conceived by the gods and the contract made it so that Arya was bound to him for at least ten years? Yet, the only thing he could tell her on why *she* was chosen was "because". What a fucking dick.

"It's all you need to know," Ivan said.

Arya rolled her eyes, popping her hip out and placing a hand on it. "What I need to know is who the fuck my husband is. I want to know why you chose me. I want to know why you have a hellscape beneath your home. I want to know why one of your staff is poisoning food, and why, of all things, am I the only one who can give you an heir." She approached Ivan, narrowing her eyes at him to attempt to intimidate the man. "Why did you choose a lowly Selkie woman who was raped and beaten before being starved and neglected? Who's to say I am even fertile after all that was done to me. How can you expect me to mother a child when I am scared of the outside world and the humans around me?"

She watched Ivan's gaze harden, not sure if Arya had gone too far with expressing her torment from the past. However, it was true and he needed to know. There were no secrets regarding her past.

Ivan lifted his hand, Arya preparing for the hit that would be coming. She flinched, closing her eyes and tensing to prepare for impact. Waiting, she felt silly as the time passed and there was no sting of his hand across her face.

Then, finally, she felt him on her skin. It was not a hard impact as she expected, in fact, it felt nice.

Arya relaxed as Ivan ran his hand over her cheek and across her jaw. As he got to her chin he took hold firmly. She opened her eyes quickly, watching as Ivan twisted his body so that he was leading her backwards. Her back hit a wall, letting out a puff of air from her lungs as the impact. His head was only inches from hers, the heat of his breath dancing on her skin.

"If I wanted someone else, I would've gotten them. I want you and only you, Arya." His thumb brushed over her bottom lip, mouth moving toward her ear. She felt the brush of his lips, getting a better idea of what this man looked like without seeing him. In her ear, he whispered, "I have waited too long for you to not be mine. No one will take you from me now."

Arya's heart pounded in her chest, mouth going dry as she leaned forward. That's when she felt it. His lips pressing softly against her cheek. Her entire world shifted, head spinning as she realized what she felt beyond that kiss.

Pain.

It was not the type of pain that hurt, but one of sorrow, envy, anger. The sort of pain that Arya dove into in those dungeons to get out of her mind for a little while. The one that allowed her to escape life as she knew it and harness the power she once believed to have forgotten. The same pain that was there when she killed that rat and led to her agreeing to marry a man she didn't know.

Pain.

Pain.

Pain.

She wrapped her arms around Ivan's neck, getting onto her toes to reach as he stood up, surprised. Refusing to let go of the embrace, Arya stood there, her head burrowing into Ivan's chest, tears coming down her cheeks.

"I wish I could make all of it go away," she whispered in a weak voice. "But I'm not even sure how to settle my own."

She heard Ivan let out a breath of surprise, Arya never letting go of him. That was when she felt his arms encompass her. It was not a tight squeeze, but one that felt cautious, as if she was a fragile piece of porcelain he was scared to break.

It was then she understood why Ivan chose her. He was lonely and in pain. He had first seen her with blood from a rat on her lips and frail from maltreatment. She was his project to keep himself sane, ignoring the pain that rolled through his body. Not healthy, sure, but she was okay with being his distraction. So long as Ivan kept her safe she would be his savior.

"We'll be married in a week tomorrow night, wash the blood from your skin." Ivan turned, leaving Arya stumbling back from the sudden absence of his embrace. Her skin became cold, missing the warmth he had provided her in those brief few seconds that had felt like years.

She watched him walk down the hall, disappearing around a corner before relaxing her shoulders.

"*Don't worry, love, you'll both be back together soon,*" Siion's voice echoed in her head.

"Fuck off, Siion." Arya growled her disapproval at the god infiltrating her mind once again. Wasn't anything sacred to them?

Clutching the book in her hand, Arya walked back toward her room. The one thing she was looking forward to was seeing Leif in that mirror again. Maybe this time she could talk to Winslet too.

Whatever happens, she did know that she needed to wash the blood that was caked on her body off. It was beginning to become uncomfortable. She just prayed that she never had to go into that river of blood again.

10

Arya stared at the entries, confused. She had never seen a book written in first person like this before. It felt gross reading, like she was eavesdropping on someone else's thoughts and desires. Arya fell back into her chair as she read from a distance. Her eyes felt heavy, but she was desperate for answers. Ones she had a feeling she would not find within this book.

The mirror was a failed attempt for contacting Leif, only her reflection looked back at her. She wondered how the magic of that mirror worked. If he had the control over it or if it was simply through the gods' will they spoke. It made her think of Idoh and Mies and Zephyr. What were they doing in that moment? Were they thinking of her? Was she ever a thought in their mind like she thought of them? Leif had told Arya to stay clear of Ivan, but why? He was the only one who was willing to help her. Sure, the marriage and baby clause was not ideal, but she would willingly help him with that if it meant her freedom. The gods wouldn't lie to her about that, Siion was supposedly the most trustworthy of the bunch.

Arya squeezed her eyes shut, pinching the bridge of her nose. Everything was so much, she just wanted to be freed. Outside the window of her room, the sky swirled with the threat of rain. She didn't like the look of it, worried that the dreaded thunder and lightning would come with it.

"What does a girl got to do around here to get a drink?" She muttered. It was not really something she wanted, but the stress and anxiety that filled her when thinking of what tomorrow would bring drove her to the beverage.

The marriage was coming sooner than she wanted. Something she didn't know if she was ready for. Just like her dream, a partnership was being thrust upon her without her feelings being considered. Would Ivan be okay with waiting to consummate their union? Fuck, the simple idea of her enjoying sex was not something she could imagine. It was only a year before that her body was pimped out by Roderick, his little friends doing anything and everything they pleased to her.

She didn't want to have no say in intimacy. It was important to her that Ivan understood that, yet she was obligated to provide him a child. Just one, but the only way children are made is through intimate situations she wanted no part in.

A headache began to form along the crown of her head from the vicious thoughts. Her joints stiffened and mouth was dry. The rain began to fall, pattering against her window with a warning roll of thunder. Arya jumped from her seat, pinning herself in the corner of her room, guarded by the desk and night table. A flash of lightning illuminated the room, the candle going out so darkness consumed her.

If anything was a testament to the warning she was receiving for the oncoming wedding that was supposed to happen, this was it. Another hit of lightning and boom of thunder shook the manor and Arya couldn't help but scream.

She rocked her body, the self-soothing gesture not working as her fear made her legs go weak and mind go numb to anything but the chaos of the weather. Her breathing quickened and her heart pounded, mind finding each shadow on the wall a threat ready to destroy her for good.

At the next flash of lightning, Arya swore she saw Roderick in the room with her. That caused a scream.

Fight or flight kicked in, legs moving before her mind could catch up. She hopped over the bed, rushing to the door and ran down the halls. Tears clouded her vision, unable to clearly see where it was she was going. The flashes of lightning made her body move faster, legs pump harder, running into walls as she attempted to escape the storm that threatened her sanity.

"Arya!"

The voice was worried. It was not the same lurking darkness that she had come to recognize as Ivan's, but something softer hid through the concern. Arya halted, body swaying at the sudden motion. She turned, looking at the darkened figure of Ivan in the faintly illuminated corridor. He held a candle in front of himself, the cloak she was becoming accustomed to missing from his body.

Shadows still hid his face, but she could see the soft gray of his shirt and the suspenders that held up his pants. His hands were clear, a single blue ring decorating his left hand. Lightning flashed again, this time, showing something behind Ivan.

It crawled slowly over the floor on all fours. Silent and unnatural. It would've almost been mistaken as human, if not for the misplaced and backwards joints, and hairless, loose white skin. Somehow, even in the darkness, the creature was illuminated enough where Arya could see the features of it, even though the darkness consumed Ivan. It rose up on its back legs behind him, mouth opening in a vertical slit where two spider-like fangs protruded. Arya's eyes opened in horror, body once again moving upon instinct.

The window behind Ivan shattered with Arya's summoning of her element. The glass shards were carried by the stream she created from the droplets, littering the thick skin of the creature trying to assault her soon to be husband. It howled out an ungodly sound, something mixed between a dying cat and angry whale.

Ivan twisted at the sound, rushing forward to place himself between Arya and the creature.

"How the fuck—."

He wasn't able to finish his sentence before the thing advanced on them, leaking a neon white goo from the wounds Arya created. Ivan growled, a sound that was unearthly and did not sound human. The shadows around the room wavered as if threatened by the noise, the beast stopped its oncoming advance.

Ivan smirked, the first time Arya was able to see it in the light. There was something primal about the anger behind that smile, and, strangely, it invited her in. It was a smile she'd seen before, one that haunted her waking hours. She stepped forward, clutching the back of Ivan's shirt. It was a simple move on her part, a play at victim when her mind could not handle being the hero for much longer. Not when the storm crashed around them and there was a shattered window thanks to her quick movements to buy Ivan some time.

A quick huff of air left his nose, almost as if he was laughing at the idea of her hanging on him. She ignored him, turning her attention back to the gangly creature in front of them.

"Friend of yours?" She asked with a quiver in her voice.

Ivan clicked his tongue. "Wouldn't call him a friend per se, but comes from that lovely hole in the ground from yesterday."

Arya rolled her eyes. "I wouldn't have guessed, not like he is oozing glowing blood or anything."

113

That got Ivan to chuckle before he gave his full focus to the threat in the room. Arya knew she wasn't hallucinating when she started seeing the shadows move around them for a second time. They crawled off the wall like undead beasts, inching over the ground toward the monster. It seemed to know what was happening, backing away from the slowly approaching darkness. Every drop of glowing blood the shadows touched was muted, the light disappearing from the eye, leaving a random blob of goo.

The first shadow clutched onto the foot of the monster, causing the beast to howl again. This time, sounding in pain. Arya was horrified as she continued to watch, seeing each separate shadow latch onto the beast and slowly absorb all its color. The light within the creature began to die, fading until there was nothing left but a muted husk of the once vicious threat.

It fell to the floor with a thump, light gone and the illumination from the ongoing storm exposing the body to Arya. Anger filled her. Not just any anger, but the type that filled her body in boiling water, forcing tears to her eyes and a roar to her throat. She ran toward the creature, using her bare fists to strike the monster. The sickly flesh gave way to her impacts, splitting and coating her skin in black. She knew the thing was dead. Knew there was no reason to continue the torture of the corpse, but she couldn't stop.

A hand gripped her shoulder. Arya lashed back, screaming with the action as tears flicked from her chin. This wasn't how her life was supposed to be. She was supposed to be with Idoh, Leif, Zephyr, Winslet, and Mies. She was supposed to have healed from the traumas forced upon her. Have her first consensual kiss. Experience friendship for the first time. Yet she was there. In that fucking manor with this stranger who dared to touch her while she was getting out all her frustration.

"Don't touch me!" Arya screamed at him. She stood, allowing her damp hair to cling to her skin. Her fists, covered in the blood of the creature, clenched at her side. That boiling inside her was quickly losing its momentum, being replaced instead with the guilt of what she was doing. Lashing out at someone who didn't do anything to her.

Arya's shoulders began to slump, shaking with her effort to try and control her tears, but it was too late. They flowed down her cheeks, her mouth opening to let in a gasping breath. Through her blurry tears, she saw Ivan take confident steps forward. Arya stepped back, slipping on the blood that had leaked onto the floor. Gravity was against her, pausing her hysterics to have momentary fear. The fall didn't come, however. Instead, Arya found herself clutched against the firm chest of Ivan, his arms wrapping around her like she would try to hurt him if he allowed the smallest amount of freedom.

"Let me go," Arya begged, not having the energy to fight him, and partly not wanting to.

"No, not when I just got you back." His arms tightened around her.

She must have been mistaking it, but there was an accent. One she was familiar with...

Arya pulled back slowly from Ivan, looking up at the darkness that obscured his face. Her hand reached up, disappearing behind the fog, connecting with a face. She closed her eyes, feeling along his squared jaw, fingers brushing over his lips. Reaching higher to feel the soft fluff of hair hidden from her.

"Who are you?"

Ivan grabbed her hand, kissing it behind the mask before returning it to her. "You'll see." There was a pause, like he didn't want to part with her. Like he was eager to explain everything to her. Instead, he said, "Be ready to travel, we're going on an adventure tomorrow."

Without waiting for her reaction, Ivan parted, leaving Arya alone with the corpse of the creature from the darkness.

11

Estelle had assisted Arya in getting ready. The dresses were still too loose on her body from the malnutrition she'd endured. It was only small amounts of food she could consume, so long as Estelle wasn't the one making it. Arya waited outside the manor, closing her eyes as she felt the breeze toss her hair. She longed for the moment when she could swim again, feeling the breeze that held the essence of salt and sea on it. Humans wandered about their duties, none paying much mind to Arya as she stood there. The carriage had been prepared for them, the horses nipping at the other's neck. Trunks were piled onto the back of the buggy, telling Arya she would not be coming back anytime soon. A long journey ahead of them.

Arya was not told of their destination, just that she was to get ready. Paranoid, Arya packed a small bag with her coat and a knife she'd snuck from the dining table after breakfast. A meal that Ivan did not join her in. She knew there wouldn't be a large chance of escaping him, something that still rang in the back of her mind. If they were close to Teielmor, Arya didn't know if she would continue to travel with this band of human-fae people she didn't fully trust.

"That knife won't help you in the long run," Rook's bored voice said from behind her.

Arya turned, seeing the woman sitting on the railing of the stairs, swinging her leg and eating a very red apple. As her teeth sank into the fruit, it gushed a bloody burgundy liquid, dripping down her lips. It was not something Arya had ever seen before, making her nervous that Rook would be joining them.

Much to her relief, Embry exited the servant's entrance, rolling his eyes with a smile as he saw Rook. "You just had to scare her, didn't you?"

Rook winked at Arya, blowing her a bloody air kiss before jumping down to the main floor. Embry spoke softly to Rook, Arya barely making out their whispers, though Rook did not look pleased.

"He's fucking insane if he thinks we'll make it past the check points," Rook growled. Embry looked up to Arya who was not being sly in how she was watching them. Rook turned her head, staring daggers at Arya. Embry pulled Rook away a few steps further, his face all business, showing why Ivan kept him around.

"Fine, but I'm not happy with it," Rook puffed, stomping past Arya and slamming the doors behind her.

Embry walked up to Arya, providing her company she didn't ask for.

"What was that about?" She asked.

Embry sighed. "Rook is not a fan of traveling, and Ivan is making her go with him."

"Where are we going, exactly?" Arya questioned as casually as she could.

"I don't know. Rook just went to see where she is needed to scout." Embry leaned against the railing, crossing his arms.

"You don't know shit, do you?" Arya challenged with a laugh. She'd assumed Embry would know more given his appearance, but it wasn't like that at all. He was just as clueless as Arya was in Ivan's intentions.

Embry raised a brow at her. "What makes you say that?"

"The fact that you're here as a messenger yet your message is go see the boss. The way you were scared of the gods visiting. That nervous twitch over your right eye like you want to say more but can't." Arya pointed out.

Embry opened and closed his mouth a few times. She was right though, and knew as much when Embry let out a frustrated grunt. Estelle was tight lipped, Embry didn't know anything, Ivan was secretive, and Arya wasn't sure she could trust Rook after the book incident. She just wanted answers, and eagerly wanted her freedom. The days couldn't pass by quick enough.

A crow flew from one of the manor windows, squawking to alert them of its presence. Embry and Arya looked up, watching the bird fly in a circle before it took off toward the road. Embry nodded, somehow taking that as his signal to load Arya in. He offered her his hand as he descended a few flights of stairs. Arya did not accept it, not seeing any worth in his friendship when he didn't know anything. Loneliness was not something she was unused to, so why be friendly with the employees of her owner?

Arya's door was opened as she walked toward it, a human setting up stairs to assist her into the carriage. She moved to the furthest side of the sitting area, assuming that Estelle, Embry and Ivan were to be joining her. Rook as well if she were to be a scout. Only, the door closed behind her. Her brows furrowed, pushing aside the curtains to see Ivan talking with Embry and Estelle on the steps. Their expressions were grim, but Embry nodded like a soldier receiving orders. Whatever was going on, Arya was getting increasingly nervous.

She pat the bag around her body, assuring herself that her skin was still with her. There was something else going on that she was not being told, which seemed to be a habit for all the people around her in life. Then they wonder why she has horrible trust issues. Arya rolled her eyes, scooting to the middle of the carriage where she slumped, crossing her arms. Fuck everything that has happened to her, and screw Ivan for forcing her into this marriage contract with a child clause. She didn't want to touch him with a five foot pole in that moment, even if he did save her from a strange monster from the depths of his manor.

The carriage began to move, Arya slyly taking a look out the window to see Ivan riding on the back of a black horse. She huffed, realizing that even if she was angry with him, she wasn't going to be able to do anything to express that to him being separated. It was going to be a long ass journey and she would have to deal with this shit on her own. God, what she wouldn't do for a monster to fight at that moment.

* * *

Idoh was covered in blood, his teeth shown in a deadly snarl as he decapitated another human who dared to attempt to attack him. His swords were ignited with flames against the setting sun, illuminating him and the bodies he stood upon. Too many men and fae have died for this stupid war, but he had one purpose for being on the front lines. He was away from Zephyr and his continuous bitching.

Idoh had left the same day Leif and Winslet did. He couldn't take it anymore in the castle that once felt like his home. Now, it was an empty husk without Arya there. It was the longest time they'd ever experienced without her, and he wasn't about to sit and stew in his own emotions like Mies or Zephyr did. He was loyal to his flame, and without her, he would burn down each human until found. The frontlines was just a starting point.

Emeric had disappeared after Idoh requested his help, that lowlife taking his freedom without a care for Arya just as Idoh knew he would deep down. It was a lost cause now, blood and death the only thing keeping Idoh occupied with his life. One battle after another, his magic growing with each kill, anger fuming when he thought about what Arya was going through in Kulessa. What these grubby humans were subjecting her to.

He had promised to protect her in that fucking dream, and now look at him. Failing at a promise he never was able to deliver but still wanted to.

Thunder cracked through the sky, Idoh looking up to see the dark clouds that began to cover the half lit moon. The sprinkling of rain came soon after, hitting his skin and sizzling upon impact. He growled at the thunder, knowing it was Zephyr's favorite way to scare people in submission, but never him.

Walking to the river that parted the two societies, Idoh grabbed a handful of the salt water, washing it over his face. He smelled of sweat and iron, burnt flesh from the few wounds he had gained throughout the battle that he cauterized himself to keep going. There was no time to pity the poor work of those burns that were quickly turning to scars. Not in the middle of battle.

He took off the armor over his body, stripping off his top to further evaluate himself for anymore wounds that he could have missed with the adrenaline. Idoh closed his eyes, sliding his fingers delicately over his muscled abdomen. He checked for any indents or pain when touched, avoiding the three lacerations he'd already treated on either side and across his chest.

That was until a cooling burn erupted from his back, throwing Idoh to the ground. He hissed on all fours, twisting his neck to see the culprit of the burn that he faced. Behind him was a woman he was all too familiar with. Fyorr.

"I have news for you," she said without much care for the wound she'd created on his back. Her blue flamed sword burned away the blood that he unwillingly donated to the goddess.

"A little warning next time," Idoh growled, composing himself as he stood to face the woman.

She was shorter than he was, taking a humanoid form so no one else on the battlefield would suspect a goddess in their presence. Especially the goddess of war and flame herself. She tossed her silky blue hair over her shoulder, evaluating Idoh as if he was a conquest from her most recent battle.

"Why would I warn you? Pain drives a battle, son, don't forget how well you fight when thinking of your dear Arya."

It was supposed to taunt him. He'd dealt with Fyorr enough to know her tricks and tactics. Anger couldn't help but boil in his gut, Idoh forcing it away as he returned his attention to the real questions he should be asking. "What do you want?"

Fyorr smiled, her pointed teeth the only sign of her true form, beside the red dragon eyes.

"I've come with an opportunity for you, though the others might also be going to their special creatures as well," Fyorr said casually. "Arya will be close soon. A fortnight, if they make haste."

123

Idoh's anger extinguished when hearing the news. Instead, a small cooling flame ignited in his core, flickering with the memory of her. The reason he was fighting. Fyorr laughed at his sudden change and softness, causing Idoh to replace his outer shield. Fyorr went on her tiptoes, cupping Idoh's cheek like a mother would her son, only, Fyorr gripped hard. Her face hardened, accompanied by the menacing smile she held onto.

"This is her last lifetime, conquer her heart like I know you can. Leif has the upper hand this time with gifts Arya got from Raena. The dream Lir gave you all to insight this bullshit is to be used to your advantage. Do not fuck this up."

"This game you all play is fucked up," Idoh hissed, pushing Fyorr's hand away from his face.

The insult only made the goddess smile. "You really want Arya to be with Zephyr? Be a queen and have all her needs ignored? Or Mies? The drunkard he had become since Lir's interruption on his life. What about Leif, who'll use his magic on Arya to help her fall in love with him. You're at a disadvantage, my sweet stupid boy."

Idoh looked away, wishing for once he could love Arya without the pressure from gods. However, he knew everything Fyorr was saying was true to some extent. It's happened before. Zephyr especially.

"I'll be ready," Idoh said with hesitation. It was not a matter of getting Arya to love him that he needed, it was the knowledge that she was safe in Teielmor with him.

Idoh glanced at Fyorr once again, finding the goddess had disappeared. Vacant from the spot she once stood. His head pounded with the lack of water and nutrition he'd received while fighting, and the incoming stress of fighting for Arya's affection once again. New place, new time, new life, same wonderful woman he'd fallen for time and time again. Fyorr had shown him as much, though he knew Arya would never remember like he did. Something that made it harder to express his desire and dedication to her.

Idoh looked into the water, seeing his faint reflection upon it. "Water and fire makes the most wonderful steam, don't you think?"

12

Ivan didn't have much care for the horses this time around.
The journey was long, riding through the night and into the
early morning. It didn't make sense that he had insisted they
stop that first time, yet risk harming the horses on this
journey.

Arya pressed her forehead to the window as she
watched the rain come down around them. It was nice to be
able to experience the storm without fear of the thunder. She
cracked the window, summoning a few of the drops to twirl
in the air, practicing her ever growing magic. It was strange,
the ability to feel her magic grow each time she used it, the
power flowing through her blood like nothing could stop her
once she reached her full potential.

The droplets danced in the air, hopping between
themselves. More of the rain came to collect into a stream of

never ending water. Hair on the back of her neck stood as she summoned from the liquid. Arya watched with interest as the strange metallic sheen coated the water. Then, an eye. It was sudden, the lid flicking open to expose a white glowing orb, then another. Scales formed on the end of the creature, shifting and moving with the flexibility of the water. Arya lowered her hands, witnessing the serpent shift from floating, to slithering right above her dress. It solidified, curling with its finned tail tucked in the center of the vortex.

Arya raised her brows, leaning forward to observe the creature. Did she just create life? Her hand reached out to the being, its triangular head dipping down like it wanted her to pet it. She smiled, laughing a bit at the eagerness of her new friend. One she could trust as it would not talk and did not have reason to betray her.

As she touched the creature, a pulsing of magic came from the contact, the snake's eyes glowing brighter. It worked its way up her arm, sliding with the summoning of her power. It throbbed in the most pleasant way, relaxing the muscles that had been tense through the journey. It wrapped around her neck, squeezing slightly. Arya allowed her eyes to flutter shut and leaned back into the carriage seat.

Then it stopped.

Arya furrowed her brows, attempting to feel where the snake had gone. To her shock, there was nothing left of it. A slight residue appeared where it had last been, the rest of the creature gone from touch. She was disappointed in the realization, upset that her new friend was gone when she was having such a good time with it.

She attempted to draw more water out of the storm again, managing to create that swirling stream, but unable to form that same creature. No eyes came from the liquid, neither did scales.

"It won't happen again, you only manage to make one serpent in your lifetime."

Arya dropped her focus, the water splashing over the ground, soaking the floor. She cursed, staring at the intruder in her carriage. Unremarkably, this person seemed like an average fish monger. He was straight off the Asitan coast. His grey trousers were held up by suspenders over his large belly, royal blue shirt sleeves rolled up to his elbows. His white hair was thinning, yet kept long and tied back in a blue ribbon as was tradition for Selkie men. Braided bracelets decorated his wrists, old and worn like they had been there for centuries.

"Assuming by the way you entered my carriage, you're a god?" Arya greeted coldly.

The man smiled, his cheeks flushed red flush. "I am. Lir, god of the Selkies."

Arya watched as he extended a hand to her, his blue, faded tattoos of sea creatures flexing. Even as an older man, he looked well built. A man from the sea, as her father would say. Reluctantly, Arya shook his hand, finding it calloused and rough, not the hands she'd expect from a god.

"What are you doing here, Lir?" Arya asked, nervous this was going to be another trick or proposition.

"I've come to give you answers. I know you have many questions, so I am going to provide you with what I can," he said.

Answers? How could she trust this man—er god—with anything?

"First, I want to tell you that everything I say must stay between us. You must not tell the others, especially Ivan or Rook," Lir said, "you're not supposed to know to keep the playing field even."

"Playing field?" Arya asked, unable to help herself.

Lir nodded. "Centuries ago, the other gods and I were bored with fae and humanity. There were always wars, traditions, needs and wants that were so basic." He rolled his eyes, sitting back in the chair. "Eventually, Raena came up with a game. One that I didn't like if I was honest. One woman was chosen and between the other provinces, she was to choose which person she wanted as her mate."

Arya raised her brows, leaning back into her seat. This was starting to sound very familiar from things she had experienced in the dream.

"When the fun was done, the choice was not favored by the other gods, and the winner gloated most arrogantly."

"Let me guess, Raena?" Arya scoffed.

Lir shook his head. "Xarius." The god of air? That was a shock, yet knowing how much praise she'd given Zephyr it wasn't a shock. If that man was anything like the sweet man she'd experienced in her dream, then she wouldn't blame the girl for her choice.

"So what? The gods can't take a sore loser?" Arya asked.

Lir snorted. "They are gods, my dear, they don't lose well. So, finding this to be more fun than I anticipated, I

129

suggested we go again. Once the five souls died, we relocated them into new bodies. Their parents were influenced by the names of the first, and thus created a cycle. However, there was a slight change. The male candidates could remember their past, but something happened with the woman where I misplaced her past memories, making her brand new in the process again."

Arya narrowed her eyes, the story becoming menacing. Gods were playing with lives that weren't there's to fuck with.

"It became another game, this time ending with a Salamander winner," Lir smiled as if remembering a fond memory. "But after that, there was the war between humans and fae, splitting the group among the battlefield. *That*," Lir emphasized, "is where things got good. It became about heroism, grief, death, torture, a real prize. So we teamed up with another god, Siion. She created 'enemies' for the group. They too were reincarnated, the woman, like you, not knowing all her memories until later. Thrilling."

Arya scowled, narrowing her eyes at the god. "Like me?"

Lir's smile vanished, open as if he hadn't meant to say those words exactly. Arya, however, was pissed. She sucked on her teeth, tilting her head to the side with a venomous stare. "You're telling me that you watched as I was held captive in Kulessa, tortured, raped, mutilated, and broken to the point where I cannot have the pleasure of touch without worry of being hurt again. You made it so my life had been spent a slave and did *nothing* to help me? After

I prayed for saving? After I *begged* to die in that fucking cell? It was just fun for you?"

He pulled the collar of his shirt, squeezing his lips tight. Obviously, the god was oblivious to how this conversation was to turn out. She didn't care about the past lives or the need to be matched to one of the men she dreamt about. She did care about being left to the hands of the humans.

"So why are you telling me this now?" Arya demanded, lifting her chin.

Lir sighed. "This is your last reincarnation. The last go round. Whoever you choose in this life is going to be the last person you choose, meaning the gods are all cheating and telling their boys what to do."

"I'm not here to court the gods, Lir." Arya allowed the hatred to burn through her voice. "I am here to find my safety and heal from the bullshit you watched me go through. If you think for one minute I am going to be courted willingly, you're sorely mistaken. If you, or any of the other gods, try to influence me to do something I'm not comfortable with, I will go after all of you."

Lir shook his head. "You're mortal, what could you do?"

"Just because I'm mortal does not mean I can't make the gods pay. I learned a lot from my human friends, Lir, remember that."

Arya watched the man swallow, clearly intimidated by her. It was strange, the power she felt from threatening him allowed the flicker of that snake to appear again.

Emotion was unleashed with Arya now. Romance was dead unless deserved. Sweet talks and fancy outings were not an option to win her over now. No, Arya wanted something more. She wanted revenge. Death. Torture of the people who wronged her. She wanted to taste the blood of Roderick as she sat on his throne with all the men who assaulted her screaming in agony.

"Go away now," Arya ordered, done with the conversation with this phony of a god. She was too angry. Too fucked up and broken to not attack him right then.

He vanished in front of her eyes, Arya gritting her teeth as she sat back in her seat. The visits from Siion and Raena were understandable now. Raena played on Arya's need for familiarity, giving the mirror so she could speak with Leif. Then Siion with her contract of marriage in exchange for freedom.

Arya let out a breath, thinking about what Lir said. He mentioned the other gods being in on it. Each of the elements represented, but why did Siion come to her and tell her to marry Ivan? Arya's leg bounced as she thought of everything. The darkened room where Ivan had rescued her. The monsters that lived beneath his manor. The strange friends he kept that had magic of some kind but Arya couldn't place them as fae. Was it possible Siion had another race of humans that she didn't know about? The Lux was supposed to mean light and demented cleansing of the humans, but what if there was more to it?

Arya looked behind her, spotting Ivan trotting along on his horse behind her carriage, disregarding the rain that came down on him. His hood shielded his face, refusing to let Arya see who was beneath. What he was. If he had come from that place below the manor, is it possible he was just as gruesome as the monsters she'd faced from there?

What the fuck did she agree to?

As soon as she gets answers to some of her questions, several others pop up. Arya wanted to know things for certain, not to have stories told to her by gods and influenced by humans. She was done with trust, finished with that pathetic mannerisms that came with being a prisoner by anyone who had her. Arya was a prize that multiple gods were looking to win, so it was time she acted like it... and that started in Kulessa.

13

The carriage pulled into a tavern Arya could've only pictured in a nightmare. The windows were boarded up, the ones exposed left cakes in soot and mud. The rain had stopped hours back, Arya's mood darkening significantly, eager to tell anyone a piece of her mind. As the carriage stopped in front of the tavern's door, she saw the footman run inside before returning to speak to Ivan. She strained by the carriage window to listen to their conversation, throwing herself back when she failed to do so. She had half the mind to throw open the carriage door herself, and prove that she was still a force to be reckoned with. Fuck, it had been hours since she had been able to stretch her legs.

The footman opened the door for her, refusing to look her in the eye. Arya rolled them, taking it upon herself to exit without the help of a man. Ivan dismounted his horse,

134

walking forward to escort Arya inside, but she decided to ignore him. She strutted forward with determination through the mud and grime, entering the establishment. Humans scurried around, preparing for their arrival, except for one. A gruff bartender polished a glass, narrowing his eyes as she entered. A brief tingle of familiarity floated over her, a sense of community with this stranger.

Arya looked upon his arms, worn with scars and faded tattoos. She had known those inked marks, however. She'd seen them on the sailors in the markets and docks by her house growing up. The blue of his eyes mixed with the fading blond of his greying hair did not lessen the beauty he held.

Without a second thought, Arya walked right up to the man, sitting on a stool in front of him.

"What can I get ya?" His Selkie accent had not faded. Arya smiled, putting her bag on top of the counter and opening it enough to show him the contents inside. Including her skin. His eyes widened, forcing the bag closed quickly before leaning in toward her. "Are you insane? Showin' that is your death 'ere."

Arya buttoned her bag closed, hanging it at her side. "Who has yours?"

The man stiffened, continuing to stare at the pristine glass he held. It was like he was scared. Arya wondered if he was in a similar predicament as she had been. Forced to serve and those scars a part of his discipline.

Arya leaned forward, placing a coin on the bar. "Give me something strong and information written down."

The man nodded, turning to the liquor on display behind him. The drink he made smoked and sizzled reminding her of the marriage she'd had in the dream. It was how she felt Fintan's drink tasted. It became a red color, bubbling from the core, something she hadn't seen in many years. A tang of homesickness riddled her insides, squirming around like a worm that refused to let her forget that she was still alone.

He set the drink on top of a napkin, the writing barely visible beneath the concoction. Arya took a sip, focusing on the writing beneath. "Grey hair, woman, owner". She picked up the cloth, dabbing her mouth with it as Ivan came behind her.

"What the fuck was that?" He scowled.

Arya ignored him, smiling to the Selkie man in front of her. "Do you have anything to eat? I'm starved."

The man nodded, retreating away from her and Ivan. As soon as he was away, Ivan slid into the seat beside Arya, facing her. He was expecting something from her, but he wouldn't get it. She was done being his little plaything. His to keep information from.

"I want you to buy that man off his owner," Arya said in a low voice so no others could overhear.

"*Buy* him?" Ivan scoffed.

Arya looked at him, face shielded again by his hood and a slight reflection of a silver mask. "That man is a Selkie. His skin is trapped by the woman with grey hair."

Ivan snorted, leaning back in the chair with his arms crossing. "What do I get in return?"

136

"You asking that is truly diabolical. He is a fae in need of help. *My* people. If you don't help him, I will without you, and I will not stop at just stealing his coat back, *dear husband,*" Arya hissed, leaning close to Ivan with a sinister smile. "You gave me my freedom, let me assist him in getting his."

"He's a man," Ivan laughed, "How do you know he doesn't want to be here?"

Arya couldn't stop the fury from encompassing her. She watched as her hand rose, slamming into Ivan's masked face so hard the piece of silver fell to the floor, his body slumped to the side. She summoned the water from a barrel to the side. It slid over the top of the bar, creeping into Ivan's hood where she commanded it to choke him. His sputtering coughs told her it had listened, his hands going to wrap around his hidden skin.

"Listen, Ivan. I like you, but let's get one thing straight. Gender doesn't matter when it comes to my people. We have been tormented and abused because of our weakness. I have my power back, and whether you help me or not, I will avenge those who were kept and tortured by humans just like I was. Man, woman, it doesn't matter to me."

"Who the fuck are you?" He sputtered through a wheezy voice.

Arya smiled, patting his cheek over his hood. "Arya fucking Abano."

She swore she could see a glimmer of his eyes through the darkness beneath his hood before she turned away with her new friend's arrival. He came with a plate of bread, stew, and cut fruit, obviously special care and thought put into the meal. Arya nodded her thanks, digging into the first meal she'd had in hours and devouring it. She hadn't realized how hungry she was, not caring that the meat was tough and the fruit was half rotten. Shit, she'd gone weeks without moldy bread before, so this was a step up for her—and it wasn't poisoned.

"What's your price?" Ivan asked with a hard tone.

"The lady already paid," the man said.

"No, for your servitude."

The question was asked loudly, drawing the attention of the matron of the bar. She waddled up, her skirts hiked so that her peg leg could be shown and her bosom out to attract any poor soul who wanted a quick fuck. She may have been pretty when she was younger, but age did not compliment her features like it would have a fae woman.

"Sir, this 'ere is my husband. He's no servant," the wench lied through smiling teeth.

Arya pursed her lips, raising her brows with the statement. This unsettled the woman, her weight shifting from her solid foot to the wooden peg and back. As if trying to convince them, she wrapped around the bar, kissing the man on the cheek. He stood still, allowing her to do what she wished upon him, neutralized by years of torment and hopelessness.

"So why is it he is behind the counter and you are up front greeting guests?" Ivan asked. He did not show any signs of Arya's previous threats, acting like the stone hearted man she knew him to be.

Arya didn't know much of human culture when it came to outside the castle walls. She assumed all human men were heads of households, keeping their women safe until it came down to selling them for whatever was needed. It was assumed they were thrown into marriages for money, as Arya had seen it done time and time again at court, but she didn't know for sure if it was the same further away from the capital's reach.

The woman opened her mouth to respond, closing it when she knew the lie was not going to pass with them. Arya heard some shuffling from above her, seeing two teens with blue eyes and blond hair watching the interaction. She wondered if the woman had bore his children, though they would only be humans since they were not born in the province of Asita. Human children or half breeds? Phobus had not been born in Dunia yet was confirmed to be a half breed in her dream... was it possible there were a lot more half breed children of fae than she originally thought? Was there even a place for them? Not fully fae, so dismissed from Teielmor, yet still fae enough to be used in Kulessa like she had been. It was not a battle she knew the answer for. A place where either side was punishment for these creatures who did not ask to be born.

"He is mine, for all rights and purposes as far as the laws of Kulessa state," the woman objected, narrowing her eyes at Arya. "Same as yours there."

Arya grit her teeth, attempting to keep her anger minimal for the sake of the children watching.

"That wasn't the question," Ivan grumbled. "How much for him?"

The woman was quiet, contemplating too long for Arya's liking. "Fine, we'll take them instead. Half breeds suit our purpose better." She turned to Ivan, mouth agape. "They're young, good for the castle staff, and whatever else Roderick would like to do with the girl."

It was a bluff, hoping the woman would treasure her children more than the man who had helped produce them.

"Seven gold for him and his papers," the woman said in a rush. "You can have his skin an' everythin'."

At least she wasn't a horrible mother.

Ivan placed seven gold pieces onto the counter. The idea he had that sort of money shouldn't have shocked Arya as much as it did, he did buy her off Roderick and then told her about the manor's renovations. Still, she looked at the glittering pieces like they were rare gems.

"I'll go with you to the office to sign over paperwork," Ivan said, rising from his chair. The woman nodded, swallowing hard as she gently picked up the pieces like they would break at the slightest touch. Arya looked up to the children who had been watching, both missing from the balcony they had once stood on. The man, however, had tears in his eyes.

He leaned over the counter, allowing himself to take deep shaking breaths. It was strange to see, someone just like her, trapped in a place and forced into slavery because of his

140

skin, freed. She had not felt the same when given her papers. Had lost trust in everyone, yet here was this sailor, crying before her because she was letting him go.

"What is your name?" Arya asked gently.

He looked up to her, a single drip marking its way down his cheek from the corner of his eye. "Porter Marina, may I ask yours?"

Arya nodded, holding out her hand to shake. "I am Arya Abano, lost daughter of Asita."

* * *

As was expected, when Ivan returned with the documentation to prove ownership of Porter and his skin, they were not welcomed to stay at the tavern for the night. Porter was allowed to ride in the carriage with Arya, who handed him his skin and the meaningless human document that proved he now owned himself. Porter was an interesting man, telling Arya about his childhood on the ocean and stories of sea monsters he'd seen. Each of his faded tattoos related to some experience he had while at sea, Arya devoured the new tales like she was a child sneaking sweets. She had learned that Porter hailed from the southern isles of Asita, only ending up in Kulessa upon his ship being captured by human pirates. He didn't know what happened to his crew, where they were after he was sold at an auction to the wench that kept him. He confirmed the children were his and he had no feelings toward them. They were only reminders of the criminal acts upon him.

Arya felt a connection to Porter, allowing him to know some of her story, leaving out the gods and influenced courting they were forcing her to be a part of. She did tell him of her restraint to trust, but her unwillingness to let any other fae be trapped in Kulessa.

"If I may say, Miss Arya, you did what a lot of others wouldn't dare to," Porter said, giving her a weak smile. "I lost all hope and expected to die in that tavern until you came."

Arya nodded, biting her lip. "The thing is, I can't find myself through the torment I was put through. I was barely into adolescence when I was tortured. I don't know who I am, and I know what is wrong and right, so I guess me saving you is a bit selfish."

Porter snorted, shaking his head. "I have never thought I'd hear someone call themselves selfish for doing something selfless."

Arya opened and closed her mouth, unable to deny him. He reminded her of her father, his emotions worn on his sleeve, yet he also reminded her of herself. The way he was so grateful even though he didn't know her. Assuming she was his savior when Arya wasn't even sure if she did something to save him or to satisfy her need for company. It was the same, very real, feelings she had when surrounded by her friends in her dream. That twinge of guilt rattled through her gut, threatening her with the ball of emotion that formed in her throat.

"Miss Arya, may I ask you something?" Arya looked up to him, nodding as she was worried any verbal confirmation would show her emotions she tried to keep hidden. "May I stay with you? I may be old, but my loyalty to you is unbreakable."

"I'd like that," she whispered. It was a different situation with Porter that allowed Arya to relax. She was with another Selkie, a man who knew of her troubles as he had the same ones. The one thing she remembered from her childhood was the loyalty of Asita sailors. Especially for other Selkies. Having someone in her corner specifically would be detrimental to her success in getting them back to Teielmor. Getting to safety.

The ride was silent from then on, Arya allowing herself to fall asleep on the bench of the carriage. Her dreams were filled with swimming seals and the aged faces of her parents and brother. Three people she missed more than anything.

Her dreams of water and seals were quickly changed, however. Her mind was consumed in darkness of shadows, flashes of purple and red bouncing back and forth.

"Hello?" she called into the cavern of darkness.

Arya attempted to move her feet, finding it difficult. She looked down, seeing the heaviness of water to her knees. Only this water was not deep navy as she was used to, reflecting red and staining her white dress as she attempted to move forward.

"Hello!" She called out again. This time, her call was greeted with screaming. Horrible, threatening screams of battle and pain.

"Is this what you wanted," a voice hissed, not one she recognized from her head. "The destruction. The torture of all your people? Is that your goal?"

"Who's there?" Arya responded, stopping her movement to look around. The voice came from all directions, with no body to connect to it.

"Prepare for death, then."

Arya was ripped from the dream, sitting up in a panic and panting. Her hands balled into fists, posed in front of her like the assailant would be there, waiting for her to wake. Instead, the silent bump of the carriage continued, setting down the course onto their unknown destination. Porter was asleep on the floor, wrinkling his nose in response to his own dreams. Upon Arya's hand, was a red mark. She held it closer to her face, allowing the soft light of the moon to reveal the symbol closely. A flame. One that was tinted gold, getting brighter as the carriage moved, the red pulsing with a metallic sheen.

"Idoh," Arya whispered, brushing her fingers over the mark. It was then she knew she would get her chance. She just had to be patient.

14

While stopping at a rest, Arya was able to bribe one of the slaves of the house to give her a map and point to where they were. She drew over the map, calculating with Porter how far from the border of Teielmor they were. It was a painstaking process, figuring that Ivan was traveling more west than she would like. It didn't bode well for the plan to escape, Porter suggesting they steal a boat if they get close enough to the ocean. She'd laughed at the idea. How would two Selkies steal a god damn boat?

She had hidden the map while they travelled through the land, Porter watching the rise and fall of the sun and the movement of the stars to navigate which way the carriage was moving. Arya did her best to mark what he was saying, ending with a bunch of scribbles on the back of the map.

Days and nights moved slowly as they made their journey, Ivan still refusing to speak to her after rescuing Porter from his captor. He could be pissy all he wanted, but refusing to help one of her people put him further on the "do not trust" list than he already was.

It had only been Ivan that Arya had seen on the journey, Estelle and Embry nowhere to be found while Rook had not come to check back in. It created a dark feeling in her gut, telling her something was very wrong. Unfortunately, that feeling only grew as the days progressed and the carriage moved closer to where she originally came from. The center of Kulessa, Roderick's castle.

The castle loomed in the distance, the carriage luckily taking the road that led away from the structure, but Arya was still on edge. She sat on the floor, hiding from the monstrosity like it would reach out and snatch her back up.

"You mentioned some friends you have back in Teielmor," Porter had said, watching Arya with pity as she hid away from the castle. "Can you tell me about them?"

Arya tucked herself into the corner of the carriage, holding her pack tightly to her body. "There is Leif," Arya began. "He's from Tiras, the next Duke. He's funny and makes me laugh a lot." Images of Leif's strong jaw and quirky attitude played through her mind. Even if it was just a dream where those things had happened, they were still real for Arya. "And there's Idoh, he's the second son of the Fintan Duke and Duchess. He's a hardass and trains like there's no tomorrow, but down deep, he's a sweetheart." She thought of the way Idoh held her when she had cried in her dream.

How he had saved her time and time again, allowing her petty nature to take over around Mies and his encouragement in her training to fight. Something she transferred over to the real world.

Her heart ached at thinking how far away they still were, wishing it was them with her instead of Porter and Ivan. It made her feel guilty, craving the company of others, but it was true. She missed them.

"Then there's Winslet," Arya continued, determined to keep her mind off them. "Winslet is a Selkie like us, but currently resides in Tiras with Leif. Those two are like peas in a pod. She's sweet, but will kill anyone who hurts her friends. Honestly, I would never get on the wrong side of Winslet."

Porter chuckled. "Sounds like my sister, Merriweather. Not a sailor in the town would try to mess with her, soft face but steel heart, that one."

Arya smiled, temporarily forgetting about the danger of the castle's proximity. "Winslet is one of my favorite people. She knew something was wrong with me the first second she saw me, and it felt good to confide in someone."

Porter nodded, looking at his intertwined hands. "I know the feeling. My crew was like that, not a bad mouthed man or woman aboard the ship."

Arya cocked her head to the side. "You had women on the crew?"

Porter laughed. "Of course we did. Some of the finest sailors to roam this bloody sea."

147

Arya smiled softly at the thought. Her upbringing was proper, forced to learn politics and arranged to be married without a second thought. Then, at the same time, there were women and girls boarding ships to be sailors and merchants alongside the men without another idea of what life would be for them. The ocean calls a Selkie like a tempting whisper of a god, and Arya had confined her life to that of the land and people. How different would it have been to be one of the sailors she'd watch leave on the ships out her window as a child? What adventures could she have had if her fate had not been confined to society and human politics.

There were many what ifs in life, especially hers, but not one of those thoughts could change their fate to what it was now. Porter was still stranded in Kulessa, and there would be no saying if Arya would have a different life than what she did.

"I feel betrayed," she admitted aloud, her voice cracking. Porter stared at her, furrowing his brows. "I was a daughter of a Duke, and instead of my parents coming to rescue me and my sister, they let me suffer in Kulessa."

"Surely they don't know you're here," Porter soothed.

Arya shook her head, curling her knees to her chest. "My friends knew where I was. The prince of Teielmor knew where I was. All of them knew but never came. They closed the border and refused any trades between humans and fae. They kept me locked here while I was used and abused to whatever the humans felt fit for a woman of my breed." Porter looked down, biting his lips together. "I asked for death so many times, Porter. I wanted it to all be over. They took my sanity and sense of self with each day. All I have left is anger and pain, what sort of life can I have with that?"

There was silence between them, Arya refusing to look at her new friend. She wiped a tear away from her cheek, resting her forehead on her knees. Misery was a dark company to keep, yet it felt like the only company she had sometimes. The thoughts and fears which plagued her mind, competing with the emotions she contained inside her chest.

"I feel like I could have fought back," Porter said after a while, Arya sneaking a peek at him. His face was twisted with pain, chin dimpled and nose scrunched. "I am a man, a sailor, someone who'd spent years fighting in taverns and pubs all along Teielmor coasts, yet a mere human woman took me." His fist balled beside him, head shaking. "All it took was a pair of sissors to my coat for me to listen. She would hang it on the rafters of our bed, tying a string to it that would drop a blade onto it and tear it apart. I would stare at it as she did what she wanted with me...but I finished. Each time I allowed my seed to fill her and I couldn't help it." Tears fell down his cheeks, finally looking at Arya. "Did I want it? I keep telling myself I didn't, but I gave her two children. I gave the woman who stole me away from my family and life children because I couldn't stop myself from releasing into her."

"What happened to you was not your fault," Arya said, letting her own tears fall.

"So why is it so easy for you to tell me this, when you can't accept it for yourself?" Porter asked, wiping away his tears. "Anger and pain allow you to remember what is good and right in the world. Don't think yourself unworthy if you feel it more than others. You've been through more than others."

Arya sat back, shocked that Porter would say something like that to her. Using her own words to contradict the helplessness that she felt with each memory of the men who'd use her for their benefit. The nights alone where she would cry to the gods and ask them why they didn't help her. The numbness she felt after being tortured and thrown back into the dungeons. All just because she was fae.

The same treatment that Porter saw.

The same terrors that countless other trapped fae men and women experienced in Kulessa on a daily basis.

"I want to burn it all to the ground," Arya hissed.

Porter nodded, leaning back in his seat. "That is your right. Maybe, that is what your friends can help you with?"

Arya thought back to the dream where Idoh promised to come for her if she was ever in Kulessa without him again. He would do it. At one request Idoh would burn down each and every person and place that tortured fae. At least she hoped he would.

15

Ivan had directed the carriage to stop at an inn. Arya was thankful, hoping to get a decent night's sleep in a real bed instead of the uncomfortable seat of the carriage. It'd been just over a week since they began their journey. As she exited the carriage, taking Porter's hand to help her down, Arya smelled something that was unmistakable.

"Is that—."

"The sea," Porter agreed quietly.

Arya looked around, unable to see much in the dim light of the evening sky. Ivan was instructing humans on where to put their horses and trunks, Arya wondering if this was their final destination. There was a small garden off to the side, a chimney that plumed with grey smoke, and ivy that wrapped through the rock wall that stabilized the inn. It was pretty compared to the other placed they'd stayed at, though that dark feeling continued. Arya snuck a look at her hand, the flame almost completely gold, the center containing a single dot of red. Idoh was close. She was close.

Upon entering the inn, a plump woman came and greeted them, her red hair throwing strands of grey through the locks. "'ello, I'm Leenore, I'll be your host during your wedding and honeymoon."

Arya's blood ran cold, her face paling. She had forgotten she'd agreed to marry Ivan. Forgotten his promise of a quick marriage. It explained the sea smell, Rook was able to perform a fae ceremony, and Arya needed salt water in hers. But why there? He could have kept them far from the border. Did Ivan want to tease her with the proximity?

Luckily, Porter was able to help her. "My lady is thrilled, just nervous. You know how marriage can be."

The woman chuckled, placing a small hand to her lips. "Of course. Don't worry, deary, I was married four times. If he gets on your nerves, just poison him."

Not the response Arya expected from the woman, furrowing her brows. Perhaps the treatment of women changed the closer to Teielmor it was. No way a woman from court would be caught dead saying something so scandalous.

"I'll take you to your room," she said with a smile.

Porter forced Arya to follow the woman, partially dragging her across the inn until getting to a room the furthest from the entrance. She did not notice any other people in the place, empty save for Leenore. Something felt wrong. Very, very wrong.

"I have your room over here," Leenore said to Porter. He reluctantly let go of Arya's arm, finding it was colder without his presence. There was comfort with Porter, companionship she so desperately craved after years of isolation, yet he was being torn away from her.

Gritting her teeth, Arya walked into her room, closing the door quickly behind her. She pressed her head against the wood, taking in a deep breath. She didn't want to do this. Marriage to Ivan was off the table now she knew who had concocted the plan. The decision for her loyalty and love should be hers, not some god who believes they'll win with a fucking contract for her freedom. Something they had no right to tease her with.

When Arya turned around, she saw the bed was covered in flower petals. She cringed as she walked forward, seeing a letter in the middle with her name written in a fancy swirling font. This was something that other women must love to get for their weddings, but Arya hated it. It was honestly disgusting to witness.

However, when Arya opened the note, her breathe caught in her throat.

"Want to escape? Follow the sound of the water".

The sound of water, mixed with salt water smell. She was near the ocean, or at least the river that separates Kulessa and Teielmor. Crossing that river means freedom among fae. Safety in one form or another. Ivan was not going to be happy, but she was ready to go. To take her freedom back and not be bound to another fucking man for another ten years. Especially one who is in league with Roderick.

A knock sounded on her door, opening to reveal Ivan holding a tray of food. "I come with a peace offering."

Arya bit her lips together, nodding as she shoved the note into her dress. No way she'd let him know what she's planning. Ivan set the food on the bed, gently sitting upon it. The silence between them was awkward, the air hanging with a heaviness that made even the roses feel too intense.

"I know this isn't ideal," he said with some hesitation, "but I promise I'll be a good husband."

Doubt it, Arya thought.

Arya stared at the food, not tempted by it when she knew she would be back in Teielmor in less than a few hours. Ivan, however, took her hesitancy as worry it was not edible. He took a bit of salad onto his fork and consumed it. At least she assumed he did. The fork disappeared beneath the darkness of the hood, not returning. Watching him eat was unnatural. Like he wasn't supposed to eat to survive. It would make sense as to why Estelle didn't know how to cook.

"Why do you wear the hood?" Arya asked.

Ivan coughed, choking on the lettuce he was attempting to consume. "Well," he said, "it's a long story."

"If I'm going to be your wife, I would like to know." Arya countered.

Ivan sighed, rubbing his head over the hood. "If you must know, I didn't want to spook you."

"You're that ugly?" Arya snorted.

"No, I look like someone you know."

That intrigued her, cocking her head to the side. Who did he look like?

154

"Years ago, I was commissioned by your friends, Idoh and Leif to find you," Ivan admitted, moving his fork around the plate of food. The words twisted her stomach, teeth clenching. "They know me as Emeric, though I was not in your little dream as they were. The gods are cruel, are they not."

"Who are you?" Arya scowled, more threatened now that she didn't have a firm idea on who this man was. How did he know about the dream and her friends?

"As I said," he said disgruntled, "my name is Emeric. I do not come from the fae world, but do not come from the lands the humans claimed either. I am from beneath the soil, in the darkness you caught yourself in." Arya shook her head, shifting away from him. "I come from people who did not know of the upper ground, and am one of the last of my kind."

"I don't understand," Arya hissed.

Ivan—or Emeric—whatever his name was, reached up, lowering his hood. As Arya stared at him, her body froze, fear riddling her body. Brown hair curled around his pale skin, silver mask revealing yellow eyes with no sign of the whites anywhere. His cheeks were sunken, eye sockets deep in his skull like he was the epitome of a skeleton. She had stared into those same eyes time and time again, the pain and horror she felt then, coming back full force.

"There was no other torturer, was there? It was you." There was no doubt in her mind. It was criminal what he had done. Nothing could repair that, not even magic.

Emeric shrugged. "It doesn't matter now, does it?"

155

It fucking did matter. It only solidified that Arya needed to run as fast as she could. There was no way she would even consider marrying a man who took pleasure in torturing her for years before taking her away from the pain of the castle. He hurt her, and he shrugged it off? No. He was not allowed to do that.

"Was that your plan all along?" Arya asked. "Make me so weak that I accepted anyone who came to help?"

She summoned as much water as she could as stealthily as she could. It collected behind her, growing with each passing second. Meanwhile, Arya continued to be aghast and horrified by Emeric's appearances in her life.

"Not exactly," he said, taking another bite of salad. She watched him eat, unable to help the scrunch of her nose and mouth. He disgusted her. "I had to get into the castle somehow, Zephyr had banned me from leaving Castle Lofta, so by making a deal with Leif and Idoh I had my chance. It was more to see what I could get away with outside of Teielmor than anything. Nothing personal, just a bit of payback."

"Payback?" The water collected was almost enough. She could slaughter him, but she needed to be sure he couldn't use that darkness he tore apart those creatures with at the manor on her. She was too close to Teielmor for her to fail now. To injure herself with this horrible person.

"You never looked at me like you did them," Emeric huffed like a child.

Arya shook her head, she gripped the pack that held her skin, ready to escape. It was time. "Maybe because you did the whole Stockholm shit wrong, asshole."

Emeric jerked his head back, like he was shocked at her outburst. Arya stood, throwing the water in his direction. Two cones shot from her hands, stabbing him in the shoulder, the other blocked by a shield of darkness. He scowled at her, Arya taking that opportunity to run. Hopping over the bed, she grabbed the pack with her skin in it, hitting the doorframe with her shoulder as she ran out the room. The throbbing from the impact did not cause her to waiver, crying out to Porter.

"Porter!" She screamed. "Porter, time to go!"

The Selkie appeared from behind a door, his shirt off and pants low on his waist. As soon as he saw Arya running, his eyes widened. "Ah, fuck."

He soon joined her, his skin in his hand, Arya's in her pack. The light of the day was completely gone as Arya and Porter made it outside. She listened, desperate to follow the instructions on the note. Trees swayed, hushing the world and silencing any hope of hearing the water.

"This way," Porter urged, pulling Arya's hand as he led her through the thicket. Branches and leaves crunched as they ran. Their breath came out in puffs of steam, the weather around them going cold. Not a good sign.

"He's gaining on us," Arya panted.

Porter shook his head, trudging on harder. The water was their only chance of escape. The only way they would have their freedom from any human or variant of human there was. That's when she heard it. A soft rushing. The sound of water over stones. The smell of salt in the air.

"This way!" Arya screamed, changing their direction toward the sound.

Beside them, branches broke. An unseen force chopped at the trees, tearing them from the ground. A giant trunk was launched through the air, crashing into the ground beside them. One after another, more trees threatened them, almost like giant hands controlling their progression. The ground caved beneath the pressure of the darkness. How the fuck did he have such an intense power like that?

Arya looked behind her. She saw him walking at a quick pace, dancing of black tentacles behind him like he was intending to scare her. Fuck, he didn't need to try, she was already scared.

The smell got more intense. The sound almost drowning. They were so close, but so was he.

Arya opened her pack, ready to escape at a moment's notice with only her seal skin on her body. The same way she escaped Phobus in her dream. The one true thing Arya knew she could count on.

"Get ready," Arya called to Porter.

Seconds felt like hours. Minutes like days. Their breath hung in the air like a trail to be followed, and their running more like a gentle stroll. The burning in her lungs threatened to make her slow, but her mind forced them onward, forbidding her body to be used like it had been in the torture chambers.

Then, they saw it.

Black sparkling rush of water smashing again the dark forms of sharp rocks that stuck out of the water like a warning. Porter and Arya stripped, not caring about the pace at which they ran, throwing the clothes to the side in order to put on the skin they were so desperate to wear. To have that part of them restored.

Porter dove in first, popping his head above the currant to see if Arya followed. It was only a second before she did, diving in and feeling the wild thrashing of her magic as it fully came back to her. Absorbing into her body like a missing piece of a puzzle she needed to place. Everything became clear. The anxiety and fear she experienced was nothing as long as she had the water.

Arya and Porter swam through the water. They wove through the rocks, dodging the various branches and trees that floated down the river's currant.

Arya poked her head out of the water, focusing on the man who stood seething on the river's edge. With barely a thought, a tidal wave of water slammed down on Emeric, his magic leaving and the darkened world lightening just a bit. It didn't kill him, she could feel him still pumping blood wherever he was, but he was not a threat to them. For the moment at least.

"That was impressive," Porter said.

Arya sniffed the air, still not feeling safe enough to stop. "Let's keep moving."

Porter and Arya swam along the stream, weaving through the water like the experts they were. Finally back in their element, things felt normal. As Arya continued, the build of magic was growing. It ran through her veins, collecting at each point of her body, ready to be used. All she needed was an outlet.

16

As if being in the dark of night, in a rushing river, wasn't bad enough, Arya and Porter found that joining them in the waters were bodies. They would come up for air, looking around at the floating corpses that wore both human and fae armor. War was happening and Arya didn't think much beyond the idea that Idoh was out there, fighting this battle.

They trudged to shore, nude bodies being assaulted by the cooling wind of night. Clothes had been an afterthought when chasing the high adrenaline gave them, but were a necessity. Unfortunately, the only ones available were currently residing on half decayed corpses.

"Please don't tell me you're thinking what I think you are," Porter moaned, frowning deeply.

Arya sighed, pulling one of the less decayed bodies onto the shore. "Unless you want to go naked into a battlefield."

"When the bards write songs of us, lets hope they ignore this part," Porter said as he pulled at the chest plate of another corpse.

It took more time than Arya would've liked to get clothed, focusing on pants first before moving onto a large tunic top that was far too big on her. It ate her body, leaving everything to the imagination. She stuffed her coat into the pack she'd found on one of the fallen soldiers. Arya decided to take one last thing, grabbing the scabbard from the ground and looking over the sword partially within. It was rusted, more than she wanted, but it worked. Arya just needed something to protect herself if it came to be that they wound up in the middle of a battle as these corpses foretold. Magic could only do so much.

Porter had a similar idea, wrapping a collection of mismatched arrows to his waist in a quiver, a bow already strung around his back.

"It's likely we're going to experience close combat, range weapons might not be the best choice," Arya said matter of factly.

Porter smirked. "I'm dressed in a dead man's clothes, wearing a dead man's weapons, and you're worried about the luck I'll have in a fight with a bow? I'll take my chances."

Arya nodded once, not looking forward to their journey ahead. "Which way?"

"I say follow the blood trail."

Arya and Porter followed the corpses. Blood soaked into the ground, ravens and other scavengers ripping at the decaying bodies without remorse. It churned her stomach, the smell not helping the nausea that built in her throat. There was so much death that surrounded them, threatening Arya and Porter with the possible future that awaited them as well. Would she be left to rot like these poor people? Where was the empathy that came with her fae culture? Who allowed such disgusting actions to happen on Teielmor soil?

"Is this the first time you've seen death?" Porter asked, breaking the harrowing silence that ate at their consciousness.

Arya shook her head. "I've seen more death than I would like to admit. In Kulessa it was a constant hovering possibility that I would be the next to be taken by the reapers."

Porter was silent, his face pulled tight. "I was lucky to only see five in my life."

"I witnessed my sister slaughtered. Saw multiple prisoners executed and neglected to the point of their inevitable death. I have seen babes and men and women all succumb to the disease and cold that came with the winter of Kulessa. I have seen women beaten and raped to the point where their spines were outside their bodies, skin covered in more welts and discoloration than actual healthy skin." Arya looked over the dead with dark eyes, recalling her memories in the dungeons. "I had held a human child, no more than seven, who had stolen an apple from the King's orchard. He

163

died in my arms from infections after his whipping and branding."

Porter looked down at his feet, stopping. "My first wife, Rakia, was killed when we were first captured by the humans." Arya stared at him. It made sense why he had given up fighting back. "She was pregnant with our first child. She wanted a girl, but I wanted a boy." He laughed, sniffing back the tears that threatened him. "She was in the wrong place at the wrong time, and I had been hit until unconscious because of my magic stirring."

"I'm sorry," Arya said softly, walking up to Porter and laying a hand on his arm. "You would've made a wonderful dad."

He laughed again, the sound full of hatred. "When I get the opportunity to kill those pirates, I will not hesitate."

Arya left it at that, understanding the feeling. She wanted nothing more than to feel the warmth of Roderick's blood on her hands. To watch the life of Phobus's eyes disappear. To ruin every life that had taken parts of her. Revenge was more powerful than many gave it credit for, and after the anger from it was gone, all there was left was hope. Hope that the future would be better. That life would go on and allow healing for the monstrous actions performed upon her. That one day, she would be able to look at a storm with awe and not fear.

Darkness was their only companion as they followed the path of blood to where she hoped the fae army would be. It made her paranoid, knowing the dark could be hiding a number of foes behind it. Any one of the bodies could be waiting to ambush them. Emeric could be in those shadows, waiting and watching for the perfect opportunity to attack. Each step and crunch of the blood coated ground increased those fears significantly, but the prospect of a temporary form of safety was all she needed to keep going.

Then, there was light.

It was just a small flicker in the distance, moving and swaying with each person who carried the torches. They hopped from one area to another, dancing like a beacon in the darkness. Arya's stomach flipped, warmth spreading over her. This could be it. The first fae she had seen in Teielmor. The first time she'd meet others like her outside the confines of entrapment.

Porter gripped her hand, the emotions he felt flowing through their connection. No—it was more than that. It was connection with these strangers.

"Selkies," Porter breathed.

"Selkies," she confirmed.

Healers, employed by the crown to go from body to body after the battle to help the wounded who were thought to be dead. Only a Selkie could sense the blood flow through the body of someone presumed dead. Could heal those who would otherwise be unhealable. Using their god given magic to assist others.

Arya and Porter increased their speed, eager to meet others of their kind. People they had been taken from so many years ago. Their outlines were visible through the early morning sky and the torches they kept close.

Then a voice called to them through the darkness. "Stop, who goes there?"

Porter and Arya stopped, both choked with emotion. Arya cleared her throat, though the emotion showed through. "I am Arya Abano, youngest daughter of Asita. I travel with another captive Selkie, please offer us shelter!"

"Holy fuck," the voice said, multiple people running to them. The faces were not familiar as she had hoped, but empathetic and displayed with smiles of greetings. Arya couldn't help the tears as they fell with being surrounded with so many of their culture.

"I am Lake, leader of the healers," the man belonging to the voice said. He was older than the others, coated in a layer of dried blood around his hands and waist. A satchel hung at his side, a clean rag laying over it. His sandy-brown hair was tied back messily with a blue ribbon, marking him as a high member of society. "My Lady, where have you been all this time?"

Arya choked when thinking of all she'd been through, none of these strangers knowing the dangers that layer just beyond the river. "Kulessa. We both have. Please, we want to get as far away from the border as we can."

"Continue your duties, I'll escort them to the commander." Lake waved them to follow him, Arya and Porter doing so as the others stared at them with fading enthusiasm. Lake was not as vocal on their journey to the commander, Arya and Porter sharing nervous glances. Magic sparked on her finger tips, tingling like it wanted to

166

escape. She pushed the feeling down, not wanting to reveal herself as a foe to this group. Good impressions, Arya.

As they crested the hill, Arya and Porter stared in awe at the vast expanse of the military post. Tents covered each area that had an empty space, leaving room for the community fires and walkways. Everyone had a job, walking around with their armor half on, or multiple swords to be delivered to the right person. Others played games. The air hummed with clanging metal, shouts of men and women, and laughter, though beneath the energy, Arya could sense the emotion. Pain. Longing to go home. Weakness. Sorrow. Torment. It was things she felt herself, pinpointing each one like it was a game of grief. Through it all was fear.

"How long have they been there?" Arya asked.

"Too long," Lake replied.

They ventured into the encampment, worming through the busy soldiers who didn't look at them twice. Their appearance in the camp was not their concern, and did not worry them. The familiarity between other fae and themselves was so surreal that Arya kept trying to make eye contact with them. To see if they'd know her from a different life so many years before. None did.

Lake brought them to a tent, pushing aside the curtain to reveal a small area with a table and maps spread over it. Troops and marks were labeled on the map with ceramic pieces, notebooks left open with scribbles of orders and information displayed on the pages. Candles were extinguished, though living through their last few hours of life before needing to be replaced. A cot rested in the back corner, blankets shoved to the foot like the person who slept upon it was not pleased with the comfort a blanket brought. A trunk of clothes and books. Arya couldn't help but smile as she looked upon the titles of those novels, finding them to be children's fables and fantasies from Asita. One book was her go to when a child, her fingers finding they could still remember the indented feel of the pictures embossed onto the pages by the press.

"What is the commander's name?" Arya asked, curious to see who would possess such a unique memory of hers.

"We are not allowed to say," Lake said, "he does not like his name as it is always used following hardship."

Arya knew the commander must be someone important and respected for them not to acknowledge a given name. Nothing else gave her hints to who this person could be, however, leading her to believe that they must like their privacy.

"Wait here, I am going to fetch him." Lake walked out of the tent, leaving Porter and Arya alone. She let herself breathe, finally able to defeat the tension that pounded within her skull. All she needed to do was be one step closer to going home. Allow herself to be protected by the people who knew of her and loved her. At least hoped they did.

She looked upon the map seeing the mass of forces that were piled along the Tiras and Ilmari lands. The sizes were large compared to those she'd seen of the humans they marked, but Arya had been oblivious to the war that was happening while in Kulessa. It was obvious Roderick did not think it a major threat, or didn't have the resources to provide so many men to compete with the fae. Yet, there were still hundreds dead from either side.

The scribbles upon the notebooks mentioned their residence in Tiras, giving Arya one of the answers she was looking for. Almost fifteen-thousand troops in their encampment, and a blank space left for how many were lost in the previous battle.

"Stop snooping," Porter urged in a whisper. "It'll look bad for us."

"We're dressed in dead people's clothes, it can't look much worse than that," Arya snorted.

The tent flap opened, sun of the morning shining into the room like a spotlight upon Arya who was clearly reading the journals on the table. She should've listened to Porter, but now she had to deal with the consequences. The light obscured her view of the commander, the man stopping in the entrance of the tent. Arya squinted, shielding her eyes so she could attempt to make out who this man was and explain her knowledge of the humans. She still knew a lot and could be useful for their wins against them.

"Who the fuck are you?" The man growled. It was only directed at Arya, the anger in his voice clear about his dislike of catching her snooping.

"I-I'm sorry—I didn't mean to pry—my name is Arya Abano—." The man raced at her, drawing a dagger from his belt and pressing the metal to her throat. Arya placed her hand between her and the tip of the blade, pushing it away to try and relieve the pressure it created.

"Arya Abano is dead. Try again," the man hissed.

"I am not going to claim I'm someone I'm not," she spat, showing her teeth to prove her own anger. Just because this person did not believe her did not intimidate her to change her story. Arya was Arya Hemore way too long to forego her given name.

Arya's eyes began to slowly adjust to the light, looking behind the man to Porter who was held back by two more soldiers. Lake stood at the entrance, his arms crossed in front of him, clearly not going to be of any help. She shifted her gaze back to her assailant, finding his eyes level with hers in the bent position they grappled in. The same blue as the lagoon she'd swam in as a child. The hair, the same light brown that Meriah had.

It was impossible. Unthinkable she'd meet him here. He was first born. The only child of Duke and Duchess of Asita.

"Kai?"

Kai was hardened after all these years. His eyes proved he had witnessed atrocities, scars upon his skin barely healed, signaling the use of iron weapons he had the unpleasant experience in meeting. It was not like her dream, seeing him there. He didn't recognize her, barely saw the resemblance of their stature and build, though Arya was still showing signs of her malnourishment which didn't help the recognition.

"How do you know my name?" He asked.

"You're my brother," Arya whispered, eyes wide with her realization of everything. He was so old now. Fuck, so was she. They weren't children anymore. They were adults who have seen the horrors of the world, trapped in positions of authority and trauma they couldn't escape from. While Kai was allowed to be in Teielmor, it did not prove to make his life any easier. It seemed to have done the opposite.

"Stop with the fucking act," he growled.

"You're wearing me and Meriah's sister bracelets," Arya pleaded, hoping it would remind him of the woven strings he held around his wrists. The last thing Arya and Meriah had made before the swim that fateful day. "We made them while mother talked about Meriah's marriage to Leif in Tiras. Meriah made faces while mother spoke, and you mimicked father."

Kai's eyes softened slightly, looking over Arya again.

"On your sixteenth naming day, mother tried to make you wear a hideous shirt with lots of ruffles on it and you had made a big deal about not wanting to. I took it into my room and shredded the shirt so you didn't have to wear it." The memories that came from Arya were pleasant and pure. It did not shed light onto the torment they'd experienced the last few years, only the happiness of their childhood that ended far too soon. "Meriah made you promise to behave in Tiras, but you crossed your fingers so you could say you never made stupid decisions at her whim."

Kai stepped back, terror on his face as he stared at Arya. She slouched, looking down at the blood on her hands and the cut that slipped over the skin of her neck. The physical pain wasn't there with the blood, only the wishful thoughts of her missed childhood and false promises of Kai

171

remembering her. Like he had in the dream. The one where he scooped her up and kept her safe in his arms after all that time.

"My childhood bear, what was its name?" Kai asked.

Arya laughed, a few tears falling. "You didn't have a bear, it was a dog. You named it Serpent, but Meriah and I named it crusty because of the horrible texture of the fur."

"Oh gods," Kai whimpered. The blade dropped from his hands, clattering to the ground as he embraced Arya. She hugged him back, letting herself be the support he needed as he cried on her shoulder. "I thought you were dead."

"Meriah is dead," Arya said, "she saved my life by sacrificing hers."

Kai cried harder, the soldiers and Porter giving the two room to catch up. Brushing back his hair, Arya forced him to look at her, smiling deeply. "I've waited for this moment since I was captured."

Kai shook his head. "What happened? *How* did this happen?"

"It's a long story," Arya said, knowing how hard it would be to tell him the truth now she didn't have time to heal like in the dream. It was raw. New. Fresh and teaming with emotion she knew she wouldn't be able to control.

"I have time."

"But the war—,"

"Will still be there once you're done."

Arya bit her lips together, nodding. "Meriah and I went for a swim the night we disappeared..."

17

Kai had listened intently to Arya's story, stopping only to ask clarifying questions before letting her continue. It was nerve racking to tell him about the torture and rape, but even more so when it came to the interactions with the gods and their intentions with her. Kai kept quiet, however, not showing any sign on if he believed her or not. After she was finished, they sat quietly in the tent, Kai rubbing the scruff that settled on his face.

"I know it's a little unbelievable," Arya started, but Kai shook his head.

"I have had interactions with Lir and, while not as intense, they were still fucking stupid. I believe you, I'm just angry."

"Why?" Arya asked, the stupidity of the question hitting her as soon as it left her mouth.

Kai took her hands in his, leaning forward. "I was convinced you had been in Kulessa. I didn't know why, but my gut always said so. I tried for ten years to get a search party to form, but everyone stopped me. Our parents, peers, fuck Leif himself said my quest would be stupid and get me killed, but I didn't care." He paused, a warmth blooming in Arya. Kai had tried to look for her and Meriah. He'd tried but was confined under the restraints of politics. "You have two new siblings."

The warmth stopped, replaced with a rock that rested in her gut. "What?"

He nodded. "Twins. Avonlea and Anahita. They were born three years after you and Meriah went missing."

"They replaced us," Arya muttered, the amount of hurt and betrayal pulsing in her core. Three years was all it took for their parents to birth new children after Meriah and Arya vanished. Fuck, they'd both been alive still. They'd been trapped in a constant loop of sexual assault while their parents were busy with newborns. Forgetting them.

Kai stiffened. "I resigned from my position as future Duke because of those girls. I couldn't be around them."

Arya didn't respond, still hurt by the idea of being a second thought to her parents. "Did they have a funeral for us?"

Kai shook his head. "Just a memorial placard at Briar Cove."

"I see." It was unfortunately something she hadn't thought about when confronting the idea of her disappearance back home. She'd assumed her parents loved her and wanted her around. Meriah was dead and Arya had suffered for fucks sake. Then there they were with two new babies, erasing the memories of their own lives and ruined childhoods away.

The tent flap opened, a decorated soldier in the doorway. "Sir, we need you."

"What is it? I'm busy."

The man looked apologetically to Arya before saying, "He's burning corpses again."

"Motherfucker." Kai rubbed his neck, staring at the ceiling. "Arya, stay here, I'll be back."

She stood. "Is it something I can help with?"

The soldier winced. "Ma'am, he's a soldier that is not dealing with grief well. No one can really help him."

Arya rolled her eyes, going to the door. "That's not true. Take me to him."

The soldier lead Arya and Kai back to the waterfront, a few pattons away from where Arya first arrived to shore. The bodies there were organized, fae corpses being transported by gurneys and lined up in rows. The humans were stacked. Their bodies were in makeshift pyramids, less considerate to them as compared to the fallen from Teielmor.

A group had gathered around the site, staring at the man who was throwing balls of fire at the dead humans. Immediately, Arya knew what this man was feeling. His face was pinched with anger, yet eyes lined with tears. His nose was red, snot running down into his mouth that was forced closed until he would let out the flames from his fingers. It

175

was not just his hands on fire. All up his arms were wisps of flames, dancing in different colors that did not normally associate with Fintan fire users. As she continued to stare, she noticed the colors were all the main colors of each province. A haunting of the lives of friends he'd lost during his time serving.

He let out a pained scream, scorching the humans with a blast of fire, sending black smoke up into the air. The reason he was causing an issue. It wasn't the grief, it was the loss of secrecy. Arya walked down, pushing people out of the way to get to the man. She was the only one to approach him, others whispering as she entered the circle they crowded around him with.

"Arya, don't," Kai said, reaching to pull her back to the safety of others.

She turned back to her brother, shaking her head. "I'll be okay."

Ignoring the others, Arya walked toward the man. He saw her, scowling as she approached. "Don't come any closer! They deserve to burn!"

His hand shifted to point at Arya who raised her hands to signal her surrender. "I don't mean to stop you, I want to help."

This confused him, his head jerking back and nose scrunching like she was insane. Arya took a few steps forward, the man focusing on how close she got to him. Instead, Arya wrapped around him, close to the water where she summoned multiple streams and cut into the bodies, slicing arms and legs off. It killed the black smoke of the fire, keeping the current soldiers safe while gaining the trust of this one.

"I'm Arya," she told him.

"Ember."

Ember threw another blaze toward the grouping, the light burning her face and the colors dancing on his arms.

"Are they for the ones you lost?" She asked, joining him in their crusade against the dead.

Ember looked to his arms, the colors dancing upon his skin. The anger faded behind his eyes for a minute, replaced with the most intense sorrow Arya had witness anyone display. It burned just as brightly as his flame did, the tears that followed sizzling off his cheeks and turning to steam. It gave Arya an idea. Something to stop his assault and remember his fallen comrades with.

"Would you like to see them again?"

Ember looked at her like she was crazy. "Are you threatening to kill me?"

Arya chuckled. "No, no, just some Selkie magic."

Slowly, he let down his arms, allowing Arya to lead him to the water. Once there, she felt the magic inside her stir, building up to allow the wall of water to be created before everyone. Then, she drew on the tears that he still had yet to release, allowing the emotion and memories that came with those tears to form.

It appeared slowly, showing Ember's point of view as he sat around a fire with a group of other soldiers. They laughed, the sound muted but energy clear. Each warrior was from different places, all joined together to help stop humans from invading the land they loved and called home. It became a story, going from one person to the next, showing their experiences with Ember, only to see their bodies in various forms of death. Battles and survival, the grief they were able to share and hatred that began to spew among the droplets that held his emotions. Then, a brief clip of happiness. Something sentimental shared with a person who no longer walked the same ground they all did. A secret being shared with the living.

The memories began to fade, drawing on the viewing of the last death, a woman from Dunia. It showed their final battle together. The way she pushed him out of the way only to take a wound that would've surely been his end. Arya watched as he held her in the middle of that war, caressing her cheeks as she smiled up to him and spoke words that would only be remembered between the dead and one living man.

Ember fell to his knees as he watched the scene, his shoulders shaking and head arched back to allow a scream to escape. It filled the world around them with pain, something that could not be mimicked unless felt deep inside their core. Ignoring the flames that danced on his arms, Arya hugged the man. The burning was nothing. Barely a warm sensation upon her skin. Ember accepted the embrace, dipping his head into her arm and let himself weep. She joined him.

Grief was a luxury to have, and she was so happy that Ember could have that. She wanted this stranger to heal from this. Learn and grow so he could help others too. To achieve the intelligence of emotion that so many Fintanian men and women are refused. She looked up at the screen of water, seeing that once again, the happy beginning of those friendships ended the presentation. And Ember smiled. He displayed a melancholy grin with tears in his eyes as he looked upon each person in that group.

"They were my family," he said, "the best thing I ever got in life. And now they're gone."

"No they aren't." Arya leaned back from the man, smiling as she raised his flaming arm. "Each one is represented right here, beside you. They'll always be with you, no matter how long it takes for you to meet them again."

He nodded, chin dimpling as he said, "I really loved them. I loved them so much."

"I know."

A man walked in front of them, his armor on except for his helmet. Arya and Ember looked up at him, seeing him offer a hand to Ember. "I'm here for you."

Ember considered the offer before slowly accepting. The man pulled Ember up, embracing him. Without a word, the two walked away together, leaving Arya in the middle of the circle, alone. The screen of water washed away and she simply stared at the small tears that floated inches above her hands. The only memories that saved their encampment from disaster.

"You could've been hurt," Kai scolded as he walked up to Arya, the group dispersing.

She nodded. "But he was already hurting."

Unlike in the dream, the feelings and magic that Arya felt in Teleimore was far more advanced than what she expected. Every movement was caught, each emotion projected to her. A pain shot behind her eyes, a pressure building like nothing she experienced before.

"Let's get you something to eat." Porter grabbed her elbow, leading her off toward the cluster of tents they'd come from. She didn't want to take food away from these men and women who needed it more than she did, but from the pounding in her head, she didn't have the energy to deny him.

Kai's soft footsteps behind the two gave Arya some comfort. Kai wouldn't let harm come to her. Wouldn't let Emeric near her or the others. He'd keep her safe until she was well enough to do it on her own. To be the person that could lead the army against the humans.

A bowl was placed in Arya's hands, her clothes turning her stomach as she realized the stains and smells that came off them were nothing short of death. She walked in the breath of reapers, dancing with them and narrowly missing their scythes. Each day she tested new opportunities to meet people from a dream. How could she say she loved them, when they'd never met her? How could a dream, one so dark and dangerous, be the only reason she loved?

"Eat, Arya." Kai had pulled a chair across from her, straddling the back like the heir to a crown and not like a commander of an army.

"All I smell is death," she responded, twisting her spoon through the milky broth.

Kai jerked his brows as if saying "*well no fuck*". "You have to remember where you arrived and what you're wearing. Death circles all of us these days."

Arya placed the wooden spoon to her lips, allowing Kai to release a breath he had been holding. She could sense his turmoil and anxiety of her arrival. It made her wonder if that was how the Gean-Cánach felt. Constantly feeling those intense emotions from people around them, unable to escape or tell their own from others. A harrowing existence that Arya was glad she didn't have to live with.

Kai sighed loudly, running his hands through his hair. There was something he had decided and Arya knew she wasn't going to like it.

"I can't have you here, Arya."

The words were a rejection she didn't expect from her brother. A betrayal to the familiarity they shared between them that had been lost for so long. Yet, here he was, forcing her away.

"I know." The words came from her even though it wasn't the ones she wanted to say. She wanted to tell him he had no right to send her away. He was a disgrace for leaving her when they'd just reconnected. How she'd gotten all the way there and he couldn't possibly love her if he was just going to abandon her again. Tears bordered her lids, unable to fall because, while she felt all those emotions, she knew he was doing what was best for her.

Arya was a distraction among the warriors. A distraction for Kai. One that could get him killed in battle. The lost princess of Asita had appeared only moments after the battle, wearing dead men's clothes and claiming a title she had no right to claim. She was replaced by her parents, thought to be as dead as those floating in the river outside of the camp.

"There is a group going to Ilmari tomorrow morning. I am going to send you with them. If your gods were good to you, when you get to the castle you'll be greeted by the ones from your dream."

Arya blinked slowly, processing what Kai said. "Castle Lofta?"

Kai nodded his head once, eyes searching over his sister with worry. Arya had not expected to be sent straight to the castle. Fuck, she hadn't even thought about it past getting to fae lands. Would Zephyr accept her need for asylum? Would he even know who she is enough to verify that? Arya looked down at her palm where the red mark had completely disappeared. Fucking gods and their false hope.

"Am I able to change from these clothes?" Arya asked Kai, trying to avoid the aching anxiety that rolled in her throat.

He nodded, standing from his chair. "I'll be sure to get you some clothes tonight. Sleep here, I want you where I can keep you safe." Porter opened his mouth, only for Kai to look at him and nod. "I'll get you a cot. You seem to be serving my sister well. Keep in mind, however, that one

182

wrong move, and I'll rip your throat out through your mouth."

Arya's jaw dropped, never having heard the kind, easy-going person that Kai was threaten another. Especially not a Selkie.

They watched as he exited the tent, his body casting a shadow over the fabric as he stopped to talk to two of the guards stationed outside. The men nodded before Kai walked away, leaving Porter and Arya alone.

"What crawled up his ass and died?" Porter puffed.

Arya clenched her jaw, shaking her head. The man she knew as her brother was gone. Tormented into a harder version of himself, and she couldn't blame him.

"I'm going to try and sleep a bit," Arya said.

Porter watched as she went to her brother's cot, tossing his blankets over her body. It smelled like home. The saltiness of the sea and the tang of drying seaweed at low tide. It sent a pain through her chest. That was when she realized, however, that she was finally safe. She was protected and between Kai and Porter, Arya was able to relax.

Tears came before she could stop them, floating off her face and hovering in the air around her. Through her sorrow, relief, and torment, Arya cried herself to sleep, smelling home and ignoring the threat of death that hung on her clothes.

18

It was cold along the shore as Winslet stood watching the boats leave to the horizon. They carried bodies. Many bodies of the Selkies who had risked everything to protect their way of life from humans. They would be returned to the sea just as she would be one day. Once her life had ended and the silence of death finally found her the way it always did in the end. Only this time, it would be permanent. A final rest after coming back over and over again. Her final life among these new souls who had no idea how good they had it being so in the dark.

Wind tossed her hair to the side, shielding half her vision as she continued to stare. Dark clouds had gathered to suggest snow, the chill barely registering across her skin. What was a little cold when compared to that of a lifeless body?

"You need to stop coming out here like this."

Winslet took in a breath, letting it out slowly. "They sacrificed so much for us, this is the least I could do for them."

Idoh stopped, standing beside her as the boats faded into the horizon. She glanced at the Salamander, waiting for what he really sought her out for. It was not common for them to have a moment alone like this, mostly because their different personalities countered a solid relationship. Recently, however, she believed the loneliness was getting to them both.

"Did you know any of them?" He asked.

Winslet shook her head. "No, not personally."

He nodded. "They burned a man who lived down the road from my family. Second son of an advisor."

Winslet pressed her closed fists into her pockets of her skirt, nails digging into her skin. Death was not something she found easy to discuss. Not since the dream. She had kept quiet about it, finding it hard to deal with without the teasing she was likely to endure from the others. A brush off from her desire to find the girl in the vision. A friend—perhaps more—that she had met during sleep that lasted months.

She forced the image of the smiling woman from her head, directing her gaze up to the collected clouds. "Seems like we're going to expect a storm."

Idoh looked up, pursing his lips as he gave a slight nod. "Indeed, it does. Snow, perhaps."

"It's too white," Winslet commented darkly. "Blood shows up better on snow."

185

Idoh hummed. "Without the winter, there would be no flowers of spring."

Winslet closed her eyes, letting the blonde strands of her hair to conceal her face. This winter was never ending. Filled with blood that flowed through the rivers and soaked into the soil. It didn't matter if there was snow to show it or not. Innocent lives were lost to the politics she once loved so much.

"There you are! And with Idoh too? What are you rascals up to?" Leif's cheerful tone broke through the dark silence shared between the two.

Winslet forced her depression down, feeling a smile grow on her face. "Just commenting on the weather, looks like snow, don't you think?"

Leif gave Winslet a pitiful smile, his eyes displaying his knowledge of her clear agony she tried to hide from him. Even with his magic, Leif didn't mention her clear deceit, something she was thankful for.

"It does. Hopefully it sticks so the children of the castle can be armed against the guards. Idoh, do you remember the snowball fights we were involved in as children?"

Idoh snorted, rolling his head to stare at Leif. "You mean how *Zephyr and I* had snowball fights and you cried over being cold and wet?"

Leif crossed his arms, tossing his hair dramatically. "I deny those allegations."

Winslet chuckled, bringing her fingers to her mouth the way she'd seen the ladies of court do. While she knew she was thought of as an airhead, a simple girl from a noble family, she was a watcher. She knew so much of everything, yet nothing at the same time. Not anything of importance at least.

She didn't know if her father was safe on the front lines. She didn't know how many wounded were coming back for treatment, or how many would make the journey home. The gossip of Teielmor was nothing anymore when so much more was happening outside the safety of the castle walls.

"We should prepare for the new envoy that is coming," Winslet said, turning on her heel and walking out toward the castle entrance. "Who knows what supplies they'll be needing."

Leif and Idoh didn't follow her as she left, which she was pleased with. It allowed her to drop that fake happiness and think of the things that truly troubled her. Like why she was marked for death by the gods.

19

Arya was met by a band of wounded soldiers in the morning. Some had minor injuries, their extremities bandaged. Others weren't so lucky. They laid in cots, skin a deathly shade, body wrapped in blankets and bandages that were both equally soaked with blood. They were loaded into modified carts, each person laying into shelves like a preserved jar.

"You must be Arya."

Arya looked up to see a woman walking toward her. The air of authority dripped from her more than she'd seen from anyone else in that camp. It was equal to that of Zephyr, yet without the noble edge.

Her dark eyes stared Arya up and down, a brow raising as if she wasn't impressed with what she saw. She stopped a few feet in front of Arya, sticking her bandaged hands into the pockets of her uniform pants. The top was tied around her waist, a brown wrap covering her breasts, yet exposing most of her torso and chest.

"I am, and this is Porter," Arya said motioning to her friend.

Porter crossed his arms in front of himself, narrowing his eyes like he was attempting to look tougher than the woman. Arya saw from the corner of her eye how he flexed his arms a little more and puffed out his chest. It would've been humorous if he wasn't self-proclaiming himself as her protector.

The woman glanced at Porter, her eyes dancing with amusement at his show. Apparently, Arya wasn't the only one who found it laughable. "Sure," she chuckled. "I am Eryn, I'll be your detail on our trip to Castle Lofta."

Anxiety filled Arya at the words. Even though she knew Castle Lofta was the desired destination, it was still nerve wracking to think she was a few days away from seeing her friends in person. Meet them, Arya corrected herself. As far as they were aware, Arya Abano was dead.

Shouting from different men in the convoy signaled the beginning of their journey, Arya looking to Porter for some reassurance of their journey. It would be a lot of walking, with her already malnourished state she wasn't sure how long she could last.

"Push comes to shove we'll put you on the wagon," Eryn said with a nod toward the bodies. "The benefits of a Selkie is your healing magic. Those folks need all the help they can get."

Help. Eryn did not mean to depreciate Arya's value or see her as a helpless victim. She saw her as a Selkie. A member of the resistance and a valuable player when it came to saving the lives of her people. *Their* people.

Arya nodded. "Let me know when they need me and I'll do my part."

Eryn smirked, patting Arya on the shoulder before beginning to walk with the others. Arya followed the woman, noticing the jagged scars that coated her back in a leathery pattern of previous torture. She knew those scars. Had them upon her own body, a gift from her previous betrothed. It meant that there was more to Eryn than just her ego adding to the authority. She'd seen war. Had been a victim—no, survivor. Like Arya.

"Stop staring." Porter coughed.

"I'm not," Arya protested.

He raised his brows, the dubious expression on his face causing Arya to blush. Leave it to her so called protector to make her feel so called out. "Sure."

The convoy travelled for hours, Arya impatiently walking with the group. She would catch Eryn looking back at her every so often, but her attention was on the wounded that walked with them. It was like watching a bee in a field of flowers. She hopped from one person to the next, offering water and dried meat. With the injured she was less intimidating, nurturing and careful. These people were special to her, regarded like family. It showed there were two sides to every person. That not everyone was as they portrayed themselves, especially in times of war.

Porter and Arya did not speak as they travelled, nor did the others walking around them. They marched to the sound of wagon wheels rolling, the moans of the severely injured, and shuffling steps of those walking around them. It was not a protection detail. It was in no way a convoy that would protect Arya should trouble arise on their journey. The damage between the group was monumental, and even as they travelled farther away from the humans who threatened the borders, there were other dangers that faced them.

Arya remembered her brother telling stories of monsters that lived in Teielmor. Fanged creatures with multiple arms and tails with venomous spikes. It had been years since she heard those stories, a child barely able to read. She'd remembered her father scolding Kai for telling her and Meriah such things as they laid in bed unable to sleep, terrified of those monsters coming to devour them. Those were only stories though, right? Then again, the gods were myths until they appeared to her. Where those fuckers were now, Arya would've liked to know. Always gone when danger awaited her, there when she didn't want them to be.

Wind picked up around them, twirling the dirt in the road into a vortex. Some of the walking wounded smiled, one lifting her hand and sending more air into the vortex. Petals of flowers joined the dirt, twisting around the walking group like a dog running around its owner. It changed shapes, another Sylph taking over the creation and making it into a bird, flying through the air and crashing into another man's face. Arya chuckled, noticing the narrowed look that he gave the other, moving the rocks to create a barrier the Sylph tripped over.

"Fucker!" The Sylph laughed, wrapping an arm around the Dullahan's shoulders. It was lighthearted, the two messing with each other even when they had been injured in the fight. A community built from a common enemy that Arya was allowed to witness and share.

"Arya!" Eryn called, further away near the wagon. "We need you."

Arya nodded, jogging toward the moving cart. In the narrow path she saw a man, his right eye covered with a bandage, focus on the woman who laid in the third row up. Her breathing was labored, skin pale, lips barely holding their color. Sweat covered the woman, soaking the bandages over her stomach and saturating the thin wool that served as a blanket.

It was her turn to help, she realized, the man barely able to pull a small amount of water from the surrounding sources.

"Help me in," Arya said. Eryn nodded, grabbing Arya by the waist and hoisting her into the cart like she weighed nothing. It shocked her for a moment, not realizing how strong Eryn was. Then again, Arya was severely thin.

She approached the man who had tears in his eyes, staring at the woman. "I can't save her. My-my magic is failing me."

192

Arya shook her head, touching the man on the shoulder. "You're wounded and still trying to save others. You are doing what you can. Let me help now."

He nodded, stepping back and allowing Arya to take his place. She closed her eyes, her hands hovering over the woman. She felt the rush of her magic in her blood, calling upon it with force. Her senses heightened where she felt the water all around her, ready to obey her command. Calling upon it, Arya opened her eyes, focusing her energy into the woman's wound. Water hovered around her outstretched fingers, giving off a blue glow. She touched the woman's bandages, instructing the water to go beneath the fabric, cleaning it and flushing the wound.

There was resistance from the water, feeding back darkened liquid. She furrowed her brows, never having been taught what that meant. She was in the middle of her training, when she was thrust into Kulessa's grip. Arya furrowed her brows, a pounding erupting in her chest and a knot forming in her throat.

"It means the infection reached her blood," Porter said in a low voice. His breath brushed against her ear, Arya glancing at him through her peripherals.

"What do I do?" She asked, her cheeks heating as she asked a simple question she should've known the answer to.

Porter nodded to the darkened water, lifting his hand. She watched as he led the toxic material away from the collected healing material, allowing it to vaporize in the air.

"You need help from another to get rid of the infected liquid."

Arya nodded, continuing to focus on the wound. Through the tiring efforts of healing, and with Porter's help expelling the dirtied water, the woman stopped moaning and her skin returned to a less intimidating color. Porter walked around Arya, pressing a hand to the woman's head. He nodded, smiling at her. "She's no longer feverish. You might've just given her a chance to survive."

The praise filled Arya in a way she never expected. Pride in her Selkie abilities amplified, a smile growing on her face. Never had she thought the beautiful creature she was had been anything but weak. A lowly addition to the fae that had no place attempting to be a warrior of any type. She had run each chance she got, hid when things got tough, accepted death with every trauma she endured. Yet, in that moment, she was more than that. A healer. A savior. A warrior in her own way.

Porter gave her a smirk back, pleased with the display of happiness she showed. He rose from his squatted position, smile dropping as he looked upon the person in the cot in front of him.

Arya rose, standing beside him to view the cause of his discontent. She gasped, holding her hand to her mouth. In front of them was a Selkie. Their body was mangled and cut, various pieces of iron still in their wounds. Even with the damage, their chest rose, if barely. The horror of their condition was not with their iron clad wounds or of the blood that coated the bandages. It was the object that laid over their body. A piece of them so tarnished and destroyed it would mean their ultimate demise.

Arya touched the torn and tattered skin of their seal form, the edges and bottom dried like a pelt. A tear slid down her cheek, knowing the loss of their skin would determine if they could find the will to survive. All connection to their kind was cut off. The burning sensation of loss all consuming. It was a miracle their body hadn't given out already.

"A lot of us are like that when they come onto the wagon," the Selkie from before said in a hallow voice.

Arya forced her eyes away from the lost soul, instinctively touching the skin that was tucked safely away in her bag. "How many?"

The man shook his head. "Hundreds? Thousands? Who knows. When Kulessa arrived on the shores of Asita, they damaged so many skins it wasn't even fair. A war crime by any means."

Arya's mouth fell open, a breath forcing itself out. It was Porter who choked out, "They attacked Asita?"

He was as horrified as she was. Asita was one of the most peaceful of the provinces. Why not go for Fintan or Ilmari with their surprise attack? Inflict the most damage on the ones with warriors trained at a young age. Then the realization hit her. It was because of what she could do. What all Selkies are able to do. Heal.

The man nodded, snorting as if the situation was somehow funny, yet humor was absent from the sound. "You two are the ones who escaped Kulessa, aren't you?" Porter and Arya nodded hollowly. "Figured." He sighed,

195

touching his eye as he looked to the ground. "They came in the night, no warning or announcement. It was silent, just another night and the moon was dark." Arya wrang her hands together. Her mother had told her it was not safe to swim with a dark moon, a Selkie tradition passed down from generation to generation. She didn't know how the humans found out. What Selkie they had tortured to figure out that information, dooming their people. "They came onto the shores in row boats, slaughtering the guards without raising the slightest alarm. Until one got back from patrol and found their comrades in a pool of their blood." He looked out the back of the wagon, his focus far away as he recalled the night. "There were so many screams, people gathering weapons when we heard the alarm bells tolling. My wife and three children were in the house when it happened. I told my girl to go to the shore. To swim with the children to Dunia. There was a chance there for them. Refuge. Safety. I didn't know more humans were on the shores, surrounding the water with fire."

Visions of the tragedy played in her mind, the helplessness that consumed those victims. The horrors they witnessed. She'd expected trauma and pain for so many, but it was different when it came to those back in her home. The first attack among so many.

"We couldn't take them all," he said, "there was just no time to prepare ourselves." His hand brushed through the dark curls of his hair. "Those who tried to escape were either killed, or their skins thrown into the fire."

"Causing mass suicide," Porter mumbled.

The Selkie nodded. "My wife included. Those who survived were hollow forms of their old selves. Some didn't talk, others couldn't function. I know far too many who laid crying and begging for relief from the burning." His voice shook, head shaking. Hands pulled at the exposed hair on his head. "The babes were in pain, so I did what no father should have to do. Too many having to do the same to those they loved."

Arya gasped, tears streaming down her cheeks. How could they? How could the humans be so ruthless to ruin people just trying to live their lives? There were no morals or sympathy for those innocents. War crimes thrust upon them and genocide happening on soil that was not theirs to tarnish with blood that was bonded to the ocean and water. Healers, pacifists, children, women, and men just living life.

"I'm so sorry." It was all she could say. No form of words would make it any better.

He nodded, the apology meaning nothing to him. His family was gone, and now he was unable to avenge them due to injury impairing his ability to fight. "Is it true what they say?"

Arya shook her head, unsure what he meant.

He snorted, finally looking at her. "That you will be the one to stop this madness?"

Arya opened and closed her mouth, shocked such a thing was said. She was no one. A formerly kidnapped Selkie. Nothing special. "I will do my best to help, but I cannot promise anything."

He shrugged, nodding. "It's all any of us can do, isn't it?"

20

As the sun shed orange rays through the sky, the convoy set up camp on the plains that surrounded them. Tall grass was leveled with injured Dullahan settling rock and earth over it in a large circle. A fire was created in the center, providing warmth for the cool night under the Ilmari stars.

The Selkie, who introduced himself as Aalto, relieved Arya and Porter from their care of the injured on the wagon, allowing them to relax among the others. Eryn had given them sleep sacks, nodding in a silent thanks for their work with the injured before moving on to help others set up for the night.

Porter stretched as he sprawled out on the blanket, arching his head back and extending his arms to the side. Arya, however, had the opposite reaction. She curled her knees to her chest, unable to shake the horrors that her people had endured while she was trapped in Kulessa. The bottom half of her face was hidden behind the fabric of her pants, eyes staring into the flames that danced in front of her.

Arya knew so much from her entrapment, yet she knew so little at the same time. The gods didn't tell her this. Roderick didn't discuss the war and Emeric failed to mention human attacks on Teielmor soils. Especially ones on Asita, Arya's home. What else had she missed? What didn't she know that she should?

Arya shook her head, ridding herself of those thoughts. Disappearing into the helplessness of her mind would do nothing for the determination needed to stop this nonsense. Too much needed to get done for her to place herself in that situation.

"How much did you learn before you were forced away to Kulessa?" Porter asked, his legs stretched out toward the fire.

Arya shook her head, unsure. "I was learning healing, and Kai was teaching me to make weapons from water."

Porter snorted, nodding as if the news they learned today had never happened. "I assumed your parents would've had you with special tutors and advanced courses with your status and all."

Arya rolled her eyes. "My mother had taught me herself. She always said a Selkie is only as knowledgeable as the teacher they learn from, and my mother saw herself highly trained."

Porter nodded his head to the side. "Your mother was a formidable warrior. A great healer too."

"Did you know her?" Arya asked, interested in how Porter had known of her mother's talents.

"Not personally, but I had been trained by your grandfather."

Arya leaned back, looking Porter up and down. "I didn't peg you for someone in the forces."

"Was it my dazzling smile and captured skin?" He teased, wiggling his brows.

"Something like that." Arya laughed.

Porter pulled his legs into a crossed position, leaning forward with his hands folded in front of him. He stared at his fingers, gaze fixated upon them. "Your grandfather was no novice. I know you probably never got to meet the man, but there was no better teacher for those who wanted to learn. He would put his entire life into training those who really put in the work. Always saw through bullshit, and rewarded achievements."

Arya looked back to the flames, imagining the man that had been only a portrait on the walls of her childhood home. She had never been told stories of him, her mother refusing to say much about her father. "He sounds like a devoted man."

Porter smirked. "Loved your mother, bragged about her nonstop."

Arya nodded. She wished her mother had loved her enough to look for her. Instead, she got replaced, like her and Meriah were nothing. She wondered if the gods left that information out of the dream to spare her the agony it caused. Would her parents even greet her like they did in the dream? Have they even told their new daughters about her and Meriah?

"Would you like me to train you?" Porter asked.

Arya turned her head, not expecting the offer. "Train me?"

Porter nodded. "It seems you are missing some vital information when it comes to all you can do. Especially since you are able to control a lot more from pure talent that many Selkies don't have."

"Like what?" She asked.

"Well, for one, that tidal wave you threw at Emeric."

Arya nodded, recalling the power she held in her dream and wondering if it was an exaggeration the gods concocted or if it was only a fraction of what she could really do. "I would like you to teach me, I really would like to have more control over the things I can do. I know I practiced in the dungeons, but mostly on the rats using the water in their blood—."

Porter's hand covered Arya's mouth, stopping her from explaining further. He removed it, shushing her with his finger to his lips. Quickly, he looked around, as if what she said would get her in trouble or something.

"You've used blood magic?" He whispered in a low tone that was barely audible.

Arya nodded, confused at his change. His body was tense, looking straight into the fire like it was an enemy he needed to find a weakness to.

"Arya, you mustn't tell anyone about this. Blood magic is forbidden, a crime and severe form of magic that has consequences when used."

"What sort of consequences?" She asked.

"Madness, all others who've used it went insane. Lost themselves in the power and control of others," Porter hissed, "It will consume you in darkness will never let you go. But it does tell us one thing." Arya looked at him, nervous about this power she was using in Kulessa without knowing the damage it could've caused her. "Only the strongest Selkies can perform it. You have more power than you realize."

That had to be a lie.

If she had the power he suggested she did, Meriah would still be alive. They would've never washed up on Kulessan shores. Arya could've saved her people who were slaughtered. Killed Roderick when she had the chance. Refused to be used as a toy for the humans who bought her. "Nice try."

"I'm not joking, Arya," Porter said.

"I'm tired, I'll talk to you in the morning," Arya dismissed, laying with her back to him. The ground was soft beneath her, yet her mind would not stop racing with thoughts. Her stomach held a dark rock within that refused to let her get comfortable. However, she didn't want to show Porter she was still awake.

Arya hadn't expected there to be peace when she arrived back in Teielmor, but she had expected it to be easier. Nurturing, maybe? Not so chaotic and dark. Mixing that with her own unresolved issues that dove deeper than she cared to explore. She wanted to train. Act like nothing was wrong with her and find happiness again. Only, a small voice in her head kept telling her that happiness was not something she deserved. A faded memory that would never be relived.

Tears welled in her eyes, her hand covering her mouth as she cried. Arya didn't want anyone to ask if she was okay. She wasn't, no one there was. They were all fighting their own demons. All that mattered in that moment was that she was back in Teielmor and soon she would see her friends again. If they were even still alive... no, she couldn't think like that. Arya shook her head, clearing the thought from her mind.

Eventually, the exhaustion of those dark thoughts and use of her magic consumed her. Dreams filled her mind, reliving the things she'd seen, mind processing the best it could, but burying the parts she needed time to be able to heal from.

A clattering woke Arya from sleep. She blinked away the drowsiness, lifting her head to look around. Their group slept around her, no signs of anyone missing from their spot. The noise happened again, this time back toward the wagon. An unorganized rhythmic pattern of coins dropping on metal.

She looked over to where Aalto slept, his body curled, and face contorted into a pinched expression. Slowly, Arya rose from her spot, rubbing her eyes. There was a tightness to her joints, sleeping on the ground having an impact like that of the dungeons in Kulessa did. Stretching out her arms and leaning back, she attempted to soothe those aching muscles as she walked to the wagon.

Opening in the back, Arya looked inside, squinting to try and see through the darkness. Nothing seemed out of place. The injured were in their spots, moans virtually silent, only the sound of hushed, wispy breathing. Arya furrowed her brows as the hair on her arms stood up. Everything inside Arya screamed for her to run. Yet, there wasn't any clear reason why. She chalked it up to not being used to being in Teielmor again. Arya grabbed onto the side of the wagon, lifting herself inside. Summoning water, she hovered it over each of the injured within, checking on their stabilization. That's when she heard the noise again. This time from behind her.

The tall grass hid its location, wind tossing the strands to make it look as though it were a sea upon the land. Arya turned fully, letting go of the wagon as she hopped to the ground. The steps she took sounded too loud against the quiet of the night, the warmth of the fire fading the longer she strayed from its blaze. Curiosity, however, got the better of her.

Pushing through the grass, Arya approached where she heard the sound. Grass concealed her path, the thought of struggling to find her way back crossing Arya's mind. The jingle sounded again, closer than it was before. She increased her speed, pushing until she came to a clearing. In it was a raven with a bag of coins tipped to the side. Beneath it, a piece of discarded armor. Arya furrowed her brows. How did a raven get this far into Ilmari without any forest around to nest in. Not only that, but the armor it was spilling the coins onto was far too large for it to carry.

That's when it looked at Arya, cocking its head to the side. The red eyes looked back at her with a twinkle in them as if it had expected her.

"Oh fuck," Arya breathed, stepping back. She had assumed crossing the river had kept her safe from those freaks. Nothing was safe, she needed to remember. Safe was a myth.

From behind the crow, the grass parted, shadows darkening the clearing. "Are we done with our little game of chase, Arya?"

Emeric.

"You've made it far," he said, brushing the feathers down on the bird. It had to be Rook. No other being could share the bloody red tint of her eyes. "Impressive, though it's time to come home now." Arya shook her head, taking another step back. "It's not a suggestion, Arya."

There was no way Arya would be strong enough to fight Emeric in the middle of the land. Not enough water to give her time to escape. Running would need to be her only option to attempt to evade him. There needed to be a distraction for her to get the opportunity to run, though.

As if the gods were attempting to make up for their mistakes, Rook took to the air. She cawed several times, circling the two before escaping. Emeric furrowed his brows, and in the next second, another entered the clearing.

206

The thing that entered was nothing short of hellish. String like hair hung off the scalp of the creature, skin coated in dried dirt and powdered with a white substance. Its small eyes were black, blinking slowly as if not expecting the two to be there. Opening its mouth, Arya's blood went cold. Hair rose on the back of her neck as she looked at the rows of sharp teeth that filled the opening, extending to the back of its neck. Talons dug into the earth with each step it took, its arms almost human if not for the insanely long proportions. A forked tongue flicked at the air, head tilting to the side as if sensing which of them would be the best to devour. It let out a barking hiss, waiting for either of them to respond.

Slowly, Arya took a step back, the crunch of the grass beneath her alerting the creature of her movement, its head snapping in her direction. Lips parted, showing off its teeth once again in a deadly smile. Cold sweat dripped from her temple, mind attempting to process how the fuck she would be able to get away without Emeric going for her as well.

And so, taking a chance, Arya ran.

21

Barking chased Arya, the grass whipping her face and arms as she darted through. There was no time to see if it followed her, hearing the barking all around her. Apparently, that thing was a pack hunter. There was no sign of Emeric anywhere, Arya grateful she at least didn't have to worry about him at that moment, only the unknown number or vicious creatures that hunted her. No big deal or anything.

Her lungs burned with the exertion, paranoia leaving her unable to tell if the sound of grass crunching was her, or something coming closer.

"Porter!" She screamed, praying those things wouldn't target the injured in the wagon. "Porter! Monsters!"

"Arya!" She heard, her direction changing to follow the voice. "Arya, where are you?"

Her legs pumped, working harder than she could afford to. From her right, the grass parted as one of those creatures jumped at her. She slid, body falling back, narrowly missing the claws that swiped at her. It tumbled to the ground, once again obscured by the vegetation. Not willing to let the thing catch up to her, Arya picked herself up, stumbling into a run again.

Light appeared ahead, peeking through the strands of straw. Shouting got louder. Orders of weapons thrown into the air. Breaking through the grass, Arya found herself in the circle that made their campsite. Unfortunately, the creatures found it first. Aalto laid with his eyes permanently transfixed into an expression of horror. His skin paled, blood continuing to drain into a pool around him. Arya gasped as she watched as one of the creatures clawed at his stomach, digging into the flesh and devouring the contents within. It pulled up, snapping a piece of intestine that hung out of its mouth, face smeared of in red.

"Arya!" Porter yelled. He was across the field, helping Eryn defend the wagon of helpless wounded. Others fought the onslaught of monsters, taking swords to them and archers firing arrows. The creatures seemed unaffected by their weapons, even with the magic of Salamanders, they were immune to the flames.

That's when she noticed the Dullahan and Sylph that had been so jovial the morning before back-to-back. Creatures surrounded them, the two barely holding off attacks. One of the monsters lunged at the Dullahan who successfully blocked it with a sword, only for another to bite down on his arm. He screamed out, his Sylph friend looking back, allowing another to lunge at her and grab hold of her leg.

Arya ran at them, picking up a sword from another victim of the creatures. She chased the creature that had begun to drag the Sylph away, knowing if it made it into the brush, there would be no escape for the fae. Her body pushed through the agony it was in, getting to the monster and slamming the sword down onto its spined back.

It dropped the Sylph, biting where Arya stood. She jumped back, the sword embedded into the thing. It thrashed, attempting to shake the metal free. The distraction gave the two enough time to escape, running back to the wagon where others huddled inside.

It was a bloody massacre, those things ripping into the flesh of the unlucky. The Sylph woman cried out as she passed by her friend, who was now being fought over by two creatures. She struggled against Arya, attempting to go toward his corpse, failing to do anything against the frail woman in her injured state.

"I need to help him!" She protested.

"He's beyond our help now," Arya said, "only the gods can give him peace."

The Sylph cringed, nodding as she forced herself forward, the last two to reach the wagon. Arya helped the woman in, Eryn and Porter lifting her by her arms.

Then Arya was hit. Air left her body as it was jerked to the side, pain erupting through her stomach. She landed on the dirt, rolling until coming to a complete stop. Moaning,

Arya attempted to rise, pain shooting through her arm as she attempted to rise. Arya screamed out, gripping the limb, looking up only to see one of the creatures slowly stalk toward her. Blue oozed from a wound in its back, Arya realizing it was the same one she had saved the Sylph from. Apparently, they hold grudges.

It gave off a low growl, Arya doing her best to crawl backwards. This had to be her end. Nothing killed these things, the dead warriors in their camp proved as much.

Arya looked back at those huddled in the wagon watching what could be her final moments. "Go!"

"Arya, no!" Porter yelled.

She ignored him, meeting Eryn's eyes. "Go."

Eryn pressed her lips together for a moment before nodding and turning to the driver. The wagon took off, the oxen thrusting into motion as fast as they could. Arya saw Porter get shoved back into the wagon, Eryn using her entire body to force him down. Arya was thankful that Eryn understood her desire to keep Porter safe. She was a goner, but Porter deserved to live.

Arya looked back at her creature, grateful the fear consuming her replaced the overwhelming guilt of leaving her friends behind. Closing her eyes, Arya waited for the impact of the creature. The pain that would mean the end of her life. At least she'd die on Teielmor soil. Would be against fae creatures and not that of humans. She thought back to her friends, wishing she could've told them how much they meant to her. Sure, she'd sound like a crazy person, but it was worth it to her. There was so much left unsaid. She wanted to tell Mies that she forgave him. That she was willing to marry Leif. That she always wanted to feel what steam she could make with Idoh. To have several more late night swims with Winslet, and to tell Zephyr he's worth more to her than just being her prince. Arya sighed, too bad she never got to kill Roderick.

The moment became too long. The creature should've lunged at her by then, her guts in its mouth as it devoured her. Yet, she was still breathing and insides where they should be. Tempting fate, she peeked, seeing the creature turning its attention to a new threat. Something these things didn't like, which Arya was not to fond of finding out what that was either.

Mist rolled in, covering the road in waves. The creatures barked, giving their attention to the new thing that threatened them. Many barred their teeth, growling low. Some slunk back into the grass, staying as still as they could to not be spotted by whatever came.

Arya took her chance to hide, shifting herself backwards to conceal herself in the brush. She had a chance if she couldn't be seen. The sound of hooves echoed over the road, followed by slicing. Heaving breaths accompanied the shrieks of the creatures as they were slaughtered. Arya looked out from her hiding spot, unable to see what saved her, but noticed the splatter of blue blood decorating the ground.

The creature that Arya injured fell before her, splattering her with the juices of its insides. However, unlike the minor wound Arya inflicted upon it, the entirety of its head was gone. An oozing pool of bone and flesh in its place.

The clopping of hooves stopped, a horse's snort announcing itself in the eerie silence. A pair of boots came from the horse's back, walking a few feet before stopping. They bent down, Arya seeing the riding pants and thick coat that were signature for Dullahan riders.

Arya eagerly left her position, pushing through the weeds with her good hand. The man stood quickly, holding out a sword that seemed to be made completely of mist. Arya held her hand up, the other cradled to her chest. "Please, I just want to get back to my convoy."

The sword lowered slowly, Arya meeting his eyes. There was a sense of recognition as she stared at him, but no idea where she knew him from. The sword disappeared in his hand, the man falling to his knees before her. A smile appeared from beneath his untamed beard, brown eyes sparkling behind the long locks of chestnut hair.

"It can't be," he laughed.

Goosebumps rose on her body, eyes widening as she placed where she knew him. His face was covered in creature blood and dirt. Unkept appearance was different from how she remembered him. Arya approached slowly, reaching out her hand to touch his face. She needed to prove he was real. That this wasn't some trick or illusion.

Warmth hovered where she touched, his hand covering hers. Her blood livened with the contact, flushing quickly and giving her the energy she thought was depleted.

Ignoring the pain, Arya wrapped her arms around his neck, unable to help the sobs that came from deep in her core. The crying was the type that accompanied screams, the sound muffled by his jacket. His arms wrapped around her, head tucking into her shoulder.

"I've looked everywhere for you," he whispered, voice breaking.

"I'm so happy to see you," she choked, "I've been through so much—."

"I know," he whispered, brushing a hand down her face. "I'm here now, Arya, I'm here."

Her embrace tightened around him again, that homely warmth enveloping her just like it had before. No, not like before, it was better. More intense. A feeling she would never forget. It felt as though their souls merged in that moment, Arya unable to imagine being without him again. History and timeless devotion shared between them in an unspoken connection.

She needed to say his name. To hear it aloud. One she'd only said in the solitary confinement of her Kulessan cell. A spell to prove he was really in front of her. "Mies."

22

It was impossible to let go of Mies. It was strange, her memory going back to what Leif said about him being a drunk. He did not smell of liquor, but of smoke and earth. A small scent of pine clung to him as well, Arya wondering if he had recently been in the forest.

Mies helped her onto his horse, the red eyed stallion nodding his head up and down and stomping his feet as if impatient with them. Situating himself behind her, Arya leaned back into his chest, giving a small sigh of relief. She'd imagined reuniting with her friends again, each scenario hosting a different person who discovered her, but it was never Mies first. In many of those instances, she'd punched Mies in the face for what he did to her in that fake prophecy. Now, all she felt was relief. Arya was coming to find the gods mettle where they shouldn't, making her believe in things that weren't actually real.

Mies whipped the reins, pulling the horse to the direction of Castle Lofta, mist consuming them.

"Arya, you need to know I would never force you into something you didn't want to do," he rushed as if unable to get the words out fast enough. Not what she was expecting him to say.

"You had the vision too?"

He was silent, but his knuckles whitened as he held the reins tighter. That's all she needed to know. It was all fake anyway, the gods playing with their pawns to perform a demented game of match maker.

"I believe you," Arya said finally, running her fingers over the fabric of his coat. Something inside her felt as though Mies wouldn't lie to her. That his words and affirmation was true. An unspoken vow between them that denied him that right.

"What were those things back there?" She asked, wanting to focus on anything other than the gods.

"Cavernlings," he said, "luckily, their one known enemy is Dullahan horses."

Arya furrowed her brows, looking back to Mies. "Are the horses carnivorous?"

"Omnivores, but all horses are under the right circumstances."

"Huh." Arya had assumed horses were all herbivores, but considering her lack of knowledge of the

Cavernlings, it was possible her animal studies were not up to par with the world.

"Arya," Mies said hesitantly. She glanced to him, knowing something terrible was about to come out of his mouth. "Why didn't you come to Ilmari like you were supposed to?"

It was a topic she hated to think about.

"Phobus prevented me. Someone convinced Roderick that Phobus was right to forbid me from going." Arya focused ahead, her skin crawling as she remembered how Phobus had his way with her that same evening. The whispers of his anger sent shivers down her spine and made her stomach ache with the memory of his cane against her body.

"Did they..." he trailed off, unable to finish the sentence, but Arya knew what he was going to ask.

She nodded. "My price depended on the person and their rank."

A dark growl came from Mies, the mist picking up around them. She leaned back into him, breathing deeply. Even the mist smelled of pine, but also the soil before it rains.

"This is so much better than that fucking dream," she mumbled, allowing herself to relax into him. For once, she could imagine herself safe. There was no Emeric or Roderick or Evelyn. It was just Arya in a seaside cottage that danced with wildflowers. Children's laughter echoed over the fields, and Mies in the sand of the beach wearing Selkie clothes, splashing water at the children who were the sources of that laughter.

"Arya."

She blinked, seeing that the sun blazed in the noontime sky. It was still dark when they started on their journey. How long had she been asleep? When did she fall asleep?

"Where are we?" Arya asked, stretching.

"A mile from Castle Lofta."

Arya paused. What happened to being a few days out? Where was the convoy of injured? "You used the mist to get here faster, didn't you?" Mies nodded. "Mies, there are sick and injured who need to be here more than I do!"

"Your safety is our main priority," he grumbled, "the convoy will get here just like any other did."

Arya narrowed her eyes, scowling at Mies. "They need help. They fought to keep humans out. *Those people* are heroes. *Injured* heroes."

Mies grit his teeth, temple popping. "I can't go back for them, however, I will send others to assist them faster."

It was the best she was going to get. If all her friends had the same dream, there was no way they would leave her, just like she refused to leave them. A link binding them together.

"Fine," she said, "I'm holding you to that."

"You have my word."

It was only minutes later that Mies turned into an opening marked with the change of dirt roads to that of white gravel. The clean lawn and pristine stair entry like she had seen in her vision was missing. People rushed without care of who the newcomers were. Wounded sat upon the stairs, a maid scrubbing blood from a step a distance away from them. Selkies rushed in and out of the main entrance, most likely healing those they could. Others went around with refreshments, providing the best support they could in the situation they were in.

Mies stopped his horse in front of the open doors to Castle Lofta. Arya's stomach flipped, nerves getting the best of her. This is what she had wanted. The thing that kept her alive. Now that she was here, finally able to see those she loved without meeting, she didn't know if she could do it.

"What's wrong?" Mies asked.

"What if they don't like who I've become?"

Mies snorted, tussling her hair. "Come on, let's go see your family."

Taking her hand, Mies led Arya through the doors, the foyer opening up around her. Painted Sylphs decorated the ceilings, resting on storm clouds. A giant crystal chandelier hung from a golden chain. Unlike her dream, however, the halls were lined with cots and blankets. Wounded soldiers laid upon them. There was a buzzing energy around her, Arya feeling invisible among the chaos that encompassed the castle.

Mies stepped around the chaos, Arya taking in all that was around her as she followed. So many were there. Hurt. Dying.

Arya stopped. In the corner, a small boy hugged a tattered bear, laying on the side of a soldier. Blood had saturated his bandages, skin pale. She went toward the two, letting go of Mies's hand. His protests were nothing more than whispering of wind as she approached. Her stomach sank the closer she got, sensing only one heart. Placing a hand to the injured soldier, she only felt cold. No sign of life. She hovered her hands over his wounds, finding no amount of healing will work. Selkies cannot bring back the dead.

Arya turned her body, staring at Mies with tears in her eyes. She shook her head, Mies bowing his as he understood what she meant. Her attention then went to the boy.

"Honey," she said in the sweetest voice possible. The boy's head rose, face turned in her direction. Arya gasped at the sight of him. His face was scarred, sliced with iron no doubt, but his eyes were what made the anger inside her boil and a scream build in her throat. Gray orbs were all that was left to prove the child once had sight, a mask of red offering Arya an idea of the attack he faced.

"Are you talking to me, ma'am?" he asked in the smallest voice Arya had ever heard. He didn't deserve this. He was a child. A baby.

"I am," Arya said, attempting and failing to keep the quiver hidden.

"What can I do for you?" A proper little gentleman.

"Sweet child, is this man your friend?"

Arya's heart sank as she saw the boy look past her, unable to tell where she was, only knowing the direction her voice came from. "No ma'am, he's my pa."

"Where is your mother?" She asked, hopeful he would have one parent left.

The boy looked down. "Ma went with the gods when I was born."

Fuck.

Arya looked around her for help, unable to be the one to tell this poor child that his family is gone. She locked eyes with a Dullahan, the desperation in the stare encouraging her to come closer.

"What's wrong?" She asked Arya.

"His father is gone," Arya whispered, "I cannot be the one to tell him. I can't handle it."

The woman sighed, placing a hand on Arya's shoulder. "Just arrived?" Arya nodded. "Go on, I'll take care of it."

Mies once again took Arya's hand, leading her away from the boy and his dead father. She forced herself to look away, unable to watch his life be destroyed by war. As they turned down a hall, escaping the sight of wounded and dead, Arya heard the young boy's protests and screams. She closed her eyes tightly, pressing a hand to her mouth.

"It's not your fault," Mies soothed.

She shook her head. "None of this should've happened. The attack on Asita. The wounded and dead. Orphans and childless parents."

"We're at war, Arya."

Mies held a hardness in his eyes that she hated to see. Darkness had infiltrated his soul, the sight of death the only cause to hide away behind fact.

221

"Who died?" She asked, fearing the answer.

"Ila."

Arya fell against the wall, mouth dropping open. The lively woman who had been her penpal throughout the years of her childhood. Mies's sister. "How?"

"War." He did not elaborate, walking down the halls that she'd known so well from the gods' vision. Reluctantly, Arya followed, hollow and filled with sorrow. How many others have died that she knew?

Familiar wooden doors greeted Arya with a sign. "*Closed for Construction. Dangerous, do not enter.*"

She touched the door, tracing her fingers over the carvings she never paid much mind to. A flash of Winslet's broken and bloodied corpse entered her thoughts. "It's just a dream," Arya reminded herself. "It was only a dream."

Twisting the nob, Arya entered. The smell of parchment and ink hit her first, just as it had in the vision. Towering shelves filled with books surrounded her. She stepped in slowly, running her fingers over the bindings. Her window was just how she'd left it, the sun outside displaying an assortment of colors where the light touched. A couch and two chairs were the centerpieces of the room, a coffee table between the three.

"I'm going to find the others, stay here," Mies instructed. Arya turned, a soft smile to encourage the action. He closed the distance between them slowly, his hand brushing along her cheek. "I still can't believe you're back." Without another word, Mies turned on his heel, marching out of the room.

Arya looked around as the door closed, leaving her alone in a place so familiar yet foreign.

"He's not too bad looking with a beard." The voice sent shivers down her spine. "Charming, in a rugged farmer sort of way."

Arya directed her gaze to the source of the sound, the god sitting upon the couch. Siion crossed their long legs in front of themselves as if patiently waiting for Arya the entire time.

"What do you want?"

"Oh, nothing too much, just wondering when you plan to stop running from your betrothed?"

Arya scoffed, crossing her arms. "Yeah, you forgot to mention the part where he was my torturer in Roderick's care."

Siion waved a three fingered hand at Arya. "Semantics, my dear."

"It's pretty fucking important to me that my spouse is not capable of torture. Specifically torture on *me*."

Siion sighed, rubbing a hand over their white face. "Either way, you made a deal with a god, dear girl. You do not want to know what happens if you go back on that promise."

"Do the other gods know you are speaking to me?" Arya asked.

Before she realized what was happening, Siion grabbed Arya by the neck, lifting her into the air. Air refused to enter her lungs, mouth gaping open and closed like a fish out of water.

223

"Tell them, and I will make your little pathetic life hell, girl. Remember, I am still a god!" Arya drug her nails over Siion's leathery hand, the action nothing to the god. Finally, Siion let Arya go, her body falling limp to the floor. She heaved in a long breath. The burning in her chest faded, air never feeling so good. "I look forward to you holding up your end of our bargain," Siion said casually. "And do keep our little secret between us."

Arya felt the presence of the god leave the room. She forced herself to a sitting position, sighing deeply as she rubbed her throat. What sort of mess did she get herself into?

A hand reached out to Arya. She looked at it not realizing anyone else was in the room with her. Flowing blue fabric covered the woman, long blonde hair like golden rays of sunlight reaching down to her waist.

"It seems like no matter the outcome of fate, you always get yourself into more trouble than you should," Winslet said.

Arya looked up to her friend, grabbing her hand and pulling her into a tight embrace. The feeling of a cool stream on a hot summer's day soothed Arya's worry. With Winslet, it was like swimming with her skin. "I'm so glad you're not dead."

"Me too." Her laughter filled the space, though it was not as full as it had been in her dream.

Arya pushed her back, tucking a piece of hair behind her ear. "It got to you, hasn't it?"

Winslet bit her lips together, refusing to meet Arya's eyes. "We're losing the war, Arya. When we do, there will no longer be Teielmor like we know it."

23

"Was it worse than before?" Winslet asked as the pair sat on the couch together. They joined together, holding each other's hands for comfort and a sense of companionship.

Arya nodded. "I was tortured, and Siion is not the only god harassing me."

Winslet rolled her eyes. "Leif is having the same issue with Raena and myself with Lir. Not sure about the others, but it's likely."

Her fingers dragged over Winslet's hands, still unable to believe the woman she'd seen torn to shreds by an iron laced bomb sat in front of her. There were no wounds on her flesh now, her complexion as clear as always.

"It wasn't your fault, you know." Arya looked up to Winslet, meeting the crystal blue of her eyes. "The bomb. It wasn't your fault. It was Roderick's. I don't harbor any ill will toward you, and would've forgiven you beyond the grave."

A lone tear slid down Arya's cheek. "I spent so long in the dungeons replaying in my head over and over. It was a vision of something that never happened, yet I still felt the same guilt and pain as if it did."

Winslet squeezed Arya's hands, giving her a smile that did not reach her eyes. The ones that were now filled with sorrow and pain. "I had wished those memories were real." Winslet admitted. "A time that never happened, yet did. I lived that with you, swam with you for the first time and snuck you away to the water your first night in Teielmor!" The girls laughed through their tears. "I remember being jealous of the time you spent with Idoh and Leif and Mies and Zephyr. I wanted you to myself, to show you that even if I was small and pretty, I could protect you too."

Arya lifted Winslet's hands to her mouth, kissing her knuckles. "I know you could. In a way, you protected me from my mind. You helped me in ways the others couldn't, a bond only Selkies could understand."

Winslet bit her lips together. "Arya, there's something you need to know—."

The doors to the library burst open, cutting off whatever Winslet was about to say. Arya furrowed her brows as her friend immediately closed her mouth, displaying the best put together face Arya had ever seen on a person. It truly was a disguise no one could see through.

Zephyr was the first through the door pausing as he saw her. He was older than she'd expected him to be.

227

Wrinkles creased his forehead, cheeks bones pronounced and the flesh hollow. He wore his crown, a silver circlet that showed off the cloud and feathers that came with Sylph symbolism.

"By the gods," he breathed. He broke into a run, jumping the coffee table and throwing himself over Arya. An electrifying pulse ran through her body. The hair on her arms rose, flesh buzzing with energy. It was like she was thrust into the heart of a thunderstorm, was a part of the lightning and thunder and surge of power that encompassed the clouds.

Arya hugged Zephyr back, fingers clawing at his back to get him closer than he already was. An impossible feat, but one she'd try anyway.

"Stop hogging!" Leif protested, throwing Zephyr off Arya and picking her up. He ran with her to the opposite side of the room, his smile larger than she'd ever seen it. Arya wrapped her arms around his neck. Emotions of all sorts assaulted her, amplified within her own. She felt everything in the room, but most importantly, she felt Leif.

He had not changed a bit since the dream or their conversations through the mirror. Sex appeal oozed from the man, though Arya noticed his figure was fuller, more muscular than before. The tip of a dark marking hid beneath the opened collar of his tunic, her fingers pulling aside the material to try and expose more. Leif stopped her, pressing his forehead to hers. "Another time."

Gently, Leif lowered her body, nodding away from her with his chin. Arya turned heart pounding in her chest. Leaning in the doorway, swords latched onto holsters on his hips, was Idoh. His hair was pulled into the regular bun, tied with a black ribbon. He did not approach her, staying in his spot in the doorway.

Years of pain and suffering built in her throat. *"I want to protect you, and I know I can in some things, but I also want you to experience life and all its joys."* He had said once upon a time. In a dream world that was so real in the moment. The only person she'd ever wanted to defend her.

With her chin quivering and tears falling down her cheeks, Arya ran to him, burying her face into his chest. Fire. It encompassed her body. A cooling flame that started in her core and licked at her limbs like serpents lashing at a threat. Idoh wrapped his arms around Arya, tucking her into him like he was her personal suit of armor.

"I'm so sorry," he choked in her ear.

Arya looked up to him, smiling against the horrors that threatened to show to her friends. "Never leave me again, Idoh Spitfyre, or so help me gods I will do more than just pin your ass."

He smiled, showing his teeth for Arya. "Gods, I fucking missed you, Little Flame."

Strangely, Arya's chest became tight. She coughed, attempting to take in more air. The attempt failed, pushing Idoh away to get more space. Unlike the dream, Arya could feel each of the swirling connections within her. It was like they fought for space, snapping and threatening each other. Her hand pressed to her chest, wheezing a breath she barely had.

"Fuck," Zephyr said.

Arya stumbled to the center of the room, pain erupting throughout her body. She could feel each bone, organ, muscle, everything. "Make it stop!"

Leif touched her gently, guiding her to the floor. "Easy now, just let it happen, Arya dear."

Grabbing his collar, Arya pulled on Leif, all too aware of each movement of bones, muscle, tendons, and skin. "Help me."

"I am, Arya dear. It's what needs to happen." He soothed, brushing back her sweat slicked hair.

Nothing felt worse. Thousands of hours of torture was endured in Kulessa. Millions of men tormenting her body to prove something to themselves about their fragile masculinity. Each death and unfortunate circumstance she faced was nothing compared to what she felt in that moment.

Arya gasped. No air. Why didn't they help her?

She looked over to her friends. All looked away, unable to see her as she was, yet not helping her either. She did so much to get back and be with them, and this is what they reward her with?

Arya's vision blurred, the edges darkening.

Then nothing.

Arya gasped taking in the air she missed, shooting upright. White light surrounded her, too bright to be indoors, yet too white to be caused by the sun. Looking around, there was no one around. The library in Castle Lofta missing, along with her friends. She stood, unsure where the ground stopped and sky began.

"Hello.?" She called out. It repeated back to her, echoing through the empty space.

Turning in her spot, Arya noticed an object in the distance. She approached it, looking for any answers to what could be going on. Was this death.? The afterlife they promised or something far more sinister than that.?

As she approached the object, she saw a person. "Hello!" Arya waved, seeing the person did the same. She slowed, realizing it was only a triple sided mirror. A reflection of herself bouncing back threefold. It was the first time Arya was able to see herself fully after the torture and neglect she faced in Kulessa. There was a disgusting mix of protruding bone and outlined muscle. Her cheeks were hollow, eyes dark and expressionless.

"You look like shit."

Arya looked into the mirror, noticing a woman looking back at her over her left shoulder. She had dark curls tucked into a sloppy braid, brown eyes and golden skin signifying that she hailed from Dunia. However, her clothes were older than what she was used to seeing. Pleated green skirts with a bustle and a corset top.

Turning quickly, Arya did not see any sign of a woman. Was she going crazy.? How would anyone be able to hide in a place like this.?

"Let her be." Another woman stood on her right side, a cloth dress held at the hips with a silver chained belt. Jewels glistened anywhere she could manage to situate them, including her silky gold hair.

"Who are you?" Arya yelled, twisting around. "What do you want?"

"We're you, Arya Abano," a woman who was eerily similar to Zephyr said with a smile. Golden wings stretched out behind her, glistening in the white of the room.

Arya shook her head. "No, this has to be a trick, or madness." That must be it. Arya officially went mad, trapped in her mind with nothing but a mirror with women trapped in her reflection.

"Don't be scared," a Finta woman said. She was dressed in black armor, a scar crossing over one eye, making it completely white while the other continued to be a bright orange. "We don't mean to harm you."

"I don't understand," Arya whimpered. It was too much.

"You are our last chance," The dazzling blonde said.

"The only one who had found them all." The Sylph said.

"Found who?" Arya pleaded for any of it to make sense.

"There's not enough time to explain," the Finta woman hissed. "Evelyn is coming. Prepare for war and conquer your lands from those pitiful humans!"

Arya shook her head.

"The coming days will bring horrors beyond your years. Know, life and death is an element in its own right." The Dunian woman stated.

Life and death? What the fuck was going on.

"Good luck, Arya."

232

The women reached out to her through the glass, gripping her shoulder. She felt each of their hands on her body. Looking down, mummified remains of each woman stood behind her, corpses that hosted the same clothing and features of those in the mirror. The difference, however, was methods of death were displayed upon their rotted flesh.

A spear pierced through the Finta woman's chest, dried blood staining what was left of the skin of her chin. The jeweled woman's throat was cut open to the bone. Rope hung from the Dullahan woman's neck, and the Sylph was covered in wounds and bruises that never got the chance to heal. The main injury being a head wound that caved in part of her skull.

"Don't end up like us," they said in unison, "kill Evelyn no matter who she is to you. This is your last life."

They pushed Arya through the glass of the mirror, shattering the pane and forcing her into darkness.

Sitting up, Arya grabbed her throat, scanning her surroundings for signs of the living corpses. What she did find was her friends sitting in the library, waiting. The light of day had gone, Winslet and Leif leaning on each other as they dozed. Zephyr sat in one of the chairs, crown in his lap, head tilted to his chest as he slept. Mies occupied the other chair, dangling his foot over one of the arms, a book covering his face. And in the window seat, Idoh looked out through the glass, a ball of fire dancing through his fingers.

Rising from her spot, legs shaking beneath her weight, she went to him.

"It happens to all of us at some point in our lives," Idoh said without looking at her. "Different versions of ourselves giving advice and warnings from their experiences in the past."

"They were me?" Arya asked, having a hard time believing each of those different women had once been her. They couldn't be more different than the girl she felt she was.

Idoh extinguished the fire that he had been playing with, turning his gaze to her. "Arya, you have no idea who you are, and you never do. The rest of us, we get memories of the past lives we lived. Always the same provinces, never the same story except for the desire to find you."

"Why me?" She asked, unsure she wanted to know the answer. Those who came looking for her never ended up having good intentions in the end.

"Because," Idoh said, "No one else in the world can make us feel as whole as you do."

Arya sighed, sitting on the bench beside him. Folding her hands in her lap, she rubbed her thumbs over each other. "Even if I believed what you said, I'm far more damaged than I was in that dream, Idoh. I was gone longer, tortured longer, and in different ways than before." She paused before locking her gaze upon his sunray eyes. "Spite is the only reason I survived this long."

Idoh shook his head. "No, it was because we were all in the same spot and the gods needed you to come to us."

"For their demented courting game?" Arya puffed a laugh. "Leif doesn't even cross the types of boundaries they did with the stupid game they play."

"Fuck, Arya, listen," Idoh hissed, "All of us are connected. That feeling you get when touching any of us, the flames that erupt between us, it's what brought you back to me. Something greater than the gods keeps bringing all of us back together each lifetime."

Arya didn't object to his idiotic fantasy, not willing to have Idoh upset with her. "What is the threat, then?"

"Evelyn. She appears every lifetime, controlling the Lux and aiming to kill you."

Her brows furrowed. "Why?"

Idoh shrugged. "In each lifetime I either died or didn't get to meet you before you passed on."

"Lovely," Arya mumbled. Whether or not she believed it, Idoh was convincing with his delusions. The mirror room was simply a dream after she passed out from a panic attack. Overwhelmed by seeing everyone in person and the bond they shared. None of it was real, just stress playing with her mind.

"Well, you have to promise me something," Arya said, giving Idoh a slight smile.

"Anything," he said.

"In this lifetime, don't go dying on me, alright? I need you."

Idoh chuckled, pulling Arya into his chest. "I'll do my best."

235

"You better, I'm sort of in bigger trouble than you realize."

Idoh looked down at Arya. "Oh? How so?"

"It's a long story, let's wake the others so I don't have to repeat myself."

"Let them sleep, and you need yours as well." Idoh stood, offering her the bench. She nodded, sleep the last thing she wanted, but knew it was required if she were to help the injured the following day. That was a task no one asked, but she needed to do.

Arya watched as Idoh slid down the wooden side of a bookshelf, dipping his head and closed his eyes. Doing as he asked, Arya laid down upon the bench, her back to her friends. She looked out the window, watching the sea wash upon the shore in the light of the half-moon. Stars winked down at her, inviting yet still so far away. Beckoning her as if they had the answers she so desperately wanted.

Who were those women really?

Why did she have the reactions she did to all her friends?

Would Roderick come to collect her like last time, or would Emeric?

Who was Evelyn really? And why did she want Arya in Kulessa so badly?

Arya took in a deep breath, eyes unable to close. In the distance she could see the forest that Idoh had learned her real identity in once upon another life. The same thicket that Phobus disappeared into when he threatened Arya and Winslet. She could see the dunes that Arya had run down so

236

many times, yet never at all. The location of her wedding to Mies and the flavors of the liquids dancing over the memories of her tongue. Her first swim was in the same waters of the sea twinkling below her. The drunken escapades with her boys that lead to her admitting to Leif that she wanted him.

So much had changed. Those memories a distant dream and never able to come to fruition. Gone like the innocence she once had.

Those rolling thoughts were too much. She needed air.

24

Arya was lucky that the gods had been accurate with their layout of the castle in her dream. She walked the halls without the need of a map, almost as if she had really been there for months before disappearing into the dark world that Kulessa was.

Candles burned on their final essence of wax, the flames barely a flicker. It was just enough light to let her make her way down the halls and stairs and zigzagging corners. Getting to the small servants' door, Arya pushed it open, the wind and smell of salt greeting her. The cold touched her skin like small fingers brushing what it could, like it needed to be close to her.

Arya closed her eyes, embracing the energy it provided, stepping slowly onto the well worn path. The stairs came upon her, using the limited light of the moon to navigate the narrow stones down to the one place she knew would be safe. The barrier engulfed Arya, like a second skin that stuck to her until it popped. After, silence consumed her. Her feet danced around the mossed over markings of the old ritual space, unable to help but smile. Leif had taken her here for the first time. When she'd feared she had hurt those who were trying to help her. At that time she was so lonely and scared. A mouse hunted by a hungry cat. Now, there was no cat and Arya was no mouse.

Finding herself at the edge of the ritual space, the open air of the cliffside the only separation between life and a plunge into the unforgiving water below, another memory came back. One of freedom. The day she got her skin back and against all odds, beat Phobus to the water.

She wanted that freedom back. To not have to look over her shoulder with each passing day. Have an opportunity to explore those mysterious feelings that came with each of her friends.

Slowly, Arya sat on the edge, dangling her legs off the side. She leaned back on her hands, tilting her head up at the stars. It was warm for how early in the season it was. The ground was still chilled, but the promise of warm air lingered with each pass of the wind through her brown curls. It was a wonder to be there again. A feeling she never thought she'd get to experience without utter pain and torture. Then again, she'd survived just that.

Her hands toyed with the hem of her pants, lifting the fabric to feel along her skin. The scars that were left upon the area were barely able to be recalled. There were so many times she'd been harmed. Her legs, back—fuck they'd even ripped out her hair a few times. Broken bones and lacerations. Burns that never really were able to heal fully before another assault to the area happened.

Yet, through it all, she had forgiven herself. Something she hadn't been able to do in the vision.

The swim had not been her fault, nor the storm that swept them away. The escape that killed Meriah was the only opportunity they'd had for help that never came. Nothing that happened to her was due to her own errors, just poor judgement and fate being a bitch. Did she still hate Roderick and those pretentious humans with all her heart? Of course. Nothing would change that anytime soon. But hate herself? No. No, she didn't.

The silence around her broke, Arya spinning quickly, summoning the water from below to her hands. Leif rose up his palms to face her, giving a sheepish smile. "Sorry, I would've announced myself but I wouldn't have been heard through the barrier. If you'd like to be alone I can go."

Arya lowered her hands, letting the water pool on the stone. "No, no, you're okay. I was just caught off guard."

Leif lowered his hands, giving Arya a weak smile. "You know I'd come out here almost every night just to see if I could feel some sort of sign of you being real."

"You had doubts?" Arya asked, grateful she wasn't the only one who second guessed her encounter with the gods.

Leif laughed, walking to stand beside Arya, his focus on the unending sea before them. Arya turned, facing the water, but attention stuck on Leif.

"I did," he said, "It sounded like bullshit, but honestly, I'm glad it wasn't."

Arya nodded. If her friends wouldn't have been real, she wouldn't know what to do with herself. Her entire goal of escape was to get back to them.

"I didn't expect you to be here, if I'm being honest," Arya said.

"Where else would I be?" He mused.

Arya shrugged. "In the mirror you and Winslet were in Tiras, it only made sense to me you'd be there."

"Mirror?" Leif was acting like their conversations through the gift from Raena was nothing. That was no dream, it was as real as Emeric and the stone they stood upon.

"Yes, the mirror Raena gave us so we could talk to each other while I was being held at Emeric's." Arya insisted.

Leif shook his head, pressing his fingers to his closed lids. "Fucking Raena. I never got a mirror Arya. I'm afraid it's one of her manipulations."

Faint laughing bounced in her head, Arya scowling at the invisible god who clearly watched them. Fucking bitch. Arya should have seen it coming.

"I should've known better," Arya muttered. "You'd never willingly live with your parents."

"Of all the things Raena exaggerated about me in that dream, my feelings on my parents were not one of those things." Leif laughed, shifting to sit beside her.

241

Arya cocked her brow, staring at Leif. "She exaggerated things about you?"

"Oh gods, yes. Winslet and I were never as flirty as in that vision. I also would've never ruined my image by dropping you on a dance floor in front of everyone."

Arya laughed, nodding. Leif rewarded her laugh with a dazzling white smile, sliding his fingers over her palm. She looked down, watching as he laced them through her own.

"I hope this is okay," he said softly.

Arya nodded, her throat going dry.

It felt right.

Part of Arya wanted more. To explore this connection with Leif and these amplified emotions that came with his touch. She wanted to meet the man who was real. Beneath the façade that Raena created to encourage their courtship. In reality, Leif was someone she was eager to reconnect with the most. Between him and Idoh, the memories they formed and care they showed her was intense, in a good way.

"I'm glad you're back," Leif said gently. "I was nervous I'd never get to see you again."

Arya sighed, allowing herself to lean onto the arm that connected their hands. "Me too. For a minute, I didn't know if I'd ever make it back to Teielmor."

While some sort of cosmic destiny bound them together, or the working of some very cunning match-maker gods, Arya was still nervous of everything. Leif felt right. Safe and peaceful. She knew he'd never hurt her, yet a small voice in her head told her to be wary. There was something more that she didn't know about him and wasn't ready to confront just yet.

"I was going to go looking for you," Leif admitted, drawing Arya out of her anxious thoughts.

"You were?"

"Mmhm. I was the one who convinced Mies to go first. I knew no one would try to fuck with a Dullahan. Me, well, let's just say I'm easier to get to." Leif chuckled.

Arya rolled her eyes with a smile. "That makes two of us."

"Not anymore," Leif said, "Not now that you are with us."

Arya swallowed, thinking back to the threat that Siion made. "Leif, can I ask you something?" Leif nodded, his smile fading as he faced her question. "Do you know Emeric? Mies seemed like he knew of him, but I don't see how it's connected."

The sigh that came from Leif was a mix of a groan and growl. He rolled his eyes, free hand scratching the back of his neck. "So, a few years ago, like twenty—I think—Emeric came to Castle Lofta. Zephyr, Idoh, and I were all children, visiting family for holiday." He took in a breath. "He came to my father as a man. Probably looks the same now as he did then."

"That's insane, it'd make him older than our parents if so," Arya said.

Leif nodded, a frown never leaving. "He said something to the King and my father that left them nervous

243

for days. Emeric was allowed to stay, but bound to a darkened room in the castle we were forbidden from." Leif swallowed. "The day we had the dream, it was the same day you were supposed to arrive in the carriage. Obviously you never made it, and when Idoh and I went to Zephyr to insist we investigate your location, he denied us."

"Zephyr denied finding me?" Arya whispered, pain riddling her body. How could he have left her in Kulessa like that?

"He was trying to protect us, but it risked you. Now I realize he figured Evelyn wouldn't kill you, but at the time, I didn't. So, Idoh and I went to Emeric. We struck a deal with him to have you returned, only he didn't come back." Arya stared at Leif, bewildered he had let loose her capture and torturer.

"Did you know he was dangerous?" Arya asked.

Leif nodded. Regret tugged at her stomach, though she knew it was not her own emotion. The swirling discomfort travelled through their touch, originating from the hand he clasped around her own.

"I didn't realize how dangerous until I set him free. That's when creatures that were supposed to be myth began to appear and we lost all contact with him."

So Emeric was the cause of the Cavernlings leaving their homes. What other animals did he introduce to the world? Arya thought back to the two creatures that escaped from the darkness beneath his home, shuttering at the thought of others like those being loose and preying on unsuspecting people.

Arya decided it was best not to let Leif know that Emeric had been the one to torture her in the dungeons and that she was being forced to marry him due to a stupid deal with a god. She would eventually let him know, but not while he touched her. The amplification of her own emotions along with feeling all of his was too much, and he barely knew what she'd gone through. It was probably best none of her friends touched her while she told them her story. No need to make a mistake while connected to one of them, especially Leif.

"Well, I'm here now, and wouldn't be if it wasn't for him," Arya said, somewhat telling a limited detailed version of the truth to soothe Leif's worries. If Emeric hadn't come along, gods know how long she'd be in that dungeon. Of course, Emeric was still chasing her, which was not part of their original deal, but she didn't need to bring that up.

"Everything will be okay now," Arya said as she looked out at the sun shedding the first rays of light into the sky. She hoped it wasn't a falsehood, but more a manifestation of what life could be. Trouble would come, but as long as she was there, she could begin to become who she was meant to be.

Leif wrapped his arm around her shoulders, kissing the top of her head. Butterflies danced in her stomach, Arya smiling as she leaned her head into him.

Things would be okay.

25

Outrage was a generous word when describing the chaos that erupted once the others learned about what had happened to Arya. She sat quietly with her hands folded in her lap, watching the back and forth that happened, Zephyr the biggest enemy. She'd learned from the screams that Idoh, Leif, and Mies had opposed his ruling. It was his influence that refused them from getting Arya when she didn't show up when she was supposed to.

"It's because of you this happened!" Mies growled, the mist coming off his shoulders in waves.

"I did what was best for Teielmor, as is my duty." Zephyr was just as angry, but Arya couldn't tell if it was because of how she was treated or the group ganging up on him.

"He's right," Winslet said causing the group to stop and look at her. As much as Arya hated what happened to her, she knew why Zephyr did what he did. "If any of you had crossed into Kulessa, you'd all have similar experiences to Arya, if not getting yourself killed."

The silence from the three men was deafening, each knowing Winslet was a hundred percent right. Would they ever admit that? Arya didn't think so. Their pride was too strong, egos amplified by their anger and desperation to show Arya how they fought for her.

"None of this matters now," Arya said plainly.

Leif scoffed. "Of course this matters! What happened to you—."

"Cannot be undone," she said, "And we will deal with that when it comes to it, but now, we have bigger issues."

The group watched her as she rose from her seat, the gown Winslet had lent her freeing compared to the soldier's uniform Kai had given her. She had let her hair down, longer than it had been last time, but they weren't attempting to make Arya look like a human which was relieving.

Standing, Arya placed her hands behind her back. "I know you know things I do not." She was right, their gazes averted telling her as much. "I want to know what you do."

"Arya, you have to understand—," Zephyr started.

"That's what I'm trying to do. Understand. I need to know these things to keep myself safe, and now that I'm here, you can finally help me do that."

The silence over the group was not what Arya wanted. She didn't want to have to pull the torture card, but if it got them talking about any of this bullshit, she'd do it.

"We're not allowed to talk about it," Winslet finally said.

Arya raised her brows, crossing her arms. "Not allowed? Who's stopping you?"

Idoh pressed his back into the shelf, rubbing his forehead. "You are."

"Me?" Arya laughed, unable to believe she would tell them something so stupid. Not only that, but Arya hadn't seen them except for the dream and there was no discussion of any of this nonsense. "Please, I would never."

"I'm sorry Arya, but you have to figure everything out yourself," Leif said, "but it doesn't mean we can't answer questions."

"Leif," Mies growled in warning. Leif only smirked, pleased in irritating the Dullahan.

Okay, what question did she want to ask first? The more threatening the better.

"Who is Evelyn?" She asked.

"All you Zephyr," Leif laughed.

Zephyr rolled his eyes, slumping into a chair. After a deep sigh, he said, "Evelyn is the leader of the Lux. She's powerful, able to manipulate a person by touching them. Somehow, she's able to break into the minds of others and convince them of things they'd never want."

Arya sat back in her seat, Leif forcing his way next to her so she was sandwiched between him and Winslet. "Is that how she hurts us?"

Zephyr sighed. "One of the ways."

"And she's Roderick's ringleader?"

Mies took a seat in the other chair, leaning so his elbows supported him by resting on his knees. "Evelyn is the leader of the Lux, she controls Roderick and two others."

"Who?"

"Emeric and Rook," Winslet cursed.

Emeric and Rook were both powerful and not human. Evelyn didn't sound human either, but she knew for a fact that Roderick was. She spent too much time with the fucker to not know if he had some sort of power.

"So why did Emeric want me to marry him, and why is Siion so insistent about it?" Arya asked.

"To keep you from us," Idoh mumbled.

"I'd always come back," Arya said, "I only feel safe in Teielmor."

Winslet blew out, vibrating her lips. "It's your home, of course you only feel safe here."

Something about the way Winslet said the sentence made Arya suspicious of the intent of her saying it. There was more meaning behind the words, but Arya couldn't place what exactly was needing more investigation. Instead, she focused on other things she wanted more information on.

"Why are the gods so obsessed with my love life?"

Leif snorted, clearly amused by her line of questioning. "Because they're bored. You know, not much going on for a god, not like we're in the middle of a war or anything."

"Careful, Leif, they might get offended," Winslet said quietly.

From the stories, Arya had heard of the gods punishing people for simply existing, and as far as she was concerned, interfering in her life was punishment enough. Especially fucking Raena. Lying bitch.

"That's enough for today," Zephyr stated in his official tone. "There's things that need to be done, get to work."

He left quickly, the doors closing hard behind him. Arya was nervous she had gone too far, but she needed answers. Things were confusing without them.

"Zephyr's right about that," Mies commented, rising. "I believe Winslet and I have a shift in medical."

Winslet huffed, leaning her head back. "Do I have to?"

"You do," Leif soothed.

"Can't you do it for me?" Winslet pouted.

He cupped her cheek, patting it softly. "Unfortunately I have somewhere to be."

Winslet groaned, rolling her eyes. "You always say that."

"It's always true," Leif countered.

Reluctantly, Winslet rose, taking Mies's hand and looping her arm into his. She stuck her tongue out at Leif, then winked at Arya. Once they were gone, Leif stood, stretching with his arms extended and back arching.

"Where are you going?" Arya asked.

Leif smirked. "As lovely as these floors are, they're awful for sleep. If you'd like, Arya dear, you can come warm my bed for me."

Arya's cheeks burned, forgetting how easily Leif was able to make her blush. She opened and closed her mouth, finally looking away when a witty comeback didn't come to her. What did come to her was the image of Leif nude beneath his satin sheets. Arya bit her lip, thinking of Leif with his hand patting the bed next to him, muscles on display, perhaps with a bit of oil on them to glisten in the candle light. She shook her head, forcing the images from her head.

"Arya and I have plans," Idoh said.

She looked over to him, not confident in the sly smirk that he held.

Leif pressed a hand to his chest. "I know I'm only a creature of passion, but you didn't have to replace me with a fiery hunk." Leif clicked his tongue. "Well, when you get bored of my cousin, you know where to find me." He winked at Arya, waltzing out of the room leaving her cheeks on fire and stomach flipping.

"Come, Little Flame, we have work to do." Idoh offered her his hand.

"I don't recall making plans with you," Arya smiled, eager to feel his cooling flame inside her again.

"Oh, we didn't, but I decided that you needed to have a refresher on your fighting," he said.

Her smile faded. "Don't say it."

251

Idoh gleamed, Arya already knowing what it was he decided to torture her with. "Balance work."

"Come on, don't tell me in those moments of isolation you failed to practice," Idoh teased, walking back and forth in front of Arya as she wobbled on a small ball.

Her eyes narrowed, determined to make him pay after she was done with this exercise. "Fuck off, Idoh."

"There's my girl."

Arya hated that she loved him saying that. She wanted to be his girl, for him to take her and hide her away. It wouldn't go over well with the others, but being his little secret sounded so appealing. Idoh inched toward her, Arya aware of his every move. The man couldn't be trusted once inside the training room. That much was true from the dream, he enjoyed besting her too much.

So, she decided to challenge his dominance.

Once getting close enough, Arya kicked out her foot, keeping her balance on the ball as she did so. Unfortunately, Idoh simply caught her leg, pulling her toward him. Balance thrown off, she fell off the ball, landing on the mat below. Idoh didn't release her leg, running his fingers over her skin in a sensual way. Arya's breath hitched, unable to do anything else but watch. The excitement in his eyes changed, a deeper desire that Arya couldn't place but felt so familiar.

"Do you remember in the dream my promise to you?" He asked in a low voice. Arya nodded. "What did I say?"

"You promised we'd make it out alive," she breathed.

Idoh knelt down, positioning himself between her legs. Arya allowed him, parting them so he would be able to move further up her body. The heat he gave off was intoxicating, like the sun after a long and cold winter. Idoh got close enough where his face was a breath from hers. Smoke drifted from his shoulders and back, clothes beginning to burn as he stared at her.

"Do you know why I am training you?" He asked.

Arya shook her head, the dryness in her mouth forbidding words to form. Glimpses of flames flashed in her peripherals, aware things around them were burning, but not caring. Idoh wouldn't hurt her if it was the last thing he did. That much she was sure of.

"Because it is the only time I know I can have you alone all to myself."

Alone.

"Why did you want that?" Arya asked weakly. She wanted him to admit to the feelings she also had.

The doors to the training room burst open, Idoh moving from her in a flash. Defeated, Arya fell back, her head hitting the mat. Who the fuck decided to interrupt them? Whoever it was, she was going to kill them.

"Wow, it's hot in here," Porter said, "Arya, I'm so glad to see you. They told me you were alive—why are you on the floor?"

"Poor timing," Arya groaned, rolling to get into a standing position. Idoh had caused a river between her legs, the first time she'd ever felt like that for a man.

Porter nodded, smiling. "Gotcha, need to train harder to get strong."

Idoh snorted, glancing over his shoulder to her. His shirt was completely gone, ashy remains surrounding his feet. Arya didn't mind the view, however. Her eyes were glued to the perfection of a body, molded with every inch of female desire carved into him. A few stray pieces of sweat drenched hairs stuck to his neck. His tongue licked his lips, moving as if in slow motion, Arya getting dizzy with the pure sex appeal he casually held, and he wasn't even Gean-Cánach.

"Are you going to answer him, Arya?" Idoh asked.

"Yes, I'd do whatever you want." Her eyes widened, hand going to her mouth. She *did not* just say that. Burning ignited in her cheeks, more intense than that of the one between her legs.

"Right," Porter said slowly glancing between the two. "I'll talk to you a bit later then."

Porter left, shutting the door quietly as he left.

"Whatever I want, huh?"

Arya stood, brushing off her skirt. "Go put a shirt on, whore." Without another word, she left the training room, the burning not stopping in both her cheeks and stomach. Finding the first dark corner, she hid behind it, placing a hand to her chest and attempting to slow her heart. That's when she knew the difference between the dream and real life. How she figured the gods were not concocting another fairytale. The gods could not make her want someone so badly all sense was lost and the thought of riding Idoh in front of Porter was a very, *very* tempting option.

"Oh gods," Arya whispered under her breath. "What have I gotten myself into?"

26

Arya was called into Zephyr's room before dinner, her clothes damp with sweat and she swore the smell of blood lingered on her like a ghost of her activities for the day. Even though she did not need to, Arya spent the majority of her time helping the wounded that lined the entry of Castle Lofta. However helpful she tried to make herself look, she did not do it selflessly. The memories of Idoh snuck into her thoughts, causing the most unwelcomed bursts of emotion when left to her own devices. Wounded were much more appealing than the tingling sensation that refused to stop when thinking about him.

Arya wiped her forehead with a cloth that was tied into her medical apron, the mixture of dried blood and other bodily fluids soaked into the fabric. She had tied her hair back with a bonnet, refusing to let the locks in her face while she worked. It was nice to be needed for something normal and not anything intense as she had been used to in Kulessa. Lifting her hand, she knocked on Zephyr's door. Silence. Arya waited a few more minutes until she finally knocked again. Again, nothing.

Taking a deep breath, Arya placed a hand on the nob, opening the door slowly. The room was only lit by burning embers in a hearth. Books were scattered on the desk in the far corner, a window open and blowing in cool air from the outside. Arya furrowed her brows, crossing the room and pulling shut the glass. Thrusting the lock into place, she turned back to the room. It was much more cluttered than she'd seen in her dream. Stacks of books sat on all sides of the bed. Tea cups and random plates of half eaten dinner sat on top of them like trophies of laziness. It was confusing seeing as there were people who worked in the castle who's one job is collecting such items and tidying rooms. Perhaps they were protesting the Prince's lack of respect for his things.

"Zephyr?" Arya whispered loudly to the empty room. Silence once again greeted her, though she didn't know why she expected anything different. She could see that he was not inside, and if he hid from her, why ask her to come to his room?

Arya sighed, dragging her fingers over the footboard of his bed. It felt like a distant world where she had spent nights in this same bed. Zephyr protecting her while she hid from Mies during the evening hours. Where he had admitted to loving her. It was so different now. Part of her

257

wished for that life back. The ability to be vulnerable and weak, to be protected by so many, yet still be seen as desirable. Now, Arya had no choice but to be her own protector. Sure, the others would try to save her as before, but Arya had been the one to escape Kulessa. They did not help her and she could not expect them to.

"Their loyalty to you does not waiver, young Selkie." Arya jumped at the voice, spinning to see a large man by the fireplace. He looked into the flames while his hands were clasped behind his back. Small feathers covered his skin, and armor shielded his torso. His face was hidden behind a helmet, though Arya could see a pair of glowing white eyes through the shadows. A white owl sat upon his shoulder, uninterested in Arya.

Arya sighed, crossing her arms as she leaned back against the foot of the bed. "And here I thought I was safe from another interaction with gods."

His eyes slid over to her, no emotion shown within. "I do not see what they have to do with our interaction."

Arya rolled her eyes. "Well, it's not every day a woman gets advice from all these lovely immortal beings."

His feathers shifted as if uncomfortable with Arya's sass. "My name is Xarius—."

"I know who you are," Arya interrupted, "What do you want?"

Xarius cleared his throat, taking a few careful steps until he was in front of Arya. She breathed in, the faint smell of storms and fresh rain coming off him. "Zephyr is not doing as he should."

258

Arya furrowed her brows. "What do you mean?"

Xarius sighed. "His purpose is to you, and he does not find interest in your existence."

"Because he is weak." Arya spun, seeing a large lizard man with full armor lounging on Zephyr's bed. Her hair flicked through the air as if on fire, the tips a bright yellow fading down to red closest to the scalp. Ancient symbols were carved onto the creature's scaled skin, other scars indicating time at war. There were more weapons on the god than Arya could count, and potentially countless others hidden as well.

Arya rolled her eyes. She was annoyed with the constant show of deities who had tempted her with a life that never ended up happening. Especially when they were gods of two of her favorites from that dream. So far, Idoh and Zephyr seemed fairly close to their dream counterparts, but she'd only been back in their presence for a day.

"Fyorr, sister, what are you doing here?" Xarius asked as if it was a pleasant surprise.

"I've come to speak to this beautiful flame, what else?" Fyorr snickered, looking Arya up and down. She crinkled her nose to show disgust of the god, but inside she was flattered. It wasn't everyday a woman was complimented by a god of war.

"What do you two want from me? I'm somewhat busy trying to figure out how to stay alive."

Fyorr chuckled. "That answer is simple. Marry into Finta, then you will never be without protection."

"Of course you would say that," Arya muttered.

"No, no, you must marry Zephyr, it is the only way you will survive another life," Xarius insisted.

There was a snort from behind Zephyr's desk. Arya glanced over, but already knew who was behind it from the smell of lavender and cedar.

"This is their last lives, Xarie, Arya must follow her heart this time." Renea gleamed, playing with the tip of one of her wings. "We all know she'd been in love with Leif since the beginning, you all just manipulate her to be with someone else. Isn't that right, Dusnia?"

A woman walked from the shadows, a train of green leaves and vines trailing her. She was the most normal looking of the gods, though it was far fetched when comparing the rest of her features. Her smooth skin was a dusty green, deeper in color around her eyes and lips. Mushrooms grew from her cheeks and neck, moss creating the long collection that would equal hair on an ordinary person. Her clothing was not clothing at all, but a matted collection of leaves, vines, twigs, and mud. It split down to lead into her train, showing off her feet which looked like they were fashioned from tree branches. The goddess of the Dullahan.

"I do not manipulate, I simply influence what is right." Dusnia spoke as if there were rocks in her throat, barely recognizable compared to her fellow gods.

"What is this, a family reunion?" Arya hissed. All they were missing was Lir and all the fae gods would be present.

A hand was placed on her shoulder, a wave of familiarity and community flooding her. Arya relaxed, turning her head to see the creature form of Lir. He did not look much different from the carriage except for the fact he was made entirely of water and fish parts. His right hand was a lobster claw, while his left was like her own. Shells were imbedded into the reflective surface of his skin.

"Oh, what the fuck." Arya complained.

"Sorry I am late, I was busy with my people," Lir said.

"We all are, you're not special," Dusnia hissed.

Arya pinched the bridge of her nose. "Okay, someone fucking tell me what you all want. I am sick of you in my head and attempting to play match maker when it is unwarranted."

Renea snickered. "But dear, that was your request."

Arya jerked her head back, nose scrunching. "I never asked for this."

"Not in this life," Fyorr grinned. "But in your first."

"What are you talking about?" Arya asked, could gods be just as crazy as her friends were?

"Normally, we let you figure it all out yourself, Arya, but time is limited for you in this life." Lir said in a soft voice. "We must show you the past, if we do not, you will never be ready for the terrors of the future."

Before Arya could object, the gods surrounded her, raising their hands in unison.

"Oh, I can't wait for this." Renea gleamed.

Pain.

261

"The fuck was that?" Arya groaned, placing her hand to her forehead where the gods slapped.

Renea smirked. "Did you remember?"

"No," Arya huffed. "I only remember my life in this world and the fact that five gods just slapped me in the head."

"Perhaps we should try again?" Dusnia suggested.

"The fuck you will!" Arya backed away from the confused gods, finding they were just as useless as mortal fae. What gods didn't know how to use their powers? Stupid, pathetic, immortals. "I'm going to bed. Don't get in my head again."

Arya walked away from the group, not looking back. However, if she had, she would have noticed the vacancy of Zephyr's room, no traces of anyone other than Arya occupying the space. She came upon Mies in the hall who smiled and lifted his hand to her.

"Were you seeing Zephyr?" He asked.

"Mies, not in the mood tonight." Arya brushed by him, getting to the door that was her room in the past. A past that was a figment idiotic matchmaking gods. Not caring if the room was already occupied by another person, Arya threw open the door and walked inside.

She pressed her back against the door, allowing tears to pour down her face. She didn't understand the world. Why was it so confusing and cruel and dark? Who is she supposed to trust when so many people are keeping things from her? What is she supposed to pray for when the gods will not answer those prayers, and she had never known anything but despair and fear?

Ignoring the armor that was placed in the wardrobe and the hints of the room being occupied, Arya stripped her clothing, getting into her undergarments and slipped into bed. The smell of salt water and cool air flowed around her as she pulled the blankets tighter to her body. Her mind and body was so tired from the day that no thoughts passed through her head before sleep consumed her. A heavy sleep the dead would be envious for.

27

A knock had interrupted Arya's cry induced sleep. She lifted her head from the pillow, eyes still swollen and crusted with her sorrow. The door opened, long blonde hair hanging from the head the peeked in through the door. Winslet smiled at Arya, bright against the emotions that plagued her.

"I thought I'd find you here," she said as she walked into the room. Arya turned on the bed, watching Winslet bounce to sit beside her. "You look terrible, have you been crying?"

Arya nodded, sitting up and wiping her eyes. "It's been a lot to absorb."

"I can imagine," Winslet said, "I do think it was much easier in the dream."

Arya snorted. "You could say that again."

Winslet kicked her legs over the side of the bed, leaning back so her arms supported her from behind. "Would you like to do something to get your mind off things?"

Arya raised her brows. "What did you have in mind?"

Smiling, Winslet jumped off the bed, offering Arya her hand. Arya smiled, sliding through the blankets and onto the cool wooden floor. Winslet's brows rose as she looked Arya up and down, bobbing her head to the side as if deciding something.

"I think we need to get you into something more—appropriate."

Arya looked down at her underclothes, forgetting she had stripped before crawling into bed. "That's probably a good idea."

Tossing Arya the clothes she'd left on the ground, Winslet waited for Arya to dress before pulling her out the door and to her own room. As they entered, Arya was astonished to see how Winslet's room was decorated. Pictures of different people were pinned to her wall, sketches of animals and plants beside them. Everything was some shade of blue, and books were stacked onto a desk between papers and letters. Winslet went to her mess of a closet while Arya went to the desk, hand brushing lightly over the letter opened on the top of the pile. The Asitan crest was etched into the broken was and her mother and father's signatures were printed upon the paper. A twang of pain hit her as she remembered how she had been replaced with another child.

How her parents had chosen to forget about her disappearance.

"Here it is!" Winslet cheered, pulling a traditional Selkie dress from the pile of blue. The flowing material was embroidered with the formal curls of waves and while connected at the stomach, the dress was very open, holes in the sides exposing as much skin as it could without being deemed underclothes.

"That is a formal dress, where are we going?" Arya laughed. She couldn't imagine there would be a ball or festival worthy of such a dress during war times. If there was, it was a bad look on the King.

"Just trust me on this, Arya, you'll need traditional attire." Winslet shoved the dress into Arya's hands before going back to searching the pile for her own dress.

Smiling at the gown, Arya stripped, pulling on the dress and struggling with the multiple holes her arms were determined to get stuck in. Once it was on, however, it was one of the most incredible pieces she'd ever worn. Even though Arya was still relatively thin due to her malnourishment, the dress hugged the little curves it had while also flowing around her like water. The fabric was soft and comfortable, surprising her.

Winslet whistled as she looked over Arya. "Gods Arya, save some sexy for the rest of us."

Arya laughed. "Look who's talking!"

Winslet had dressed in a two-piece crystal blue dress that hung on her body like it was always meant to be there. It made her eyes electrified and skin seem more pink. When

Arya thought of the beauty of Selkies, Winslet was the epitome of such thought.

"Come on, we need to hurry or we'll be late!" Winslet said, grabbing Arya's hand and pulling her out the door and down the hall. The girls giggled with each other as they ran, Arya still clueless as to where they were going, but excited for any adventure that didn't have to do with gods, bonds with her friends, or humans.

Winslet stopped them in front of the door to a servant's quarters. Of all places Arya had expected to go, this was not one of them. Winslet knocked in a rhythmic pattern, pausing as she whispered under her breath, "One, two, three, four, five, six, seven, eight," then knocked a few more times.

Locks were undone, a pair of deep green eyes looking out at them. They lit up when they saw Winslet, opening the door the rest of the way and ushering them in. The girls entered, the door closing quickly behind them. Inside, Arya couldn't help but gawk.

People gathered in formal wear from each province, displaying their elements proudly. Dullahan hovered stones around them, Salamanders fire. Sylphs swirled feathers from their wings around, Selkies forming different animals out of water that cuddled against their person. Gean-Cánach occupants had a purple glow above them that Arya had never seen before.

"What is this?" Arya asked.

Winslet hung on her arm, inching them forward into the crowd. "Have you ever heard of Yepkeper?" Arya furrowed her brows, shaking her head. "Well, Yepkeper is an art event where the civilians of each province come together and show talents directly related to their heritage."

Arya's stomach bubbled with excitement. She had always wanted to experience the cultures of each of the provinces when younger, the knowledge of different traditions thrilling to her child self. Now, Arya had the chance to learn in the best way possible.

People around her stretched and did small dances using their elements. Musicians tuned their instruments in the corner, a wooden floor in the middle of the room lit with a circle of candles, bowls of water, and mounds of dirt. Winslet and Arya sat in front of one of the candles, leaning into each other, sharing the excitement of the moment.

As if sensing their eagerness, music began to play. Nothing like Arya had heard growing up. It was rugged and heavy with drums. The crowd quieted, all waiting to see who the first person up was going to be. Arya craned her neck, looking to see who would be the introduction to her first Yepkeper.

As if hearing her thoughts, a man slid into the center. A wave of ecstasy hit her as he slid to the middle of the floor. Arya squealed, watching as the green eyes met hers, a devilish smile on his lips. Dropping, Leif positioned himself on the ground like it was over a woman, waving his body like he had been intimate with this imaginary person. Arya covered her mouth, her cheeks burning as she watched. Winslet cheered, splashing out some water from their bowl onto his shirtless torso, the beads glistening deliciously as he moved.

As the song continued, Leif moved around the floor, drawing attention to his body and beautifully sculpted muscles. Women and men alike shrieked with their encouragement of Leif's dance, Arya also a major fan of his display, if the tingling below had any say to it.

As the song began to change, Leif went to Winslet, pulling her up from the floor by pinching her chin and dragging her forward. Arya couldn't help but kick her feet with the emotion she felt. Her hands covered her mouth as she watched Winslet stumble onto the middle of the floor by Leif's order. She hung in there like a puppet until the pulse of the music jumped her to life. Leif placed his hands over her as she moved, like he was the one controlling her. It was incredible, Arya never having experienced anything like that before.

Eventually, they moved together, dancing in unison and popping their bodies to the rhythm. Whistles and cheers came from the people around them. Leif hovered a hand over Winslet's chest, Winslet beginning to slowly bend backward at an unnaturally slow pace. Arya wasn't sure she'd be able to do anything like they did, but still wanted to try.

When the song began to change again, Leif and Winslet jogged out of the stage, reuniting with Arya.

"You both were amazing!" She gleamed.

Winslet laughed, shifting her weight onto Arya's shoulder. "We practiced for *hours* so we could perform that."

"Winslet is a terrible student," Leif teased.

Winslet shot Leif a playful stare before the three turned their attention to the group of Dullahan who stood in the center. The earth moved from the mounds on the side, slowly inching around the perimeter. With the change of song, they stomped with the drums, the earth rumbling with each step. It became almost hypnotic watching them, Arya's body vibrating as they moved, getting faster with each thrum of the instruments. Then, it was faster than she'd expected them to go. The earth bounced around the spectators, amplifying their strong movements. Arya couldn't help but absorb the energy they put off, wanting to learn their moves. Then as soon as they didn't seem they could go any faster, the group ran off to the side.

The music slowed, becoming more mysterious and sensual. The candles in the room dimmed, Arya invested to see who was coming next. Then, everything went dark. Screams of excitement sounded around her, the air buzzing with anticipation. Flames ignited once again, starting from farthest away from her and circling to meet in front of her. In the center of the floor was a man. He wore a crown of gold, like branches of the sun exploding from his skull. His eyes were barely seen through the narrow slit between the cloth that covered his face. On his neck was a thick collar of gold spikes that were tipped with dangling rubies. His chest and stomach were exposed, a maroon skirt held onto his hips by chains that danced with the reflection of fire.

While he looked like he shouldn't move gracefully, there was a feminine approach to the dance. His arms outstretched and hips popping to each drop and rise in

270

music. At one point, Arya watched his stomach muscles move on their own accord, as if each were controlled individually. Bursts of light blew into the air from his hands and rippled over the muscle he controlled, giving an impression that he was fire. He spun in a circle, letting her see the ribbons that trailed from the mask, until everything went dark again.

When the lights came back, the man was gone, no where to be seen in the crowd. Almost like he never existed.

"Who was that?" Arya breathed.

"We don't know," Leif whispered, "he just appears then is gone and no one can tell who or where he comes from. All we know is he shows up every time Yepkerper is organized."

"I'd fuck him, and I don't like men," Winslet laughed.

Arya chuckled, rubbing a hand over her mouth. She stared at the spot she'd last seen him, wanting to know who that man was. Winslet was right, no matter who you are, that dance does something to a person to make them want the dancer.

"Finta men are the submissives in their relationships, right?" Arya asked.

Leif nodded. "The women control most everything as they're seen as more powerful than the men."

"Why?" Winslet asked.

"Could that dance be one that's used to attract a spouse in their culture? We all wanted to fuck him, so it would make sense." Arya pondered.

Winslet shrugged, smiling as she watched the current performers. "It's thrilling to see the differences of fae when we've always grouped ourselves together. So different and yet still the same."

Arya enjoyed her time with Leif and Winslet, watching the dancers. When the show was over, Arya left her friends to retreat back down the halls that led to her room. Sleep was threatening her, but this time her mind was spinning with the different dances she'd witnessed that night. Ignoring how she was dressed, Arya fell into bed, cuddling into the blankets and consuming herself into the world of sleep.

Part Two: Remembrance

28

She loved the simplicity of her life. The knowledge that no matter what it threw at her, she had the emotional peace that came from never having to fall in love. An arrangement made sight unseen by her parents upon her birth.

Arya walked through the field of flowers, sparkling gems of all colors dancing with light from the midday sun. It was a beautiful day, the first of many once the spring rains gave way for the sweet summer breeze. Her fingers tapped over the delicate pedals of the wildflowers that bloomed from those unforgiving storms in the months past, but Arya had always found such beauty in the world, whether they be from the flowers or the storms.

"Arya!" A woman screamed in joy. Arya smiled, rushing through the field in her silver gown to get to her best friend.

Evelyn met her halfway, donned in the most stunning golden dress Arya had ever seen. Of course, it was necessary for her given she was the daughter of the Duke and Duchess of Tiras. The girls embraced, red and golden hair mixing in the collision.

"Where have you been!" Arya complained with a smile.

Evelyn blew out until her lips vibrated. "Mother is making arrangements for my marriage. It's a few weeks away and I'm so annoyed, I want more time before I'm shipped away."

Arya pulled Evelyn to the ground with her, hiding them from the surrounding spectators that may wander into the field. "At least you get to travel, Evie, I have to stay in Tiras my entire life!"

"You know people here," Evelyn pouted, reaching to play with a lock of Arya's hair. It glistened in the sun as if a gem. "I won't know anyone in Ilmari."

"But you'll be a princess," Arya giggled, "and I will come at every opportunity so I can visit my dearest friend in her new world."

Evelyn took Arya's hands in hers, kissing her fingers. "Promise you'll come to my coronation!"

"I wouldn't miss it for the world!" Arya laughed, forcing her hands from Evelyn's and wrapping her arm around her neck.

They laid back into the grass, looking up at the sky as puffy white clouds passed. It would be one of the last times that they were together as unmarried women. Innocence taken to continue the line of succession for their families. It was unfortunate, their friendship depending greatly on their betrothed.

"Are you ready for tonight?" Evelyn asked in a small voice.

Arya shrugged, sighing. "I don't have any other choice."

Evelyn nodded. "I'm sure he's a good man, you have to be as the son of the ambassador, right?"

Arya nodded, not wishing to go into more detail. Emotional peace was better than being in love. Love was a concept they crafted so there was hope in time of war. It was the Gean-Cánach way. Whoever her betrothed is, he will be a good man to her just as she'll be a good wife to him. It was arranged that way. Love wasn't required.

"You'll be there, right?" Arya asked, ignoring her question. She didn't want to wonder what would happen if things did not go smoothly.

"Of course I will Yaya! It's the marriage for my best friend, I wouldn't miss it for the world." Evelyn took Arya's hand, clutching it tightly. If there was one uncertainty in this world for the girls, it would be the next time they would see each other once they no longer lived only a field away.

"Friends forever?" Arya asked.

Evelyn turned her head, eyes glistening as she said, "you doofus, we already made that pact."

* * *

There were so many women around Arya as she was prepared for her ceremony. Golden cuffs were slid onto her

279

wrists and wrapped around her ankles, layers of chains with different ornaments placed on her neck. Silver cream was dashed over her eyes, cheeks, nose, and forehead to make her look like the glistening water in the early morning light. Purple cloth was wrapped around Arya, her hair plaited with multiple violets tossed between the twists.

All she could do was watch herself in the mirror as the women of her family danced around her like the bees in the field, pollinating her with beauty and wealth.

"What a glorious bride!" Arya's mother gleamed, walking into the room with her distinguished blue gown. While most mothers would wear lesser fitting gowns, Arya's mother never lost her figure after having her seven children. The envy of most mams in the city along with a bargaining chip used to secure Arya and her five sisters their engagements.

"Thank you, mama."

Arya's mother shooed the doting women away, each giving Arya bright smiles and air kisses as they left out the door. Her mother leaned down her cheek pressed against Arya's own. It was like looking into a mirror, the difference of a few age lines and the color of their eyes, Arya taking the brilliant green of her father.

"Look at the two of us, Gean-Cánach women of the highest regard." She bragged, petting Arya's golden locks.

Arya bit her lips together, nerves getting the best of her. "What if he doesn't like me, mama?"

"Oh, no, my sweet girl," she cooed, kissing Arya's cheek. "If he says anything of the sort you tell his mother. She was most eager for your womb to share in beauty for her family."

Arya's face dropped, her voice lowering to a whisper. "Is he that ugly?"

Arya's mother paused. She inhaled, throwing her head back and placing a hand on her stomach. Rolling laughter emanated from the woman, as if Arya had been born to be a fool instead of a bride.

"My goodness darling, you truly believe I would allow my daughter to marry anything less than a god?" She wiped a tear from her eye. "How little faith you placed on me."

"I'm sorry, I believe the nerves are getting the best of me."

Arya watched in the mirror as her mother grabbed the sheer fabric from the wardrobe, brushing it with her fingers. She walked over slowly, smiling softly at the cloth. "You have nothing to worry about, my dear girl. I was just as nervous on my wedding day."

"You were?" Arya breathed.

Her mother nodded. "I was like you, unaware of what your father looked like, his manners, if he would find me as desirable as I hoped he would be to me."

"What did you think when you saw him unveiled?"

Mama laughed. "Honestly, I was underwhelmed. Your father is the most caring and passionate person I could have been arranged to. I was truly lucky, just as you are. Life will be easy and freeing for you, Arya. Trust in the process."

281

Arya nodded as a knock sounded at the door. A small woman peeked in, smiling softly. "It's time."

Arya's mother squeezed her shoulder, more giddy than Arya was herself. She walked out of the room, leaving Arya alone with the veil ready to conceal her identity. It would be the last time she looked at herself before she was married. Quickly, she pinched her cheeks, bringing more color to her skin. Reaching up, she pulled the fabric over her face.

Walking out of the room, she followed the flowers that had been arranged perfectly. Ribbons and garlands created a mythical wonderland of red, purple, and pink, the colors of Tiras. The colors of her betrothed's house. Of her house as soon as the vial was drunk.

Her stomach rolled as she got to the spot she was supposed to stand. It was practiced so many times before yet now she felt as if she was the lead actor in a production she never read the script for.

Breathe. *Arya told herself, closing her eyes as she focused on the breaths she took. Everyone could feel her emotions if she didn't control herself. She didn't want anyone to know if she regretted the match or her disappointment if she didn't like him.* Gods, help me.

The doors opened, Arya waiting for the harp music to announce their entrance. Entering the room, Arya walked down an aisle sided by her family. The center of the room held a white arch decorated with lanterns and flowers, her dress, tussling petals beneath her.

Her breath hitched as she saw her betrothed on the other side of the room, entering like she did. He wore a violet suit, golden embroidery showing the status his family held. His veil only reached his shoulders, shielding Arya from her first glimpse of him before they were officially wed. It was tradition. Necessary for survival of their family lines. No matter what he looked like.

They met in the center of the room, a priestess in a blue hooded gown glassily looking ahead. Arya was taught from a young age not to look at the blind priestesses, but now, no one would know if she looked.

The woman was beautiful, lashes long and dark, her lips a full red and skin an earthy red. Purple paint was brushed carefully onto her face and neck, robe the only thing separating her nude body from those in the room.

Arya watched as her lips moved, but could not hear what the woman was saying. It was all nonsense. Jumbled words that were supposed to mean something, but meant nothing. Something came out about love and cherished moments and Arya couldn't tell if it was supposed to be a joke. She never met this person before, how could she have any cherished moments with him?

Her heart pounded, Arya able to feel it in her throat. The vision around her peripherals darkened, Arya only able to see what was directly in front of her. Even that began to go dark.

Then she felt it.

Emotions like her own but stronger. More hopeful.

The darkness began to creep away, Arya seeing her betrothed had grabbed her hands over the podium with the vial. *"I vow to protect and cherish this union with the blessings of the gods on my side."*

His voice was euphoric. The perfect melody to drown out her thoughts and nerves. She didn't care what was beneath his veil, as long as he spoke to her in those sweet vibrations and cared for her heart.

"Madam Arya, it is your turn," the priestess said.

"I vow to protect and cherish this union with the blessing of the gods on my side." Arya whispered like she was speaking to a lover and not the room of all their family and friends.

The priestess took their hands, pricking their fingers and pinching the skin until a drop of blood ballooned on the surface. She then raised the vial with the grace of a dancer, tipping Arya's hand first so her blood entered the chamber. Red smoke puffed as soon as the blood hit the liquid inside. The priestess then turned to her betrothed, dropping his blood into the vial. Instead of red, the smoke was blue.

The priestess swirled the vial, a snake of smoke coming out in a deep purple. Red and blue combined, Arya realized. Their blood mixing with the magic of union.

"Now, with the blood mixed, and your family bound between two, it is done." Without another word, the priestess disappeared, leaving the vial corked on the podium, swirling purple.

They were joined.

"Take off the veil!" The crowd chanted through their drowning applause.

Arya slowly put her hands beneath the cloth, lifting so it uncovered her. Her betrothed did the same, but Arya couldn't look at him. Not yet. She wasn't ready to see who she was bound to.

"My name is Leif," he said gently, "And I believe you are the most beautiful woman I could have the opportunity to gaze upon."

Arya's breath caught. Somehow she knew the words were true, her chest pulsing with warmth. Slowly, her eyes lifted, staring at the man she would call her husband. Deep tanned skin, sandy hair, a collection of freckles strategically placed over his cheeks and nose. And his eyes. Ones that looked deep into Arya's own, a brilliant hazel that she'd never seen before.

"Oh," she gasped, "my mom said you were going to be ugly."

His brows lifted, a smile spreading wide. Arya could not believe she just said that. Her cheeks felt like flames licked the blood beneath them, rushing over her entire being.

"So does that mean you approve of me?" He laughed.

Arya covered her eyes, groaning to rid herself of the embarrassment unsuccessfully. "I do."

"Well, at least we have that going for us. I do need to know one thing. It is very important you answer honestly," Leif said with a shift to his tone and smile dimming.

Arya nodded. "Anything."

285

She hoped it was something she could answer correctly. This was the beginning of an unbreakable union, if she answered wrong, would it change their entire lives?

"What is your name?"

Arya let out a breath, giving a small laugh. "My name is Arya. Arya Abano."

29

Arya woke with a grogginess about her that would not equate to the sleep she just had. She rubbed at her eyes, attempting to help them adjust to the daylight that poured in through her window. After a few moments, and with her sight finally returning, Arya pulled her brows together, trying to figure out what that dream was all about. It was so real, never having experienced a dream where she could feel the grass of the meadow and wind that rushed around her.

Then she saw him.

Arya pulled the blankets to her chest, covering what she could from the form that sat against the wall in a slump. Hands clasped in his lap with boots removed so Arya could see the brown socks he wore. His other clothes had been gently laid on the back of the chair by the window, his body bare except for a simple pair of black pants. While his muscles were mesmerizing, Arya had found there was something more shocking about this man. His red hair was let down so it hung in his face, straight, silky locks that went down to his chest.

Taking a careful step off the bed, Arya padded over to where Idoh slept, parting his hair to double check it was her Salamander. Her wrist was snatched, pain erupting from the pressure exuded. Arya gasped, the cooling flame encompassing her like a burst of a bomb. Idoh's golden eyes showed through his hair, a fiery passion behind them.

He pulled Arya into him, covering her mouth as she went to protest. "Quiet, they'll hear."

Arya's heart was beating out of control, realizing Idoh was half naked and Arya was only in her underclothes, sitting in his lap. If anyone saw them, there would be gossip of her impropriety for sure. If the others didn't know her, it surely would spread through her friends and gods forbid she get teased over it by Leif.

"Idoh," Arya whimpered. "I'm indecent."

"I know," he growled. "Look."

Idoh pointed to a shadow on the wall. Arya furrowed her brows, looking from the shadow to Idoh. He pointed, narrowing his eyes. Arya looked back again, noticing there was another shadow, moving slightly. Their bodies did not give off shadows, and if they did, the light was coming at them, not to their left. This shadow was on the wall, moving like a person walked through the room, yet no one was there.

It bent over the bed, as if looking for someone inside. Faster than humanly possible, it turned and blurred until it was out of the room. Idoh removed his hand from Arya's mouth, his face solemn.

"What was that?" Arya asked in a whisper.

"Emeric," Idoh stated. "He's looking for you."

Arya sighed deeply, putting her head in her hands. "Of course he is. I'm the most desirable person in the entirety of time aren't I?"

Idoh smirked, his eyes tracing over Arya's exposed arm. His fingers slid down her arm, goosebumps rising to the surface. "You sure are, Little Flame."

"Don't tease me, Idoh." Arya struggled to speak, focused on the gentle burns his touch caused.

"What's a little bit of steam?" He whispered in her ear. Arya breathed out, letting a small moan escape. Gods what was she becoming? "We haven't finished what was started in training."

Arya thought back to his ashy shirt and the river that was reappearing between her legs. Idoh wrapped his arm around her waist, jerking her body as close as it would get to his. His member was hard against her, his pants doing nothing to stop the pulsing it was doing. He wanted her, and wanted Arya to know it. Fingers walked over her collarbones, hand wrapping firmly around her neck. "Do you want this?"

Arya did. She wanted it so badly. Her body craved to feel what his tongue would do to her insides and how the flame would respond to him being inside her. Unlike in the dream, Arya was fully on board to experience pleasure with someone who she consented to.

"Yes," she whispered.

"Yes what?" Idoh growled.

"I—I want you."

Without a struggle, Idoh flipped Arya around so she sat straddled in his lap. His hand was still proper, placed in the middle of her back for support, the other dragging along her jaw. His golden eyes bore deep into hers, Arya encompassed in a flame unlike any other. A burning desire that was destined. Fated to happen.

Idoh gripped the back of Arya's head, his hand fisting her hair. Pushing her forward, Idoh pressed their lips together.

Arya melted.

Nothing could have allowed her to feel the way that kiss did. His body and hers merged, everything he was became her, and she became him. Pain, agony, desire, love, all emotions that were not hers circled within her mind and body. Anger. Desperation. Need to prove herself. Things she'd felt before but never at these levels. Not this dangerously.

Arya's chest was pushed, her body hitting the floor. It took her a minute to process what happened, mind and body still whirling from the connection she had formed with Idoh. A simple binding from an innocent kiss.

"What are you fucking doing?" Mies growled. Only, it was not directed toward her, but Idoh. Mies gripped Idoh's neck, knuckles white and a flowing mist coming off him. Idoh smiled cockily.

"Bonding with my favorite girl. It's our last life, why waste it?"

"And they call Leif the whore," Mies hissed, throwing Idoh back to the ground and wiping his hand on his shirt. His attention turned to Arya who watched with her hand on her chest.

Pain and anger still resided there. A dangerous combination that caused many thoughts to circle her head. Idiotic thoughts, but tempting ones too. It boiled inside of her, each minute of her existence dedicated to the suffering and torment she'd gone through. Arya growled at the horror of it all, furious at everything and everyone who had put her in those situations. She hated the gods. Their stupid fucking game. The way her friends knew about her location but didn't rescue her. Was she that pathetic? Worthless and unimportant that she wasn't worth the effort it took to take her back home? Fire burned inside her, thinking of how easy it would be to kill them. To end *everyone*.

"Arya, are you okay?"

She shook her head, tears welling in her eyes. How could she be so horrible? "I'm having thoughts, bad ones." Her eyes settled on Idoh, a stream of water falling over her cheek. "Make them stop."

Idoh's smile faded, skin paling. "You stopped it too soon."

Mies crouched in front of Arya, Idoh pushing to get in too.

"Arya, what are you feeling?" Mies asked.

"Can't you feel it?" She pleaded, her nails clawing at her chest, nails tearing at the surface of her skin in an attempt to rid herself of the heat that burned with fury.

Pressure built within her. She longed to make it stop. To feel something other than the agony and frustration in the world. Gods, she wanted it to stop. Arya called out, gripping her hair and curling into a ball. Everyone failed her. Dismissed her as a weak Selkie who was worth nothing unless given to them. Emeric thought he deserved her, forcing her hand and taking no regrets in torturing her. The secrets that were kept ruined her motivation, sending her into darkness unknown.

"You're nothing."

"Roderick should've killed you, not Meriah."

"You're not worthy of your friends."

"No one loves you, not even your parents."

"You're wrong!" Arya cried, pulling at the strands of hair she held.

Voices filled her head, overlapping with negativity and hate that she never processed. People who hated her for being a Selkie. Humans who wanted her as a trophy. Self-doubts that she had hidden in the recesses of her mind.

Her arms were pulled away from her hair, Arya screaming as the voices drowned her thoughts and consumed her mind in darkness. Burning continued to rip through her, tensing her muscles as if being struck by lightning over and over again.

"Please make it stop!" She pleaded. "Please, please make it stop!"

But it did not stop.

It only got worse.

"Embrace the pain," Leif's voice broke through the tormenting thoughts.

Arya listened to him, doing her best to relax her body. She allowed the pain and anger to consume her. The burning erupted, fire encompassing not just her outsides, but insides as well. It filled every crease and roll, every cell that made her who she was. Arya couldn't focus on anything but the anger.

How dare the world treat her as it did? Where did the gods get off on denying her a right to choose her own way? Why did no one trust her with anything?

Then a noise.

A nasty buzzing noise that increased her fury to another level. Arya couldn't feel the pain anymore, launching from her laying position toward the irritant. Her hand wrapped around a neck, her eyes burning as she stared at Zephyr. He stared at her with wide eyes, mouth open in awe.

"You *left me to die*!" Arya hissed, tightening her grip around his throat. "I *needed* saving. *You* failed me."

"I was doing what was best for Teielmor," Zephyr struggled.

"Arya, let him go," Winslet insisted. Arya didn't look to Winslet, the one person she had no anger for. "This anger is amplification from your bond with Idoh. Not you."

Arya let go of Zephyr, feeling the fury subside. Pain left with it, giving her back herself. The room swayed, her hand pressed to her forehead to try and stabilize her vision.

Leif's soothing touch pressed against her arm, Arya allowing herself to lean into him. He wrapped her in his arms, tight, yet not constricting. It was like he knew her and what she needed in that moment. It was only when he had embraced her that she remembered the dream from the night before. An arranged marriage to Leif. It wasn't the worst situation she could've accepted. This time around was nothing like her dream, and marrying Leif would be more of a relief than anything.

"You could've sent her into madness!" Winslet screamed at Idoh, her finger in his face. Arya forced her attention to the commotion, finally processing that she was not alone with Leif in that moment.

"She needs to start bonding or she won't survive! I was only doing what was best for her—what you all should be doing too." Idoh narrowed his eyes, but a sly smile tipped the corners of his mouth.

"She's supposed to bond when she's had the dream, not whenever you feel like it!" Mies growled, his eyes narrowing at Idoh.

Arya was quiet. While she could process that somehow Idoh had caused that surge of anger and that Arya was bonded now to him, she didn't know what that meant. Overall, she was just exhausted and wanted to leave. It didn't feel safe in Ilmari anymore, and with the stress of everything she just wanted time to escape. To be Arya for once and not some lover for multiple people.

Idoh looked at Arya as if he knew her thoughts, hurt flashing through his eyes. Arya turned her attention to the floor, refusing to feel bad about the situation. At least her friends were able to stick up for her.

Without dismissing herself, Arya left Leif's arms, listening to the silence as she left. Footsteps trailed after her, Arya spinning to see the group following.

"Leave me alone," Arya stated without the presence of emotion in the words. She was too tired for that. She just wanted the ocean and silence.

30

There was an outcropping of flat rocks a few miles from shore of the Castle Lofta beach. Arya had laid with her seal skin flattened to her chest, allowing the water to splash on her, eyes focused on the passing clouds above. The water was chilled with the early start to spring, but Arya didn't care. It felt nice to just have a few minutes to herself. Even with her nature to seek companionship with other Selkies, Arya enjoyed this fleeting treat.

It had been decided while she swam that she would believe the others and the gods in the past life idiocy. While she struggled to understand it and accept it as truth, it would make her life a whole lot easier if she gave up her notion of what she believed to be true. Facts tended to be skewed in favor of one person or another, and with her recent encounter with Idoh, she didn't trust anything.

Unfortunately, it seemed as though the world revolved around Arya and her "bonds". The dream of being with Leif had left her with many questions, but one thing was certain. The woman in the mirror was the same woman she'd seen with the slit throat. If she was one of her past lives, Arya wanted to know how she'd gotten that wound. How all those women died. If she knew, it may help her uncover how she could stay alive. Maybe more.

Arya sensed him before he came to her spot. The dark water parted to reveal his large black eyes looking up at her, skin slick with the sea.

"Did they send you?" Arya asked.

Porter dove into the water, surfacing once again with his seal skin in his hand. "No, but they're all worried about you. Did something happen?"

Arya shrugged, sitting up so Porter could sit next to her. "Have you ever felt like things never turn out how they're supposed to?"

He snorted, petting his skin as he settled on the rock. "Constantly. I think that's a curse of life." Arya nodded, pulling her knees up and hiding her face behind them. Porter rubbed her back, sighing deeply. "Tell me what troubles you."

Arya shook her head, attempting to banish the tears that threatened her. "Do you remember when I told you about them? How they were my only chance of happiness?" Porter nodded. "I think I was wrong. Idoh *bonded* with me, whatever the fuck that means, and the anger I felt when it happened scared me. I wasn't me, but a version that even the

297

humans would fear." Porter stayed quiet, looking out across the expanse of black. "They keep telling me I'm not ready, I don't understand, that I need to wait for them to explain when the time is right. The thing is, if I do, they're risking everything! The lives of the people, the invasion, Evelyn, Emeric, Roderick. They're all out to get me and it puts everyone I love at risk."

"Did you ask the gods for help?" Porter asked.

Arya let out a crude laugh. "They just want me to promise to marry their pick. It's like nothing matters but my acceptance of their bet."

Porter nodded his head to the side. "Sounds about right."

"What do you mean?" Arya asked, looking over to him. He was unusually calm for someone learning the gods were real and Arya was the focus of a matchmaking attempt they concocted.

"Myths always end up like this, Arya, you should know," he said, "the goal is for you to break the mold of those traditional stories. Fuck what they expect and how the heroes typically succeed. This is reality, and sometimes, it takes suffering of others to encourage change in fate."

Arya narrowed her eyes. "You sound eerily knowledgeable in this topic."

He shrugged. "I've seen you sacrifice yourself for others mentally and physically. Your heart is pure and your intentions are good."

Arya blinked, never thinking of herself as pure and good. She was disgusting, a whore. Not someone who deserves such titles. No one wanted it as badly as Arya, but there were dark things inside of her. Ones that ached to be freed and she refused to let them.

"Do me a favor, Arya," Porter said as he stretched. "Let yourself be you. No restraint, no overthinking, no regrets."

"What if it turns out badly?"

"What if it doesn't?"

Arya was still unsure. She didn't want to be left alone when she'd spent so much time in solitary. All Arya had wanted was to get back to her friends that she'd seen in her dreams. However, these people weren't like those dream versions. Their attitudes and actions were different. They were more desperate.

"Do you see that?" Porter asked as he stood on the rock.

Arya furrowed her brows, tracing to where he looked. In the distance a dark shadow of a ship stood. It was tall, easily a cargo ship. However, when Arya continued to watch, she noticed the white flag whipping in the wind. The flag that she'd seen multiple times over her stay in Kulessa.

"We need to warn them," Arya whispered, fear gripping her to the bone. Roderick had come for her.

Porter nodded, joining Arya in jumping into the water, their skins on as they rushed to shore. No matter their intentions or goals, Arya needed to prepare the castle for an attack.

31

The castle was a mess. People ran, helping the wounded to carriages and carts to escort them off the property. Dunian horses were being prepared for battle, Ilmari wings prepped with armor. The few Finta soldiers able to defend the castle armed themselves with multiple jars of explosive powder and weapons. The Selkies were determined to go with the injured who could not fend for themselves.

Arya and Porter had jumped into helping get the injured into the carts. Evacuation practices obviously expected as the group was able to rid themselves of the injured within thirty minutes. For the first time since arriving to Ilmari, Arya had seen the King and Queen, unfortunately bidding each other farewell as the Queen got into a carriage.

"Arya! You need to go!" Idoh shouted.

Thinking about what Porter said, Arya scowled and raced up the stairs. "Get me armor."

"You are not fighting."

That surge of anger came to her again, Arya marched over to him, grabbing Idoh by the collar of his shirt and shoving him to the wall. "Stop looking at me as weak. I survived more than I had to, let me fight for the people I love."

Arya swore she saw the corners of his mouth twitch before he nodded, grabbing her hand and running through the halls. Arya kept up the best she could, the pair slowing when getting to a door beside the training room. Idoh took the lead, going inside the large closet and pulling Finta armor from the drawers. He piled the items over his arm, occasionally holding pieces up to Arya.

"Put these on and fast," he ordered.

Arya nodded, stripping her dress and putting on the pants and shirt Idoh had started with. He gave her socks and boots next, followed by a chest piece, and leather thigh holsters. Finally, he gave her arm bracers, each holding a small throwing knife in a built in sheath. Idoh took a minute to run his fingers through her hair, twisting the locks into a single braid.

"When did you learn to braid?" Arya asked, attempting to lighten the mood.

"I used to do it to my hair as a child." There was no sign of emotion in his voice, just a hardened exterior. It was like the Idoh from that morning had disappeared and was replaced with this person. One closer to the man she had seen in her dream.

Idoh pulled at the straps holding Arya's armor on, double checking its security. Then, unexpectedly, he pressed his forehead to hers. "I'm sorry."

"Sorry?" Arya asked.

He nodded, eyes closed. "For this morning. I shouldn't have rushed our bond."

Arya slid her hand up his cheek. "Idoh, I'm angry, but I will never hate you. We'll talk about it later."

He sighed, forcing himself from her and marching out of the room. Arya followed, grabbing a sword from the wall on the way out. If magic failed her, she needed a backup plan.

The castle shook as they made their way to the beach, shouting announcing the arrival of iron laced cannons. Sylphs took to the air from the cliffs, their armor glistening gold in the sunlight. Dullahan sat atop their horses, mist circling their red eyed beasts who waited impatiently to ride. Salamander men and women smoked, flames igniting and extinguishing in preparation. Gean-Cánach and Selkies waited around the forest to sneak attack the incoming humans. Arya joined Idoh in the front lines, darkness embracing her.

Arya was prepared to kill to protect those around her, and if needed, use the worst magic for the best intentions. Porter said be unapologetically her, so she would be in every aspect of the phrase.

Flexing her fingers, Arya called upon the water, it obeying without hesitation. It danced around her, bubbling and collecting like a snake ready to strike. Nothing was quite as satisfying as how it felt to be in control of her element. Being away from it for so long meant that the familiarity and power was thrilling. An encouragement that Arya didn't know she needed. One she was thankful for as she saw the amount of humans who came at them.

Thousands of boats rowed to shore as they waited. It was as if the entire human army was on that single ship. Arya narrowed her eyes, refusing to show her fear in light of the updating information before her. This was the fight she had been expecting and needed.

The humans rushed through the ocean, getting to the beach where they immediately began to fight. Earth rose and fell, air whipping and twisting to throw some humans off their feet. Flames shot in the smoke and fog mixture, water hardening to ice to puncture through flesh and armor. All the while, an intense feeling of honor and determination floated through the air.

Arya joined them, thrusting her whipping water that she had collected toward the approaching foes. Idoh fought next to her, Arya grabbing one human and throwing them to the ground where his flame incinerated their head. Arya spun, flinging water through the air, hardening it to pointed ice that implanted into a human who sliced at a Dullahan man.

She collected more, drawing from the air and ocean, dancing a deadly choreography that felt more natural than walking or talking. It was within her nature to wield such a marvelous element. Once, Arya had been convinced water was the weaker of elements. Her Selkie appearance causing her to be targeted by Roderick and other humans. Now, as she destroyed flesh and bone and metal, Arya couldn't be happier with her element. Her destiny as a Selkie—a creature of water.

Unfortunately, it was only a few who were able to get the best of the humans. A shot of iron pounded into the beach, flinging the metal into the humans and fae alike. Shards that didn't kill impacted the ability to manipulate their element, allowing the humans an upper hand.

Arya whipped her water at the humans who surrounded another Selkie, lassoing them together and collectively drowning the bunch. The woman nodded at Arya, retreating to the tree line to be healed the best she could be. Looking around, the battle was turning in the human's favor.

Another round of canon fire littered iron pieces over the beach.

"Arya!" Idoh yelled, grabbing her arm and pulling her into him. Metal shards zipped by them, Idoh's armor being torn and shredded as it hit him.

"Idoh, stop, you'll get hurt!" Arya protested, but it was no use. Idoh held her tightly, refusing to let her out of his grasp.

The smell of blood hovered in the air, Arya watching at humans and fae alike sprawled amongst the sand, various sizes of iron sticking from the corpses.

"Are you hurt?" Arya asked, brushing the tips of her fingers over Idoh's jaw.

He let out a shaky breath, pressing his forehead to hers. "If you don't stop I will not be able to stop myself, Little Flame."

Arya snorted, shaking her head. "Not the time or the place, Idoh."

The fact of the matter was, they were losing.

Humans were double the amount of fae, the iron slowing the human warriors, but not injuring them as bad as it did the fae it touched. Elements weakened, wounds failed to heal.

Then a scream. One she didn't want to hear.

Across the field, Arya saw a blade puncture through a leather chest plate. His brown curls were stuck to his forehead with a mixture of sweat and blood. His horse was nowhere to be seen, yet Mies still fought, stumbling back and raising a barrier of sand to protect himself from another stab wound.

Her heart pounded in her chest. Throat closing. Flashes of another life. One where humans had attacked and Mies laid in a puddle of his own blood. Arya cradled his head in her lap, cursing the gods as she cried. Her heart ached. Broken with the memory of losing him. A different life. She wouldn't allow the same to happen this time. Not if she could help it.

"Cover me!" Arya screamed, not looking to see if Idoh followed her run. She tore through the fighting humans and fae, killing without a second thought. All she needed was to get to Mies. *Her* Mies.

A human ran at her, lifting a sword above his head, Arya twisting to gain momentum on her whip. The water sliced through the human, bone and all. He dropped in two pieces, gaining Arya the attention she didn't desire. Multiple came at her, delaying her approach to Mies.

He crawled backward, hitting the sandy back of a dune cliff. The human approached slowly, hand flexing on his sword. She wasn't going to make it. Mies was going to die.

A blaze of fire lit to her right, three humans burning before they fell.

"Go!" Idoh yelled, throwing another ball of fire to more approaching humans. Even if she ran, Arya knew the likelihood of her making it wasn't good.

Be unapologetically you. Lir's voice hummed in her mind.

It was permission, Arya realized, to do the one thing that made the Selkie so strong. A banned practice.

Arya took a breath in, letting go of all her anxiety, fear, and troubles. She felt for water in the air, arms and feet working to combine the water in the air with that of the earth. Then she felt it on the sweat of those fighting, each drop and collection on the fabric and hair. Arya reached her hands up, reaching deeper. Blood pumping, muscles contracting, organs pounding. Water was in all of them. Waiting. Luring Arya in.

She separated the people quickly, finding the sparkle of elements within the fae, leaving only the dull life source of the humans. Threading her will through each, Arya infiltrated their armor and skin, diving into their bodies without consent. Sifting through until suddenly, all humans stopped.

Mid movement, humans stilled as if becoming statues. Arya opened her eyes, bright with the magic of water. The fae paused, cautiously looking around at all the stilled humans. Strained noises came from their mouths, Arya walking through humans and fae alike.

"I think they're screaming," she heard someone say.

Good, Arya thought.

Getting to Mies, Arya clenched her jaw. The human who hurt him stood with a sword raised, ready to end her Dullahan's life. However, he forced her into a position of madness. Desperation to save someone she loved, and thus ending his own life.

Arya felt the blood moving through his body. His heart was healthy. A quickened thrumming that proved he was scared. So, she stopped it. There was a wheezing as the man died, Arya removing all blood from entering the organ. More hearts joined the chorus in Arya's head, their rhythmic beating allowing her to smile. They were hers to control. To manipulate and punish for what they did to her people.

So she did.

The humans dropped, each clutching their chests as Arya released them from her hold. Their eyes rolled back, others arching their backs as their bodies failed them.

"They're dead," someone said, "How?"

Arya knelt by Mies, ignoring the awestruck fae around them. She encouraged the water to come so she could heal his wounds. Arya didn't look at him, knowing if she did, her guilt would say it all.

"Tell me it wasn't you," Mies grunted. Arya stayed silent. "Gods damn it, Arya—."

"I saw you die," Arya whispered, her eyes flicking up to meet his. A distant memory of rope tightening over her neck made her shutter "I killed myself over it, didn't I?"

Mies opened and closed his mouth before nodding. "Yes."

"When was that?" She asked.

"Three lives ago."

Arya returned her focus to Mies's wounds, healing with what energy she had left. Idoh approached after, refusing to mention the humans' sudden deaths. She was grateful for that, finishing her work and standing. Idoh and Arya both helped Mies up, accompanying the other survivors of the battle back to the castle.

As they got to the front entry, refusing to wait in line to enter through the servant's door as the other warriors had, a carriage approached. The horses were panicked, barely stopping before the trio. Mies put his hands up to the horses, whispering sweet nothings to them so they would calm down. Arya had seen the carriage leave, however, the white curtains were now stained red.

Arya opened the door knowing what could be waiting beyond it. As the smell and vision hit her, Arya lost the little contents that were held in her stomach.

Heads. Heads of her people were piled within the carriage, topped by the frozen scream of the Queen. Arya recognized the collection to be a mix of those sent for refuge. Injured and weak fae. People who didn't deserve to die. Not like this.

Then her eyes connected with a pair she didn't want to see among this group. Blood spilled from his partially opened mouth, already drying on his skin. Arya couldn't help the tears that fell, kneeling and placing her hand on his cheek. Porter had been so alive a few hours before. Arya furrowed her brows as she noticed something inside his mouth.

"Arya, don't." Idoh warned.

Arya didn't listen, pulling out a ribbon of his skin. His seal coat cracked and turned to powder as she pulled. Each inch of the ribbon caused her chest to tighten, solidifying the fact that Porter was gone. Her crying intensified, continuing to pull the ribbons of Selkie skin from his mouth until finally, it stopped. At the end, however, a red piece of paper was attached.

Enjoy your time with my little distraction, Arya? I wonder if all your friends were too.

Evelyn

Arya stood, grabbing Idoh's armor. "Where are the others? Zephyr, Leif, and Winslet?"

"Leif and Winslet went with the carts," Idoh said hollowly. "Zephyr is upstairs."

Arya fell to the ground, head dipping in defeat. She should've known. She should have seen this coming.

"Arya what's wrong?" Mies asked.

"She has them."

"What?" Idoh breathed.

"Evelyn has Leif and Winslet."

"That's wrong," Mies said, limping to pick Arya off the ground. She furrowed her brows, looking to the entrance of the castle drive.

Leif slid his foot as he pushed forward. His hand pressing a dirtied rag to a wound on his arm, blond hair coated in a thick layer of dirt, blood, and iron shreds.

Arya didn't wait, running to him and wrapping her arms around him. She sobbed in his chest, Leif holding her with his chin resting on the top of her head.

"They took Winslet," he muttered.

Arya nodded. "I know."

"They branded me," was the next thing he said, lifting the rag from his arm. His flesh had melted and bubbled where the iron had marked him, a large E imprinted into his skin.

Not only did this bitch brand one of her friends, but she stole away Winslet. If Evelyn knew of Arya's dream, changing the trajectory of her life, she knew how much Winslet meant to her. How that devilish marking did nothing but ignite a fire of vengeance within her core.

Arya saw Leif, beaten, bloody, barely able to stand, and felt nothing but rage. A fire in her core erupted, heat encompassing her entire being as she knew what she had to do.

Arya placed her hands on his face, making him look at her. "Bond with me."

Eager girl, Renea chuckled in her head.

"What?" He asked in a whisper.

"I've had the dream of our marriage, Leif. Bond with me so I can take the pain away."

Leif shook his head, sighing deeply. "I wanted it to be special."

"We don't always get what we want, and I'll need you bonded to me when we rescue Winslet," Arya said.

Without another word, Leif fell to the ground. He rubbed a hand with his eyes, Arya meeting him on the dirt road.

"Leif-."

"Let me grieve," he interrupted. "Let me process that you won't get to have the beautiful moment I dreamt for us."

Arya nodded, brushing back his ash coated hair. "Being yours is a dream enough."

Before Arya had time to react, Leif's lips were on hers, and nothing in the world felt so right before.

32

Arya had never experienced lust like when she kissed Leif. It filled her entire body with a desire that was unable to be controlled. Clearly, Leif felt it too, his hold stronger and body pressing against hers. Arya slid her hands over his body, finding her way beneath his clothes. Her fingers traced the outline of his muscles of his chest as Leif reached down and picked her up. It was easy to throw her legs around his waist, feeling his growth against the need to feel it inside her.

Radiance and bliss enveloped Arya, no sign of the anger she'd felt with Idoh present. With Leif, all she wanted was him and everything he could give her.

While Arya was of the faint tugging and pulling that came to her, she ignored it. Nothing was more important than Leif's body merging to hers.

Flashes of passion were accompanied by glimpses of the past. Different lives and different faces, but Arya knew it was him each time. His body flexing beneath her own. The memory of how his skin felt on her fingertips. The tickle his breath gave while he whispered into her ear. It was seductive, yet safe. A treasure to be kept hidden, but displayed openly. A contradiction that only made sense if you were part of the equation.

Then it hit her. Soaring peace like nothing she'd ever felt before, yet remembered so clearly. Every memory that included Leif from this lifetime and the past ones combined into who Arya was in that moment. The final element.

"Enough!" Zephyr yelled, splitting them apart with a gust of wind that sent Arya into a tree nearby. Her head hit the trunk, pain and warm liquid following soon after. She slumped forward as she hit the ground, dazed and unable to focus on the things happening before her. As she fell to her side, Arya could hear the distant sound of fire crackling.

Screams echoed over a field of bodies, fire and ash sprinkling down around her. Fear and adrenaline fueled Arya to move, slicing through each body that came at her like child's play. She knew she was the best. Trained all her life for battles like this, yet now, being in the middle of it, Arya wanted nothing to do with this world or the anger of Finta people.

Now, Arya had one goal in mind. Protection.

Cresting on the hill, her leathers and cotton soaking with sweat, Arya looked over the source of the screams.

313

Warriors of all ages fought against these intruders from another land. Ones with wings and could steal the air from their lungs. The headless riders of the west had come to assist Finta in their separation from this so-called unity the winged ones insisted upon. They also brought their own warriors though. Ones who could heal and affect the mind during the war.

Among the chaos that was battle, Arya spotted the man she had been searching for. His light skin was darkened from soot and char, yellow eyes ablaze with fury and passion. The same ones she had stared into the night before. He fought with light by his side, hands and feet gliding through the air with such speed they did not show the flames he threw, but simple orange streaks.

Arya rushed to him, her blades incinerating each foe that forced her hand. She slid beneath the legs of one man, slicing up through his groin before exiting his body. He fell to the ground, wound bleeding and eyes dulling. It was not the first or last time she would watch death come for someone at her hand.

The Finta soldiers fought around her in elegant fashion. Their moves like dances and flames their song. Even with the mood shifters, these men and women were filled with the fury of flame and nothing could take that from them.

As Arya got to the man she sought after, she noticed a shift in the air. Almost as if the wind had halted. Ash held it's place in the air as a pair of silver wings dropped from the heavens in front of her. A man rose, silver hair having been

314

held back by a circlet falling to his chest. His eyes moved over her with curiosity, the corners of his mouth twitching.

"I have been looking for you," he said with a smile.

Arya narrowed her eyes, stepping back and raising her swords so she could prepare for the fight this winged man was about to get. Looking for her? Yeah, sure buddy.

Then she felt it.

A choking, deadly ball that formed in her gut. Arya looked past her enemy, seeing another winged man stealing the air from her love. Idoh's fire dimmed, his lips fading into a chilly blue. His mouth opened and closed, air refusing to enter his lungs.

She couldn't live without him. Refused to have the one person she cared about ripped from her like this. No matter their fancy weapons and air magic, Arya would fight for him until the end.

Fury built inside her, aching to come out since she had been allowed to learn fire manipulation. It churned inside her, increasing in force and power until Arya knew it was ready to be released.

She leaned back, crouching slightly before lifting her leg straight into the air and slamming it down. The ground quaked, splitting to reveal the lava that laid dormant below the surface. It bubbled and hissed as it touched the air, the winged man stumbling away in horror at what she uncovered, but the one hurting her Idoh did not. Arya ran at him, feeling the unlocked energy of the molten core, molding it without touching anything. It shot into the air, grabbing the winged man by the face and arms. He screamed as Arya pulled him *into the soup of fire, letting out a blaze of flames as he was consumed.*

A familiar feeling of cool washed over Arya as the pressure of another person touched her back. The pit in her stomach disappeared and she looked back to the winged man from before, her eyes pinned on him as her next target.

"Looking for me, you say? Didn't anyone tell you it isn't smart to go find Death?"

Arya sat up in bed, Leif asleep in a chair beside her, Idoh leaned up against a wall on the floor. Mies was nowhere to be seen, but by the window, his silver wings laying limp behind him, was Zephyr. He stared out into the darkness, as if waiting for something.

"Whose side are you on really?" Arya asked, crossing her arms as she noticed she wasn't wearing anything other than her underclothes.

"Yours. Mine. Whichever gets me what I want." He replied quickly, as if having rehearsed the question.

"And what do you want?"

"You. I've only ever wanted you to myself."

Arya scoffed, shaking her head. "You should've thought about that before you refused to rescue me."

Rain assaulted the window he looked out of, the storm not forecasted earlier that day. Zephyr turned, pushing Arya against the wall. His fist slammed beside her. She kept her face stoney, refusing to show him just how scared she was. How her heart picked up speed and sweat began to collect at her hairline.

"You don't scare me, Zephyr," she lied.

Their faces were inches apart, his eyes pinned to hers with the energy of a raging storm behind them. Arya narrowed her own, refusing to let this man get the better of her.

"I should," he snarled, "You have no idea what I'm capable of."

"You're capable of backing the fuck off." Mies.

Arya broke her contact with Zephyr to look at the man. His hair was stuck to his face, clothes dripping essence of the rain onto the wood beneath him.

"Go," Mies ordered.

"I am your prince-."

"Fuck right off with that bullshit, you know full well the only reason any of us are still here is for her. Your crown means nothing."

Zephyr let a growl escape his throat, pounding the wall one more time before storming out of the room.

Mies walked to Arya who took a deep breath in. "You okay?"

She shook her head, ridding Mies of his excess water before leaning into his chest. "Sometimes I wish I could've just been married off and had babies like other noble women."

Mies chuckled, wrapping his arms around her. "Now where's the fun in that?"

Arya smiled, inhaling deeply. Maybe it was easier, but fuck if she didn't think about it from time to time. It would've been Mies's children after all.

33

Arya sat at the long wooden table with a plate of eggs and ham upon it. She pushed the food around her plate without much effort, the fork heavy in her grasp. She knew the others were talking about the war and the attack, but without Winslet, Arya was left with a hollowness that refused to levitate. It was easier than how it felt when Winslet was dead, but it was still hard. A piece of her missing, and possibly in Kulessa, facing those tortures she didn't want her to ever experience. If Roderick knew what was best for him, he'd keep his grubby little hands off Winslet.

"What do you think, Arya?" Idoh asked, glaring at Zephyr.

Arya looked up from her plate, clueless at what the topic had been. She glanced to Leif, who thankfully understood her distraction. "I personally think that running to get Winslet is a good idea, but Zephyr is our prince and he is in control of us."

Arya raised her brows. They really wanted her to debate on whether or not they went after Winslet? Were they really that stupid?

"We're going after her," Arya said as she set down her fork and pushed her plate away. There would be no arguments on if they would be saving Winslet. She was not spineless and if they were, then so fucking be it. She'd go alone.

Zephyr shook his head. "As prince I'm telling you—.""

"You are not my prince," Arya snapped, narrowing her eyes at him. "You failed me as a royal when you refused me saving and forced me to endure torture that close to killed me. Exposing Winslet to such pain will not happen, orders or not. It is as simple as that, *your majesty.*"

The three men stared at Arya like she had unclothed in front of them, Arya wishing Mies had been around to steal her away. All she did was defy Zephyr, was it really all that interesting? She was sure if anyone else had done the same, they would've been thrown in the dungeons. Then again, Arya wasn't sure Castle Lofta had dungeons. She'd never heard or seen them, perhaps it was just a human thing.

As if beckoned by her need, Mies sat beside her, patting her leg. "I'm riding out." It was like a punch in the gut when Mies said that. Arya's head going dizzy and chest tightening. She didn't expect him to leave her, especially when it came to their bond not being solidified. "I'm never the first to be bonded with Arya, giving me more time to be alone. Winslet needs rescuing and I will not be a coward and refuse her like I did Arya. She deserves better than that."

"I'm coming with you," Arya said.

"The fuck you are!" Idoh protested.

"You just came back to Teielmor, who knows what will happen to you if you travel into Kulessa for a second time. If you'll come out alive." Lief argued, his fingers sliding through his golden locks. They glistened in the light of the morning sun that shimmered through the windows. A beautiful piece of art.

"I do not follow the orders of any of you fucks," Arya said, harsher than she intended, almost like someone else was talking through her. The corners of Idoh's lips twitched and she could see his eyes get wider as if knowing something she didn't. "My place is one of war since you all refused to help me before. Good intentions or not, I refuse to leave anyone in the hands of Evelyn or Roderick."

Idoh stood, smirking. "I'll get my armor." Arya furrowed her brows. "If you think you're going alone, Little Flame, you're sadly mistaken."

"You could get killed," Arya said.

"So could you, more likely you would before me." Idoh chuckled.

Arya narrowed her eyes at him, sucking on her teeth. What an asshole. She could handle herself. Fuck, it was him who almost died against the humans. *No*, Arya reminded herself. *Not in this life he didn't.*

Leif sighed, spinning in his seat and standing.

"Where are you going?" Zephyr demanded.

Leif shrugged. "To Kulessa it sounds like. My best friend and Arya are going so I have to as well. I know you wouldn't understand, you've never been bonded to her."

Arya's mouth dropped open, looking to Zephyr for confirmation on what Leif just said. He dropped his eyes to his fists that clenched into balls, knuckles white from the pressure. So it was true. Arya had never bonded with Zephyr... but why? What made it so she refused him in every lifetime? There was more she needed to know, but it wasn't going to happen in that moment.

"Are you coming?" Arya asked him.

Zephyr's jaw tightened before he spun, standing only to storm past the group. Wind brushed around her as she watched him go, a hazy shimmer of his wings threatening to expose themselves. It was about control, Arya realized. Zephyr did not have control of them when she was there. She would always overpower him.

"Come on, let's get moving. Winslet needs us." Leif said from behind her. She nodded, working on the different things they would need to prepare. If only Porter was there to help her.

34

Arya had gone to find Idoh, wanting to know more about the woman in her dream. She knew it was her, but it was a fuzzy, unclear version that he would know better. There wasn't much Arya needed to pack, her sack mainly consisted of weapons and food. She didn't have anything but her skin when she came to Castle Lofta, and when she went back to Kulessa there would be nothing more they could take from her.

As she turned into the training room, voices caused her to stop and pin herself beside the door. The voices were angry. Elevated whispers that showed the disdain for their interaction.

"*You* had said she would be delivered to me this life," Zephyr growled. "She was supposed to be only mine!"

A low cackle was the response, the hair on Arya's arms rising. She knew that cackle and the deep voice who followed it. "She is not yours to take, traitor. While you may be in this rotation between us, she will never choose you. Your soul is tarnished in every lifetime you enter."

Emeric.

He was there. Inside the castle. Talking with Zephyr. She needed to go. Find someone who could help her escape. Mies or Idoh or Leif.

Arya took a step out, the floorboard creaking beneath her feet. Her breathing stopped. Fingers slowly toying with the blade she had strapped to her waist. The voices had stopped, Arya eerily aware of the darkness that began to inch beneath the door. He was coming.

She took off down the hall, sprinting as fast as she could.

The door opened, darkness expanding out behind her like a tsunami. Arya ran as fast as her legs would carry her, the sunlight refused entry by the shadows that Emeric controlled. They extinguished light like candles being blown out, not the full force of the sun.

Flashes of the day Arya stole her skin back came to her. How Phobus had chased her, pushed her down the stairs, how she'd swam for the first time in her skin. Arya was not that pathetic girl anymore. She was a motherfucking Selkie.

Turning, Arya held her hand out as if gripping Emeric by the throat. Strangely, it was there, in her hand, the feeling of his warmth flowing into her. So, she clenched.

Emeric stopped, parting the dark tentacles that came from him so Arya could see him clearly. His hand went to his neck, smirk warning her of danger she faced if not confident in her abilities.

"I've been waiting for you to uncover your talents, Arya."

She did not respond, squeezing harder. It was strange, his Adam's apple bobbed and pulse thrummed, yet they were so far apart. Wind whipped around them, Arya suspecting Zephyr was attempting to get through the darkness.

"Do it," Emeric said, "kill me. I know you want to."

"Don't tempt me," Arya yelled, though her voice quivered, displaying the fear she truly held.

Emeric smiled. "You won't do it. You can't." He laughed as if she didn't have him by the throat. Fury built up inside her. Idoh's bond flushing to the surface. All senses were heightened, skin heating with the fire of a thousand suns. She noticed as Emeric's smile began to fade and he rubbed at the skin she was holding.

"You bonded with Idoh before you were ready. How do you have his magic?"

"It's not his magic," Arya growled, "It's mine."

Willing that fire through her, it tunneled out her hand and exploded from her arm. Fire and water circled her outstretched arm, not dimming in their combined power, but amplifying. Boiling and steaming. Emeric screamed out, clawing at his neck that began to get progressively darker. It flickered with light of embers, and bubbled as if affected by severe heat. Darkness closed in on him, then there was nothing.

Light filled the hall again, as if the darkness was never there to begin with. Bird chirped outside the open window, combined with the crashing of waves. Arya no longer felt the skin of Emeric, the dance of water and fire lessening as she lowered her hand.

"Arya!" Idoh called, running to her with Leif close behind. "What happened?"

"I felt you use magic," Leif huffed as he caressed her cheek. "Dangerous magic."

"Emerick was here," Arya said cautiously. Her eyes flicked to Leif's. "I didn't know Gean-Cánach could touch people without being close to them."

Leif opened and closed his mouth. "What?"

"I assumed it was the Gean-Cánach power I used," Arya muttered, still in wonder at what just happened. "I grabbed his throat and could feel everything—like I really was touching him."

Idoh shook his head. "Arya, you're not supposed to be able to do anything like that. Basic magic, sure, but not advanced techniques."

Arya looked at him, flashes of his former self playing with her vision. "Did you have the same eyes in every life?"

Idoh stilled, his temple pulsing.

"You've had the Finta dream." Leif said.

Arya nodded. She looked down at her hand, allowing the warmth and anger to build into flames at her finger tips. "So it's not just anger," she said, "It's passion."

325

Idoh nodded slowly, gazing at her as if seeing her for the first time. "And it's not just lust, it's love too. Deep and different for everyone." Leif let his shoulders release the tension that had been held there. Arya looked past them to Mies who hovered in the hall down the way. "What secrets do you have for me to unlock?"

He smirked, clicking his tongue. "I supposed you'll have to wait and see."

Arya nodded, remembering that Zephyr had been enclosed in the darkness. She turned, finding only a single silver feather in the corridor. "Why did I never bond with Zephyr?"

Leif refused to look at Arya, Idoh following his lead while rubbing his neck. Mies, however, stepped forward, parting the two other men and giving Arya a soft smile. "Let's get on the road and I'll tell you all about it."

The group walked out of the place that was once her safe haven. Somehow, it was different now. Not safe and cozy as the dream had portrayed, but empty and soulless. While light was let in through the windows, darkness filled the emptiness with despair. It was not where Arya wanted to end up once all of this was over.

The salt water hit her as she exited the castle, swirling petals of flowers from nearby trees. Closing her eyes, Arya let herself consume what could be the last time by the ocean for a while.

Where would she want to live the rest of her life?

Focusing on the different people she loved, Arya decided she wanted a cliffside manor. Below the manor the ocean and lava from Fintan would meet heating the rock beneath. It would always be warm and smell of salt and steam. Perhaps a garden where she could plant vegetables and herbs, but struggle with rabbits and other game eating them. Winslet could help with watering the plants and they would go for nightly swims while they looked at the stars. Leif and Idoh would do whatever they wished with their time, but were always around if needed, and Mies would cook delicious dinners. She didn't know if Mies could cook, but it just seemed like he might be good at it. There Arya would be happy.

"Arya, you ready?" Idoh asked, his hand barely touching her before the cooling flames she loved so much erupted throughout her body.

Opening her eyes, Arya smiled, leaning into his shoulder. All they had to do was get Winslet and everything would be alright. She could have her happily ever after.

And you must kill Evelyn, Fyorr said as if it was just something to add to a to-do list and not a major task that could change everything.

Arya sighed, stepping into the carriage she was sure they were stealing. If Arya was honest with herself, stealing was not the worst they could do anymore. Not when they were determined to trek into enemy territory and she was the only one who knew how to act like a human. She looked between Idoh with his yellow eyes and red hair and Leif who was practically a god with how effortless his beauty was. There was no way they'd fit in with the humans. Mies, now he was perfect for fitting in... as long as he didn't get angry and start misting.

"Gods help me," Arya whispered as she rubbed her hair back out of her face.

"Worried about being stuck with two of your bonds for too long?" Leif teased, leaning against the window.

Arya snorted. "Something like that."

"Don't worry, we'll be easy with you." Idoh winked sending heat all over Arya's face.

"That dream was right about one thing," Leif said, leaning forward to close distance between them. "Idoh and I don't mind sharing."

Arya's throat went dry, her mind fuzzy except for the implied ideas that Leif had implanted into her head.

How intriguing, Renea hummed.

"Both of you, quiet," Arya stammered. "We're going into enemy territory, we can't be distracted."

"On the contrary," Idoh snickered, "I'd like to be *very* distracted."

Idoh placed a hand on Arya's knee, his eyes flicking to Leif. Without much communication, Leif slid his way behind Arya, their bonds dancing together with her soul as if to prove they belonged there. Idoh slid further up her leg, as Leif twisted Arya's head to face him. His breath tempted Arya's lips, her head leaning forward and legs falling open to allow Idoh between them. Everything about them made her want more. Forced her to forget everything in exchange of lust and desire.

"Stop," she breathed.

They did. No complaints, no talking her into it, or forcing her to continue. They just stopped. Idoh sat beside Arya, and Leif returned to his spot by the window, but not without kissing her on the temple.

"Y-you both stopped."

Leif gave her a sad smile. "We want you to be happy Arya, no matter how much we want you, you call the shots."

Idoh nodded, taking Arya's hand. "There will never be a time where we do not obey your requests. If you tell us to stop while in the middle of the deed, we will. And if it is before, so be it."

"Why?" She asked, tears building behind her eyes.

"Because you are more important to us than a silly moment of intimacy." Leif chuckled. "Once you believe that, you'll have a much better time trusting us."

Arya didn't ask anymore questions, leaning her head on Idoh's shoulder. Leif twisted in his seat, laying his head on Arya's lap. She brushed through his hair, finding peace in the action. Memories of the past came to her doing the same thing, Leif's head in her lap and Arya feeling content with her life.

This was good. Once she got Winslet back and bonded with Mies, things would get easier. She was sure of it. It had to be.

35

Winslet could only see through the small keyhole lock of the trunk she was stuffed in when the humans had attacked. Leif was hurt in front of her, brutalized when he had tried to use magic on their perpetrators. Iron poles struck him over and over, his skin sizzling and the smell of burning flesh still something Winslet could not get out of her nose. As for herself, she was shoved into a trunk once she was tied up and left there.

These humans were smart. Refusing her water to drink and only giving her dried food. If it wasn't for them having her coat, Winslet would've crashed the carriage as they went over the river that separated Ilmari and Kulessa. Of course, that was all a guess on whether or not it was the correct body of water, but she figured it was a good guess.

Winslet could smell the burning earth and stale air that had an eerily recognizable memory attached. She was only a child when her parents had her accompany them to the war camps of Fintan. It was then she knew she never wanted to live in such a hot place. Not to mention the lack of shoreline and Selkie respect. Winslet recalled the mocking stares of the Salamander women and the pity the men gave her as she passed. Like she was weak and pathetic compared to them. That was the thing, Winslet was not weak and they were not better than her. It had been one of the pivotable moments in her life where she decided to grow up to prove everyone wrong.

Yet, there she was. In a box, bouncing through the frontlines of war with her hands tied behind her back.

There was a good chance Winslet was being used as bait for Arya. There were many opportunities to steal other Selkies, but they aimed for her. If that was the case, Winslet knew they already suspected her as weak. Possibly thinking her power equated to that of Arya without her coat.

She could use that to her advantage.

From what the dream Lir gifted her said, humans were stupid. Power hungry and misogynistic. Winslet had died in that version of history, and this time around, she had no interest in doing the same. Death was cold and unforgiving. Empty almost. She remembered the darkness that came after the explosion, and the knowing that everything was over. There wasn't fear or sadness, but nothing. Consciousness in a void. The others didn't remember death, the gods granting them their sanity in each reincarnation, but Lir wanted Winslet to remember. Why, she didn't know. What she did know was the fight to survive would be stronger than before and packages would not be opened by her.

Kidnapping her, Winslet suspected, had been a strategic move on Evelyn's part, meaning she had the same dream. The question was, which god gave it to her?

Winslet had known of the betrayal in each lifetime, the gods sabotaging their dynamic for their own power plays of Arya's mate and love story. Each time, the one Arya bonded with the most intensely died tragically. Strangely coincidental in Winslet's opinion.

The wagon came to a stop, Winslet's guard going up. She listened for the footsteps of the humans, judging just how far they were from her. If they were at their destination, she needed to know everything she could to escape.

The trunk opened, piercing light blinding Winslet. Trees were not around to shield the group and Winslet could not sense water nearby. Plains or valley of some sort. The humans grabbed her and tossed her without much care of her wellbeing, causing her to roll on a bed of grass.

"Oh, you can't be serious."

Winslet groaned as she heard the voice, knowing exactly who this was. It was also when she knew that her kidnapping was not to lure Arya to Roderick and Evelyn. This was the work of the most annoying, attention seeking, pathetic bitch the gods could've made immortal.

"You brought me the wrong Selkie!" Estelle shrieked.

The humans shrugged. "A Selkie is a Selkie. Who cares which one was grabbed?"

"I do! This one is not *my* Selkie."

Winslet rolled onto her back, adjusting her eyes to the sky. White puffy clouds floated through the blue, the moon faded, but visible. Almost a full moon. That was good, especially if Arya includes Mies on the rescue.

"Take her back, I don't want anything to do with this—*thing*."

Ouch.

"You will want to keep me, Estelle. As much as it kills both of us to be in each other's company," Winslet said.

Estelle snorted. "Why would I do that?"

"Because Arya will come looking for me, meaning she'll be coming to you too." Winslet watched the wheels in Estelle's thick skull begin spinning as she put together the plan that Winslet was leading her to. At least it was Estelle and not one of the others like Rook. They were harder to manipulate.

"Where's her skin?" Estelle asked, clearly accepting Winslet's capture. Good. That will make things much easier for her.

The humans threw Winslet's coat at Estelle who held it out like it was filthy. Winslet clenched her jaw, but refused to say anything to ruin her chances of escape. At least *she* knew her coat was clean and perfect just as it was. Estelle was just a bitch.

Once the humans left, Winslet and Estelle waited in silence. It was more than awkward, the air was thick enough to cut with a knife.

"Do you want to cut these restraints off?" Winslet asked, hoping the girl wasn't completely insane since their last meeting.

Estelle sighed. "Just don't run, the humans here are particularly horrendous."

"Wasn't planning on it, I can't sense any water nearby," Winslet said. She waited as Estelle slid a cool metal by her skin, Winslet prepared for the woman to "mistakenly" cut her. To her surprise, it didn't happen and the rope released from her wrists. Winslet rubbed the raw skin, muscles aching with the new ability to move the way they were supposed to again. "Why'd you want to kidnap Arya?" She knew the answer already, but she needed Estelle to say it herself. It was part of her new plan.

"I-I wanted her to see me," Estelle whispered.

Winslet sighed, pressing her fingers to the lids of her closed eyes. *Every* lifetime she'd experienced Estelle, she has this idea Arya will want her. The gods won't let that happen. Estelle was not in the cards for Arya and she refused to believe it. But who was Winslet to say any of that? Especially when Estelle had the upper hand in her kidnapping. Winslet didn't know where the fuck she was, and Estelle was powerful, even with her idiotic ideas of the world she'd lived too long in.

This is good, Lir whispered in her head. *Arya is coming for you.*

Not good, Winslet reminded him. *Arya is in danger here.*

Lir only chuckled, the sound fading like it was vanishing into a tunnel. While Lir wasn't the worst of the gods, Leif having it much worse than herself, there was one thing each of the gods had in common. They sucked when it came to helping them.

"So what now?" Winslet asked, falling back to support herself on her hands.

Estelle sighed deeply, clearly her thoughts interrupted by Winslet's question. "Come on, I have a place not too far from here."

"Emeric doesn't know about this place right?"

Estelle shook her head. "It's all mine. He would never approve of my relationship with Arya."

"Maybe cause it's incest," Winslet whispered under her breath.

"What?" Estelle asked.

Winslet shrugged. "I didn't say anything."

The idiot nodded, walking without looking to see if Winslet followed her. Unfortunately, it was the only option she had until she figured out where she was and where Arya was headed to intercept them. Arya wasn't ready to face Evelyn yet. She needed to be bonded to all of them first. That was the only way she'd reach her full potential. The only way they'd all be able to live their lives as they wished.

Winslet snorted at the thought. As if the gods would ever allow that.

36

Mies had stopped the carriage inside of the frontlines camp that she had found her brother in again. It was nightfall, and given the quick timing, she assumed there was some sort of Dullahan magic at play. Something she could get used to.

Idoh and Leif helped her out of the carriage just in time for Mies to collapse on the ground beside them. Arya rushed to him as he groaned on his arms and knees, head resting on his locked hands. He was cool to the touch, skin clammy.

"You've overdone yourself," Arya huffed in defeat. So much for her quick expedition to find Winslet.

"I'm okay, just need a rest," Mies protested, attempting to rise. He got onto one foot, attempting to push himself up. Standing lasted for less than a second before he stumbled again, Leif and Idoh coming to support him.

"Easy there big guy," Leif cooed, "don't wanna make our girl worry now."

"I'm fine," Mies mumbled.

"And I can control water," Idoh snorted.

Arya followed behind the three men, worry peppered into each thought that ran through her mind until it began to get dark. Death and loss of magic returned to her time and time again, Leif looking back regularly at her with each passing scenario.

"A little help here!" Idoh shouted, a group of soldiers rushing to help carry Mies into an infirmary tent. Selkies wouldn't be able to help him though. Their healing only worked on physical ailments, magical was out of their range.

"Arya!" Kai yelled as the group made it into the center of camp. Idoh stepped in front of her at Kai's approach, Leif snickering at the movement, clearly aware of who Kai was to her. How Idoh didn't remember, she wasn't sure. Obviously, family affiliations were not his strong suit. No wonder he never got very far with courting.

"Step aside," Kai ordered Idoh.

He shook his head, causing Arya to sigh deeply. Her foot swung back, landing between his legs in the most sensitive spot of a male. A wheezing cough escaped Idoh as he fell to his knees, hands cupping the area.

"You're adorable, Idoh, but never get between me and my brother." Arya threatened sweetly into his ear. Arya then ran the rest of the way to her brother, embracing him tightly.

337

"Why are you back?" He asked.

Emotion built up in Arya's throat, tears welling as she finally had to admit the taunting thoughts that threatened her sanity. "They follow me no matter where I go. I'll never be rid of them unless they're dead or I am."

"No, no, don't think like that," Kai soothed, brushing down Arya's hair. She allowed herself to cry into his chest, finally feeling like the little kid she had been the last time she had seen Kai. It wasn't fair that she had been ripped from her older brother, but all her life hadn't been fair. To know it was all planned that way by the gods as well made it all the worse.

"I don't want anyone else to die because I'm around them," Arya gasped, her shoulder shaking with the intensity of the emotion that ravaged her. "I don't want anyone else to die because the humans want me. Why do they want me so badly?"

It wasn't fair. Why was she special? What made everyone hate her so much they'd kill just to prove a point? Arya's fists clenched Kai's shirt, forcing him close to her and refusing to let him leave. He wasn't going to, his arms tightening around her like he was attempting to protect her from everything she'd faced. Protecting her like he wanted to all those years she had been away.

Breathing became harder for Arya. Her sobs took most of the air that her lungs managed to gather, mucus limiting access to it.

"I can't breathe," she said frantically. "I can't breathe—I can't breathe—I can't breathe."

Arya fell to her knees. Images of those murdered in the previous invasion clouded her mind. The wounds Leif sustained. The possible traumas Winslet was being subjected to at that very moment—and all of it was her fault. It was because of her that everything was happening and if she was dead it would be better. Everything would be better. No one would die. No one would suffer. They'd live happier and without worry. Why did she have to be born? Why was she born?

"Just let me die!" She cried. She could feel the tugging of people around her. The muffled voices of worry, but it was so distant compared to the roar of the voices of woe that sang in her head. "I don't deserve to live. They died and it's all my fault!"

Fire.

Arya could feel it around her. It kissed her skin, dancing upon her like fairies from the mythologies that Kai had read to her when she was really little. While the voices were there, they were simple hums from afar. Tears evaporated from her cheeks, feeding the ball of orange, red, and yellow that encompassed her from the others. Kept everyone else out. It was warm, like hot tea and a blanket in front of the hearth on a winter night. Something familiar but so distant.

Through the flames, a man stepped through. His skin was made of scales and metal. His shirt was missing, exposing his rippling muscles that were coated with variations of maroon scales. A hand reached out to Arya, golden claws tipping each finger like jewels the nobles in human court wore.

"Idoh—," Arya whimpered, her lip quivering.

"I know, Little Flame," he whispered.

Arya rose, rushing into his arms, refusing to allow him to let her go. He smelled of ash and molten metal, but it was so familiar to her. A smell that reminded her of home, yet it was somewhere she'd never been before. A hint of a past she'd had with Idoh that was slow to be recalled into the forefront of her memories.

"Don't leave me," Arya pleaded, feeling Idoh moving away from the boundary of fire. The air was cool on her skin, water clinging to her as if looking for wounds to heal, but the injury was not something that could be healed with magic of a Selkie. It was one of the mind, and that was harder to heal no matter what magic a person possessed.

"I'll never leave you," he promised. "I will always be here until my last breath."

"Promise?" Arya asked.

Idoh nuzzled against the side of her face, scales smoother than she had expected them to be. "Everything I say to you is a promise."

Idoh had been offered a tent to put Arya in, the soldiers recognizing the weakened woman as the one who had helped one of their own. Respect was rewarded in the camp, and Idoh was impressed with the amount that was shown for Arya. People came with offerings of blankets, food, and their own personal stashes of homely supplies to make her feel comfortable.

Arya was aware of everything, but was unable to respond. The emotion that escaped her was too much, her body void to the world as it happened around her. That was part of the reason that Arya wanted to hide with Idoh. He did not pressure her into speaking, nor did he ask her if she needed anything. It was simply an exchange and order of what she was required to do.

The sun had slowly darkened outside the tent, but Arya hadn't feared what lay beyond. She could feel Leif's heartbeat on her skin like he was laying beside her, and when Idoh left for brief moments, the dancing flame within her chest continued to bounce happily.

She knew it was not something everyone got, but Arya was happy to have them. Like a reassurance she was still worth something. Deserving of more than the claws of death.

Idoh walked into the tent after a while, Arya watching him sit upon a rug beside the cot. Leif followed in soon after, looking at Arya beneath the mound of blankets and asked, "is she awake?"

Unsure of why she did it, Arya closed her eyes, pretending sleep had taken her a while ago.

"No, asleep." Idoh responded.

Leif nodded, sitting across from Idoh. Her eyes peeked open, seeing two of the most important people in her life tired and troubled. She hated seeing them like that, wishing she could see Idoh teasing her with talk of indecency and Leif pronouncing his knowledge of her secrets to the entire group like it was a game. The dream was so much easier for their little group, Arya wishing they could've lived through that, minus Winslet's death.

"We can't let her continue," Leif announced. Arya stilled.

Idoh snorted, shaking his head. "You're underestimating her."

Thank you, Arya thought wishing she could slap Leif on the back of his luscious locks.

"I'm not," Leif protested. "Winslet being gone and Mies not bonded to her yet puts us all at risk." He sighed deeply. "She hasn't even had *those* memories comes back yet and she's emotionally unprepared."

Idoh focused on his fingers, finding something under his nails important. "If you leave without her, she will never forgive you."

"Winslet is my best friend. We've been friends in every lifetime and will continue to be in this one. Arya needs to bond with her otherwise we'll never get what's promised."

"And what about Zephyr? She had never bonded with him, does he no longer count?" Idoh hissed.

Leif snorted as if the question was stupid. "Zephyr ruins his chances with Arya in *every* lifetime. Do you not remember when he tried to steal her away from you?"

Idoh nodded his head to the side, the corners of his mouth twitched up. "That was idiotic to do. Arya is loyal to her men."

"And women," Leif corrected.

Women? Arya had not thought of females in that way before. It was always ingrained in her since she was little that women were meant for men. It was how children were made. How the succession was passed through the generations. Then again, when she had been with Ila, Mies's sister, Arya had thought about what'd it be like to kiss her. Then the dream did have very sensual moments between her and Winslet. However, Arya never thought of her as more than a really good friend.

"It doesn't mean that she needs you to possibly go into human territory alone to rescue Winslet. Especially if Roderick has her." Idoh countered.

Leif was quiet as Arya angrily thought of how rude it was for Leif to talk all this bullshit about her being unfit to rescue their friend. The thing was, Leif and Idoh wouldn't get far at all without her help anyway. They didn't know the humans like she did. Didn't know their towns or the layout of the kingdom. If Roderick did have Winslet, they sure as hell didn't know the layout of the castle like she did. Those fucking rocks were her prison for over ten years.

Arya's brows were furrowed, partially looking at the fabrics laid over her as she thought of those markers. When flicking them back to where she could watch Idoh, she noticed his golden eyes staring back at her. He had known she was awake. Wanted her to know what an idiot Leif was being so she could be prepared.

"*Sneaky, sneaky, Salamander, oh what do you see, is it fire, is it ice, is it an enemy to defeat—?*" Meriah's voice hummed through a memory Arya swore she had forgotten.

Perhaps there was some realism to each rhyme about the fae she had yet to experience.

"Stay put and let Arya figure out her own path, Leif. She just bonded to us, she'll need our strength in the coming days or all will be for not." Idoh said. Leif didn't respond, Arya hearing him move from the tent moments later. "He's gone."

Arya sat up, crossing her arms over her chest like an offended child. "What the fuck?" Idoh smirked, crawling on his hands and knees to get closer to her. "I am perfectly fine saving Winslet!"

"Little Flame, you almost drowned the camp," Idoh said softly, tucking a piece of Arya's hair behind her ear.

She jerked her head back. "What?"

"Emotion drives a Selkie's power, remember? Your emotions were strong and told your magic you were under attack. Thus, you created a giant serpent to fight those demons within your mind."

Arya opened and closed her mouth, lowering her arms to pick at the skin around her nails. "Was anyone hurt?"

"No, you didn't hurt anyone but me."

"You?" Arya asked with wide eyes.

Idoh smirked. "There was a reason I had to go into my fae form to retrieve you, my love. Such steam we create."

Arya looked down, worried he would think of her differently due to harming him over and over again. This was not sparing, this was real life and each day she felt as though she was betraying Idoh with her impulsive aggression.

344

Idoh put his knuckles beneath her chin, lifting until her eyes met his. "I adore the spark of fight I see in you, Arya. Even if those moments are aimed at me."

"Are you sure?"

He laughed, the first time she'd seen him throw his head back with the howl. "Of course, it shows me you still want to live. That you trust me to take those blows because I am getting in your way. I want you more and more every day, especially on the days you best me in unexpected ways."

Arya cupped his hand, moving it so it rested on her cheek. The flame danced within her chest, growing larger with each second their bodies touched, even as simple as his palm holding her. Leaning into it, Arya relaxed her shoulders, flashes of another time coming to her mind. Of Arya straddling Idoh, her ear to his chest and weapons circling them like a nest of war. She could still hear the thrumming of his heart from that time, however. A soothing thum-thump that she couldn't tell if it was happening in that moment or the past.

"Can I try something?" Arya asked. Idoh stared at her, hunger clear in his eyes, but restraint displayed in the tension of his limbs. He nodded once, Arya moving from the cot and blankets. "Lay down."

37

Darkness had fallen on the tent, a lantern the only display of light to illuminate the room that Arya shared with Idoh. Everything outside was nonexistent when it came to worries, all that she wanted was to test where she was. How far she could comfortably go without stopping. Of everyone, she knew that Idoh would allow her to stop when she needed to. *If* she needed to. Arya had ordered Idoh to lay on the cot, throwing the blankets to the floor beside them. The heat that came off him was thrilling, a sizzling sound coming from each touch she teased.

Arya watched Idoh as she removed her pants, eyes never leaving his to evaluate what he was seeing. To her surprise, he watched her. Measuring each movement to be sure she wasn't pushing herself. To see if there was any doubt associated with her decision.

There was not.

Arya had waited years to meet Idoh again. To feel him against her skin. To embrace his power that was teased within a vision from the gods. Arya took her time, removing the leather that protected her chest, letting it drop to her feet without much care. Idoh swallowed as Arya was left in a long undershirt, edges burnt from the dome of fire from earlier, yet wet with the collected water her body refused to leave her without.

Her arms raised, showing more of her thighs to Idoh than she had previously, shuffling her fingers through her hair. The locks fell around her shoulders and framed her face like the relaxed waves of the ocean.

Arya had one goal, embracing the woman she was from her and Idoh's past that she wanted so badly to know better. A warrior filled with righteous anger and fire. Only Arya was made of water, and Idoh should know just how powerful she was with her current element.

Standing beside the cot, Arya lifted her hand, each finger manipulating the moist collection from her shirt, summoning it to do her bidding. Idoh tensed as the water circled his throat, steam hissing as it hardened into jagged pieces of ice. Arya stepped over his waist as her water snapped each ribbon of his shirt, removing the fabric from his chest for her. As she sat on him, her hands pushed away the loose fabric, heat giving her a slight burn at each movement, like she was surrounded by hot water.

Leaning forward, Arya could feel Idoh hardening beneath her, thrilling her. It surprised her, the emotion never accompanying sensual experiences before.

Her hand wrapped around his throat, Idoh placing his on her thighs, his eyes focused and analytical.

"You're mine to control, understand?" She ordered. Idoh nodded, his mouth opening, but unable to produce anything to say.

Arya leaned down, licking Idoh's jaw until she got to his ear. Her lips circled the bottom of the lobe, tongue playing with it as her breath released. Idoh tensed beneath her. His grip on her thighs increasing as he attempted to restrain himself. She liked it. Loved knowing that he was struggling to contain himself, but still was because she told him to. Following orders like a true soldier to the crown, and she was his queen.

Her hips moved as if having done this before, grinding over Idoh's erection with each breath intensifying the feeling of domination. She moved her lips from his ear, tracing breathy kisses down his neck and across his throat. Idoh puffed out a weak moan, his hand loosening on her thigh. Arya took the opportunity to grab it, placing it beneath her shirt and forcing him to massage her breast and hardened nipple. Her other hand pressed against his chest, being used as leverage as she slid her hips over his covered cock.

"Do you want me?" Arya asked, enjoying each movement she made on Idoh. Knowing this terrifying individual was nothing when it came to her power over him. He was hers to torture and control and was happy to be.

"Yes," he growled, his dick jumping beneath her as if attempting to convince her.

Arya sat back, using both hands to remove her shirt, exposing everything to Idoh. He took a moment, looking over the body she offered him like it was the promised paradise after death. Idoh continued to massage her breast, sliding her nipple between his fingers and pinching slightly. Arya moaned, her head arching back as she smiled. There had been moments where she'd imagined this moment in the dungeons of Kulessa, but no moment of fantastical thought could've prepared her for the real thing.

"Do you want to please me?" Arya asked.

"Yes, Little Flame, I do."

Arya smiled, the confidence within her building. She lifted from his waist, walking on her knees forward until she exposed herself to his lips. Idoh did not complain, his hands gripping her ass as he dove into the offered nectar like it was a feast and he was a starving peasant.

Arya couldn't help but let out a breathy laugh as his tongue slid over her again and again. Grinding her hips into his mouth, allowing him to suck and lick every inch of her. Her hands threaded through his hair, pulling him into her as he continued to please her in a way no one ever had before.

Their bond danced in glee with their connection. Each moment being known yet a surprise. Idoh kept displaying his desire for her. Pleasing Arya with every flick, grip, and suck. It was hard not to feel such an intense desire for him. To be closer than physically allowed. She *needed* him. *Deserved* him.

Everything was beautiful and at her own pace. Slow. Erotic. Hungry. Idoh did not restrain, but did not push. He wanted her, and only her. Their flame expanding throughout their entire body—until she felt it.

Emotions came to Arya unexpectedly. She choked as she breathed in, Idoh stopped, pushing her back. Tears came down her cheeks, Arya hating herself for being so emotional during something so good. Ruining the moment for both of them. Why couldn't she have held it in for a few more hours?

"What's wrong?" Idoh asked, lifting up and forcing her to sit in his lap. "Do you need to stop?"

She shook her head, yet the tears wouldn't stop. "I want more. I want all of you and to never leave you again. I need you. I *need you.*"

He smiled softly, kissing each tear that escaped her eyes. "Let me take control?" His arms circled her waist, pressing her close to him. She nuzzled into his neck, inhaling the smell of ash and steam. Arya nodded, letting Idoh take over.

Heat came from beneath them, Arya realizing he burnt off his pants, their skin touching without any barriers. "Remember, you tell me no if it's too much and I'll stop."

Arya nodded.

She watched as his body heated, skin molting from its lively golden into the metallic maroon that his scales were made of. Arya touched his face, embracing the hard silkiness of his new features and the angular construction of his brow and jaw. The eyes, however, were Idoh. *Her* Idoh. Her legs

350

wrapped around his waist, Idoh held onto her back, smoke rising at each point where Arya touched. No—not smoke—steam.

All Arya wanted was him to give her everything. She wanted all of him.

"Are you ready?" He asked, his voice a little less than a crackling growl.

Arya nodded. "I want all of you."

Idoh growled, showing his canines and incisors that had sharpened in his transformation. His head reached down, biting Arya's shoulder, pain and pleasure spreading over her like nothing she'd ever expected before. Her back arched, Idoh holding her ass up, Arya unable to help but drip her arousal onto him.

Arya felt his cock position below her, but it was not like the others she'd experienced. It too was scaled, the tip pointed like the tail of a dragon she'd seen in mythologies. Instead of being afraid, Arya was thrilled.

Idoh placed her down onto him slowly, his girth more than Arya had ever taken before. It curved, each scale rubbing inside her perfectly. She gasped, shuttering as he continued deeper into her, his tongue licking at the blood that escaped from the wound he inflicted upon her.

"Oh gods, oh gods," Arya squeaked.

"Don't fucking bring them into this," Idoh growled, lifting Arya again and setting her back down. He maneuvered her body like she weighed nothing, covering her mouth with his when she began to get too loud. Arya couldn't help but call out her pleasure, muted only by Idoh's mouth, and forked tongue flicking against her own.

"I love how you call for more, Little Flame," Idoh groaned, increasing the speed that he moved Arya's body. Her nails carved hazardous designs into his back, her mouth moving to his shoulder so she could mute herself against those who would hear them outside the tent. "Give me your pleasure."

Arya could feel herself building to climax. Each thrust into her, each flick of the pointed end of his cock, brought her closer.

"I-Idoh," Arya pleaded.

"Mmm," he growled happily. "Say it again. Call my name when you come for me, Little Flame."

Idoh flipped Arya, gripping her waist as she was tossed to her back. He thrust his hips faster into her, eyes wild with desire and hunger that seemed insatiable. This wasn't like those humans of the past. This was Idoh. *Her Idoh.* Something inside her snapped in that moment.

It was like a shield had broken from her, allowing emotion and anger to run freely into her body. Flame and fire burned everywhere as Arya allowed Idoh to have her. He covered her mouth as she expelled, her back arching and Idoh laughing in his triumph. She wasn't done, though. No—Arya needed Idoh. He needed to be part of her. Fully.

"More," she ordered in a cracking voice.

"More?" Idoh asked with glee in his eyes, as if he hadn't expected her to say such a thing.

Arya lifted her head, meeting his eyes and wrapping her hand around his neck. "More."

A crazed smile appeared as Idoh continued to thrust, his body moving like it was designed to gift her a show in masculinity. Every thrust pushed her closer to another climax, but she could see him getting closer as well. Arya clawed at his back, forcing him down to her, licking the sweat from his neck. Idoh groaned, quickening his movements.

"Give yourself to me, my flame," Arya whispered into his ear, her nails scratching up to his neck. Idoh arched his back, roaring out as flames encompassed his body. It was a quick burst and heat shooting inside of Arya. She smiled, finding something else she conquered when it came to Idoh. After the flames retreated and all that was left was a mixture of smoke and steam within the tent, he gripped her jaw, forcing their faces close together.

"Fuck you."

Arya snorted, raising a brow. "Round two already?"

"You vixen," he laughed, flopping beside her, his scales disappearing back into his skin.

Feeling an overwhelming sense of pride and humor, she gazed at Idoh, his full—naked—form exposed just for her viewing. Nothing compared to the sex he gave her, but then again, she hadn't had much pleasurable experiences to compare it to.

"Was it good for you?" Arya asked, immediately regretting the question when it escaped her mouth.

Idoh looked at her, a frozen, open mouthed smile telling her all she needed to know. "Was it good for me?

353

That's your question after our first time bonded in this lifetime?" He rolled from his spot, grabbing Arya and pulling her into his lap. "Gods you're the most innocent gift to fae-kind!"

"Let me go!" Arya shrieked as she laughed.

"Make me!" Idoh snickered, littering Arya's head with small pecks of affection.

The flap to the tent abruptly opened, Leif sticking his head in, nose scrunching. "Why does it smell like–." He paused, seeing Idoh and Arya frozen, their clothes missing. "Oh—well then. I'll leave you two to it." Leif winked, gazing quickly at what he could see of Arya's body, biting his bottom lip.

"Go!" Idoh demanded.

Leif kissed the air, removing himself from the tent.

Arya's mouth dropped open, face burning with embarrassment. Leif was bonded to her as well, would his feelings be hurt?

"Don't worry about him," Idoh said as if hearing her thoughts. "He's just happy you opened up to the possibility."

"How do you know?" Arya asked.

Idoh smiled softly, kissing her temple one last time. "You'll see in time."

That's not ominous or anything, Arya thought.

Beside everything else, Arya was proud of herself. She was able to enjoy pleasure from someone she trusted and knew would never betray her. She watched Idoh contemplate how he was going to get a new pair of pants, Arya already having dressed herself.

"Good luck," she called to him as she exited the tent.

"Hey! No!" But it was too late, Arya jogged away from the tent, smiling at her mischievous prank she pulled on Idoh. Perhaps she had a lot more in common with Leif than she cared to admit. However, there was something Arya wanted to do and she needed to do it without distraction.

38

Water was what Arya needed after experiencing her time with Idoh. While his flames of desire were thrilling, Arya was still a water creature and needed some comfort of her element. The moon was just bright enough to light the night sky, white rays of light glistening over the surface of the liquid.

Like she was a child again, Arya closed her eyes, calling upon her element. An old friend who had never truly left her, just was not as present in the past few years. Arya fell back into a routine that Meriah and Arya was taught by their mother. She started with her hands low, water collecting around her outstretched hands, moving as Arya did.

Each movement. Each step and glide of her body was followed by the silky trail that obeyed each command. Arya felt each creature and grain of earth affected by water, continuing to sense it in the distant clouds above her, preparing to deliver rain to a nearby area. Everything was peaceful when Arya focused her power around the peace given by water, yet knew how destructive it could be.

"That's beautiful," Leif said, breaking Arya's concentration. The water dropped around her, slinking back into the earth and river where it originated. "Oh—sorry."

Arya giggled, giving Leif a small smile. "It's okay, just something I used to do with Meriah and my mother when I was little."

Leif smiled back, taking the few steps to join her. Arya and Leif continued to follow the path of the river, Arya playing with a small bit of water that snaked between her fingers. It was a comfortable silence, laced with calm happiness that she had always appreciated while in company of Leif.

"Can I ask you something, and feel free to decline to answer, but I need to get it out of my head," Leif said.

Arya furrowed her brows. "Of course, I'll answer anything I know the answer to, which is not much." She giggled.

Leif gave her a soft smile, tracing his fingers down her palm until they laced together. It was such a sweet and unexpected gesture that Arya couldn't help but get giddy over. While Idoh was intense and filled with the fires of desire, Leif was like experiencing the beginnings of affection for the first time. Hand holding, kisses, those lovely little butterflies that swirled inside her chest and stomach whenever he did something while thinking of her. If given the option of feelings, Arya preferred the simply elegance of Leif's courting.

"Did you—were you—ugh I don't know how to say it, and that is *not* like me," he stammered, clearly flustered. Arya chuckled, finding it sweet that he was so nervous around her. This was nothing like the smooth talker she'd come to know in her dreams. This version of Leif was better. Real.

"Out with it," she teased.

He shook his head with a smile, giving her a sideways glance. His emerald eyes locked to hers and everything horrible they faced no longer felt so terrifying.

He let out a long breath. "Okay, here it goes." He paused. "Did you choose Idoh as your first because he has more of a protecting presence?"

Now that was not the question Arya had suspected. Leif refused to look at her once seeing the shock that crossed her face, clearly regretting his decision to ask. However, Arya liked the boldness he displayed for it.

She stopped their stroll, leading Leif to the edge of the water. She slipped out of her shoes, motioning for him to do the same. Leif obeyed, confused at what Arya was going to do.

"When I was in Kulessa, I hated being a Selkie," Arya admitted, closing her eyes as she focused on the water around her toes, moving the riverbed around her. She could feel Leif watching her, and she liked it.

"Why?"

"I thought all Selkies were weak. That we were pretty little creatures that were worthless unless we had water and our skin." Arya opened her eyes, lifting Leif's hand out. She willed the water to circle his arm, cooling the limb, but not wetting it. "Humans poisoned my mind for a long time, Leif. I couldn't fight back, couldn't do anything without being overpowered and used. So, I hated who I was born to be."

He furrowed his brows and Arya smiled.

The water wrapped tight around his arm, Leif jumping back and attempting to rub the liquid rope off him. He was unsuccessful, eyes widening as Arya took a few casual steps forward then let him free.

"Selkies are not weak or needing of any more protection than a Salamander or Dullahan. Same with Gean-Cánach." Leif opened and closed his mouth. Arya wrapped her arms around his neck, reaching on her toes to be able to lock her hands together. "Could a Salamander or Dullahan or Sylph manipulate someone the way you could?" Leif shook his head. "Could they influence the mind to think they loved someone they did not?" He didn't say anything, standing there without a hint of emotion.

Arya sighed, realizing things would be harder to explain than she realized. She let go of his neck, kicking the water around her feet. "Would you say the person in the dream was partly who you are in the real world?"

"More or less," he admitted cautiously.

Arya smiled. "That man in the dream was my savior before the others knew. Well, besides Winslet of course."

Leif furrowed his brows. "What do you mean?"

Arya laughed. "Ignoring the part where you dropped me in the middle of the dance floor, every moment I needed something to feel safe, you provided it to me."

Leif shook his head, looking down. "No, Mies or Idoh or Zephyr—."

"You gave me a place to finally let go of all my built up frustration from my sexual mistreatment. You gifted me Tiras shoes, which was *very* illegal. Shielded me from Phobus by 'making deals' and sorting out my protection assignments." Arya placed her hands on her hips, smiling down at the blackened water. "Leif, you refused a marriage you knew you wanted because *I* wasn't ready."

Leif opened and closed his mouth, finally letting out a deep sigh. "But it wasn't anything powerful."

"To me it was," Arya insisted. "You made me laugh, overthink what your relationship with Winslet was and caused me so much jealousy." Arya laughed, covering her mouth. "From the very first moment we met, you knew I needed saving and you hid me away in the library, teasing the others of my poorly kept secrets!"

That cracked Leif's hard exterior, the memory coming back to him. "Our mysterious human ambassador."

Arya laughed. "And you are more than just a pretty face, Ambassador Leif."

He stepped closer, the warmth of his body pushing away the chill that came from the water. "Do you promise to keep a secret of mine, Arya dear?" Arya furrowed her brows, but nodded. That's when Leif wrapped his arms around her.

His head cradled into her shoulder and his back began to shake.

Arya could sense his tears falling as he cried into her, her own sorrow building with his. She didn't need to ask why or what caused the emotion, just letting Leif cry. Her arms wrapped around him, pulling him as close to her as she could.

"I thought I lost you when you didn't step off that carriage," he admitted through his tears. "I thought you wouldn't ever be coming back."

"No, no, my darling Leif, I would've found my way back no matter what."

His fists balled into her shirt, keeping her close. "I'm terrified, Arya. I can't lose you."

"You won't." Arya knew it was an empty promise. Behind those words were the unknown events of the future and Leif's fate along with her own had been riddled with death and loss in the past. She didn't know if Leif was hers, and Arya couldn't promise her death would be avoidable. What she did know is she'd try everything in her power to get back to him and the others. Gods or not, Arya was bound them and she needed them more than they realized.

"Can I show you something?" Leif asked, lifting his head just enough for Arya to see his tear ringed eyes. She nodded. "It's not pleasant, Arya, it's dark, evil even, but no one knows I can do this."

Arya nodded hesitantly, unsure of what could be so dangerous for Leif to be able to control. "Whatever it is, it's you, I'm sure we will be able to move past it. Maybe even use it!" Arya gleamed, attempting to be optimistic.

Leif sighed, closing his eyes, smiling weakly at her. Warning bells went off in her head. Something wasn't right. Leif was tense. His body pulled away from her, like he was attempting to escape.

"I love you—."

Blood sprayed over Arya. She stilled, her eyes widened, unable to believe what she was seeing. Leif looked down at her, blood dribbling from his mouth as a dark shadow pierced through his chest. The scream Arya wished would come stayed stuck in her throat, tears escaping without the help of her blinking.

Shadowy arms lifted Leif's limp ones, pulling at them until they popped and ripped. The stringy bits of flesh fell into the river, finally allowing Arya to scream.

"Leif!"

Everything inside her pushed away her fear, charging through the water as fast as she could to try to get to the creature. The dark water washed away the remnants of his blood, Leif's head finally falling to the side, eyes rolling back.

"No! Leif! Leif!" Arya screamed. The creature dropped him into the water, body sinking into the murky blackness of the river.

Arya used everything inside her to force the water to deliver his body to her, but she couldn't sense it. The water delivered waves upon waves of unsettled riverbed and floating logs, but Leif's body was gone. Vanishing without trace.

"Arya!" Mies shouted.

"Where is he?" Arya screamed. "Give him back! Give him to me!"

This couldn't be happening. He was supposed to stay with her until the end. He was hers! Hers!

A wave appeared in front of Arya, tossing her beneath the water, thrusting her to shore. She tumbled on the mud, gaining her bearings before attempting to crawl back into the river.

"Arya, stop!" Kai demanded.

"No! I need him back! He can't be gone!" Arya screamed.

Mies wrapped his arms around her, Arya thrusting a whip of water back toward him. He cursed as it hit him, but continued to hold onto her. He leaned back, wrapping his legs around Arya's waist, crossing her arms over her chest so she couldn't use the full force of her magic on him.

"You need to save him!" Arya pleaded in a scream. "Save Leif!"

Kai shook his head. "Arya, the only one in the water is you."

"No," she cried, relaxing into Mies. Defeat. That's what it was. "He was killed. His body—I'm covered in blood—shadow monster—."

Kai knelt before her, worry undeniable in his ocean eyes. "Arya, you're not covered in blood."

What is wrong with them? Where is Leif if he isn't dead? She saw the monster—saw it kill him. Oh gods... Leif was dead. He was dead.

"What the fuck is going on?" Idoh shouted, looking over Arya's slumped crying body.

Mies glanced to him, expression grim and without emotion. "Leif was killed by a shadow monster."

Idoh's jaw clenched. "You didn't sense a body in the water?" He asked Kai. Kai shook his head, still focused on Arya.

Leif was gone. Gone. Dead. No, this couldn't be right. She still felt his heart in her chest. His magic in her blood. He couldn't be gone.

Arya ripped from Mies, getting a few steps more before she was once again restrained. Arya screamed, Leif's bond getting more distant.

"I need him!" She screamed. "Let me go! I need him!"

"Let's get her warm. We will travel into human territory tomorrow." Kai dismissed.

Idoh and Mies pulled Arya along, her head craning back to try and spot Leif's body one last time.

39

The blanket that wrapped around Arya was damp and smelled of horses. A fire played with the air in front of her, Arya's eyes pinned to the light with a desperation she was unaware any person was able to feel. There was low hums of conversation around her, but Arya didn't pay attention to it. She needed to focus on the light. In the light, that shadows couldn't get anyone else.

Leif had died in front of her.

His body floating somewhere in those dark waters and that creature still among them. It was dark by the water. Only moonlight signaling their path forward when they talked. When Leif was confessing his vulnerabilities to her. She'd loved their conversation. Was calm and happy and she was so pleased to be talking alone with him. Leif knew how horrible life was to her, and felt the same way about Winslet as she did.

Arya pulled her knees close to her, hiding half her face behind them. The creature was more than a monster. It was something different. The gods felt more real than it did, yet it tore Leif apart like it was a physical entity. Her body shivered in result of the horror that repeated in her mind. The event getting worse as her mind added things that never happened. Fact and fiction was mixing and Arya didn't know which was which.

Then there was mist around her. Floating swirling tendrils of fog that had circled the fire, brightening the flames so they danced over the grey. Arya took the time to look around since she was sat in that spot, immediately finding she was outside Kai's tent. Idoh and Kai could be seen through the small slit talking animatedly and pounding their fists on the table. Pieces of war markers fell as they did, ink already tipped and slowly dripping into a wet collection upon the dirt, staining it black.

Two men stood outside the tent, strong and at attention, but it was clear they were listening to the argument. One rolled his eyes, but didn't say anything, clearly annoyed with whatever was being discussed.

Two other tents surrounded Arya, one behind her and one in front. They were dark inside, clearly unoccupied. Their entrances faced toward the rest of the camp, dots of fires and shadows of people hovering around them, picturesque in the worst sort of way. It was almost like the paintings she'd seen in Tiras when visiting their gallery. There was an entire section dedicated to war and battle, her father and Leif's speaking enthusiastically about the past conquests, but all Arya felt was sad. War wasn't thrilling. It was death and anguish and tragedy that was illuminated as glory by men who didn't fight.

Arya shook her head, attempting to clear the thought, finally seeing the only other person that stayed around her. The owner of the mist.

"I know in the dream you'd asked me never to use it on you, but I could see you struggling." Mies didn't look at her as he said it. He was dark, face shadowed with the light of the fire and darkness of what they're to face. Humans.

Arya didn't say anything, leaning against his strong arm. He smelled like fresh grass and moist soil by a river in the early morning. She closed her eyes, allowing all other thoughts to vanish and just experienced the location he took her to. Somewhere quiet and secluded. Fields of wheat that danced in the wind like waves of the ocean. A bright blue sky hosting a collection of clouds. Mies different but the same, working with a scythe, his shirt soaked with sweat and hanging on the belt of his pants. Brown skin taking the golden sun with glee.

"What are you seeing?" Mies whispered as if it was a secret between them.

Arya gave a weak smile, refusing to open her eyes. "You are working a field. There's a small house with a straw roof and no door. There's a pond nearby, but I don't see it."

Mies hummed. "Look to your hands."

Arya looked down in the vision, finding her hands were occupied. Small fingers curled around her, Arya suddenly aware of a wrap around her chest. "Who are they?"

"Wylda is the oldest. She's the one with curly brown hair and dark eyes. She probably has a collection of dried twisted grass on her wrist." Arya looked at each child, finding the girl on her right having the bracelet of grass as Mies promised. A flash of Wylda as an infant came to Arya, Mies showing her the moon and promising to take her on a ride when she's old enough. "Landon is the one with no pants on." Mies chuckled softly. "If I'm correct, he has a crown of dandelions in his hair." He was right. The boy on her left hosted an intricate crown of dandelions and wildflowers upon his light brown hair. Hazel eyes looked up to Arya as he spoke something inaudible before both Landon and Wylda ran in front of her, holding hands. They approached Mies, who smiled, crouching down to give them a giant bear hug.

"The baby was Estelle." Arya furrowed her brows, watching as she unwrapped the infant from the cloth around her chest. Undoubtedly, the white halo of curls and sparkle of freckles over her dark skin proved to be no other. She was innocent here. Sleeping with her fingers flexing as she was moved. Estelle did not look like the other children, and as if reading her mind, Mies said, "she's not mine. Our friends from the next farm over had her, but died after a wolf attack. Estelle survived and you adopted her."

"Adopted? Wylda and Landon are my children?" Arya asked.

Mies hummed. "From a long-long time ago. I believe your first or second reincarnation."

Opening her eyes, Arya looked desperately to Mies. "Please, you have to tell me what happened to them."

He picked up a strand of her hair, tucking it behind her ear. "Wylda ended up marrying a lovely man in the village and having several children. She lived until old age and died peacefully in her sleep." Mies looked down, slowly picking up Arya's hand and placing it to his lips. "Landon became the owner of the farm, found himself a wife and had a few children. He died in the bed he was born in."

Arya clenched her jaw, removing her hand from Mies and placing it in her lap. Her hair fell in front of her face as she said, "What really happened?"

Mies sighed deeply, shifting in his seat. "Evelyn found us."

Arya took a deep breath in. "She killed them?"

"No," Mies said, "Emeric did."

Arya whipped her head to Mies, appalled that the man who killed Wylda and Landon kept Estelle like a pet. Mies nodded as if he knew how she would react.

"Why?" She asked.

Mies bit the inside of his lip, giving her a cynical laugh. "She wasn't yours or mine biologically. It's the only thing I could think of."

Arya thought back to the other women that were past incarnations of herself. The woman who looked like she was from Dunia had the rope around her neck. Dread filled Arya as she thought about it. "They killed you too, didn't they?"

Mies didn't respond.

"So, I hung myself."

"It was the only time you took your own life."

The air was heavier than minutes before. The weight of how her life with Mies ended was tragic, but how those children's lives ended was worse somehow. They were innocent in everything except who they were born to.

"How do we know this is the last life?" Arya asked, a question she'd been holding off asking for a while.

Mies snorted, clicking his tongue. "Because we all met each other before we met you."

"Sounds like a stretch," Arya mumbled thinking on how Leif was dead and Winslet possibly being tortured as they spoke.

Mies bumped her shoulder, the attempt playful but without the positive energy behind it. "Wanting to get more time with us, Ambassador Arya?"

Arya turned her head, gazing into the golden discs of Mies's eyes. For a moment, Mies was that same man who had walked her to the dining room her first time in Castle Lofta. The dream version of Mies became horrible, but right now, he was the version she originally wanted to escape with.

Mies looked away first, taking in a deep breath. "I've been wanting to apologize, but I never got the opportunity before."

Arya furrowed her brows. "Apologize? For what?"

"How the vision ended up. Married to me through the mist and upset. I just want you to know that is not me. I will *never* force you into a situation you're uncomfortable with."

Arya had left her mouth open, but the words she was looking for became lost behind her laugh. Mies jerked his head back in shock at her reaction, the cackle growing into a full bought of hysterical laughter.

"Arya?" Mies said nervously.

She patted his arm, wheezing and clutching her stomach. "The gods did you dirty."

Mies allowed a slight smile onto his lips, chuckling with her until they both were howling in laughter. Arya pressed her face into the cloth that covered Mies's arm, and he arched his head back, announcing their humor to the stars.

To anyone who passed, they were seen as having drank too much mead, or perhaps finally broke through the psychological torture of war. However, to anyone who knew the story behind Arya and Mies, they too would probably laugh.

Mies wrapped an arm over Arya's shoulders, gripping her tightly to his side. Arya smiled, wrapping him into a hug. The vision didn't mean shit to her anymore. Life didn't make sense, much less a series of sped up months where she only was able to know what could've happened.

"I've forgiven you a while ago," Arya admitted. "While realistic, it was not real."

Mies nodded, inhaling the top of her head. Arya waved her fingers through the fading mist around them. The feeling was so familiar to her, allowing the memory of killing for the first time to reenter her mind. It was not real, a part of the vision when she rid their group from Phobus for good, using Mies's mist to summon him to her. It was a vital tool.

"Can I ask a favor?" Arya said.

Mies nodded. "Anything."

"I would like to wear your mist again."

Mies paled, Arya looking up at him worried she'd over stepped a boundary. The vision had told her it was overly personal for a Dullahan to share his mist with another person, basically tying them together.

"Are you sure you want to risk that?"

Risk it? He was worried about her. Not societal notions or worries, but how Arya would feel knowing Mies could control her whenever he wanted.

"I want to know that if something happens out there, and we get separated that I can tell you where I am. I want to feel that extra presence of you around my neck to tell me I'm not alone if things go wrong and I end up in isolation again." Arya bit her lips together, looking down at Mies's strong hands lightly holding hers. "I want to know it won't be another ten years of torture and if needed, you can wipe that from my mind."

Her eyes flicked to Mies, his jaw tight and eyes focused on the ground around them. "Okay."

She watched as he moved from her, the earth splitting and bits coming from the cracks. They collected in the air, Mies holding the earth in the fire, Arya amazed as it began to liquify. He molded and formed the metal in the soft wind, cooling it with the air and forcing it to bend and twist where he wanted. A red chain pulsed as it laid on a rock beside them, a collection of sand floating into the flames next. She watched as the sand was heated and compressed, turning to liquid. Something she didn't know could happen with sand. Mies warped and spun the molten glass, creating a circle with his fingers and blowing into it. As if he had done it through the tube, the liquid expanded, filling with an air pocket he created. It spun in the cooling air until finally solidifying to where it looked tacky to the touch. Mies then summoned a collection of the mist around them to enter the newly created container, sealing it shut with a pinch. He summoned the metal to the air, molding them together.

"It's not perfect, but if Idoh sees this, he'll freak out."

Arya shook her head, bending so Mies could melt the jewelry around her neck. "He doesn't need to know."

"Are you sure about all this Arya?" Mies asked lowly. "We could go right now."

Arya sighed, lifting her eyes to his. She smiled weakly, cupping his cheek. "I'm done running."

40

Getting into Kulessa was easier than Arya expected. The
horses they were gifted from Kai were fast, and strangely
undetectable through the human territories. She suspected
the beasts to be Dullahan, but without their riders, the mist
wouldn't accompany them.

Arya kept the hood of her cloak up, shading her face
as they passed the different towns that Kulessa had along the
border. Idoh and Mies did the same, not willing to risk
anyone seeing Idoh's eyes or the haziness that accompanied
Mies on a horse so close to a full moon.

It felt as though they were skipping through portions
of Kulessa, their arrival to the capital happening in the early
evening. Arya, Idoh, and Mies stopped along the edge of the
forest, looking out among the bustling city. Arya had never
seen it from this angle, always among those being forced into

different directions by the king's guard. It was primal. Poorly maintained and the people angry. Nothing like a fae city.

"I say we wait until nightfall," Idoh said.

Arya crouched down, rubbing her hand over her mouth as she thought. "If they have Winslet, they'll be using her already. A Selkie is always put to work as soon as they can. I don't want her to suffer more, or risk us missing her because she's being held in another room."

"If we don't make a plan, we risk our own safety," Mies countered.

"What about *her* safety?" Arya protested.

Idoh growled a sigh, crossing his arms over his chest. It was clear he was uncomfortable where he was, whether that was because of the clear lack of elemental power in Kulessa or just being around so many humans in general, Arya didn't know.

"Look, we have a slim timeframe to get Winslet and get out. Once they know she's gone, they're going to come looking for us," Arya said.

Idoh nodded, squatting next to Arya and began drawing with a stick. They mapped out the castle and city, finding what exits they could use and how to make their way around without alerting the guards.

"Someone will have to stay behind," Idoh said with a grumble. "If we all get captured, what the fuck was the point in all of this?" Arya and Mies made eye contact before looking at Idoh. "Oh, no. It will not be me."

Arya nodded her head to the side. "My flame—."

"Nope, you're not going to *my flame* me."

375

"Arya and I look the most human. Even the blind could tell you were fae. If not for the eyes, it'd be the hair," Mies stated bluntly.

"What's wrong with my hair?" Idoh huffed.

Arya winced. "Humans don't have hair *that* red. It's—unnatural for them."

Idoh shook his head. "I'm not letting you two go in and wait to see if you don't come back. I lost Arya once, I'm not doing it again. Especially now we're fully bonded."

Mies choked, coughing and covering his mouth. "You waisted no time with that, did ya?"

Idoh gave Mies a narrowed glance, Arya rolling her eyes. "Listen, Idoh, you're staying here because you can get more troops together from my brother for rescue if needed. Mies is coming with me because he looks almost identical to the other guards in the castle. He'll pretend to have seized me, bringing me to the dungeons or Roderick, someone. Once they dismiss him, Mies will find Winslet and help her escape."

"What about you?" Mies asked.

"Roddy and I have unfinished business."

Idoh snorted. "Can't that wait until after? What if Evelyn is there?"

"Then I'll kill her too," Arya said. Mies rolled his eyes and Idoh stayed silent. Arya sat back, huffing. "You both don't think I can do it."

"You just don't know exactly who you're dealing with," Mies said.

Idoh shrugged. "Evelyn is a tricky creature."

Arya crossed her arms, hating that both these men who were supposed to be bonded to her felt she was too weak to take on Evelyn. She was just a human, how bad could it really be to kill her? Even if she wasn't just a human and like one of those strange hybrid creatures like Phobus.

"Fine, I'll just distract them until we find Winslet."

Idoh smirked. "Now that is something I can help with."

41

Fire.

Of course it was fire that Idoh had ended up using to create a distraction. Arya was surprised at the rang that Idoh was able to manipulate the flames, a single lit lantern left unattended in the stables was all it took. The hay used for bedding and feeding took up immediately, then the thatch roof, which ignited the wooden beams that held the structure. The stable hand had let the horses loose just in time for the fire to catch onto the armory, which connected to the castle. By that time, workers and civilians rushed with water and blankets to try and put out the flames. The perfect distraction for Mies and Arya to break in.

A door on the side of the castle led into the guards' chambers. Lumpy beds stretched across the long hall, each having a trunk at the end and blanket laid on top of the cot. The room was empty, Arya leading Mies in.

She went through two of the trunks before finding one with a neatly folded guard uniform inside. Blood was stained onto the collar of the blue cotton, not enough to be noticeable, but Arya knew it was likely the man who owned this uniform before was dead. Perfect.

"Put this on," Arya ordered.

She turned, dancing on the balls of her feet over to the door that led to the castle to be sure no one was coming. Arya turned to see the progress on Mies's attempt of putting on the uniform, the poor man fiddling with the buttons.

"On the gods Mies," Arya huffed.

Rushing over, she began to button the coat over his white top. The uniform fit him better than she liked it to, and the scratchy material was nothing like the handwoven fabrics of Dunia.

It's just for a little while, Arya reminded herself.

The last few buttons were giving her trouble, slipping out of the holes as she attempted the next, and repeating. "These fucking things."

Before she knew it, her body was pressed against the far wall, hands held above her, both within Mies's hand. With the other he gripped the back of her neck, forcing her head to the side. His lips attached to the sensitive skin of her neck, trailing sloppily down to her collarbone.

"Mies what are you—."

"Alright! This must be the new recruit," a man said with a cheerful accent. Luckily, she didn't recognize the voice. He pat Mies on the shoulder, giving them the biggest smile. "Rule one, make sure you don't get caught doing that when the commander walks in."

Mies grinned back. "I thought with the fire I'd have some time. She was too irresistible." Mies with a human accent made her skin crawl. Combined with the way he looked her up and down, she knew he would not be suspected as fae by these humans.

Arya pulled into her previous life as a trained human. She dipped her head low, covering her body with his shirt. "My apologies, my lords."

The guard lifted Arya's chin, licking his lips as he stared over her body. "Damn, rookie, where'd you dig this one from?"

"Can't give away all my secrets," Mies said, giving Arya a smack on the ass. She jumped, cheeks burning with embarrassment, even if this was just a ploy.

"Please excuse me," Arya mumbled, scurrying out of the room. Arya stopped right outside the door, listening to be sure Mies could handle himself. Pleasantries were exchanged between the men, all promising to show Mies around if he gave them some tips on bagging ladies that looked like Arya. The footsteps signaled their exit, meaning Arya was the only one to find Winslet.

Arya stopped by the maid's quarters, slipping into a veiled outfit meant for the mute workers. Humans believed the mute to be holy, and employing them at the castle was Roderick's sick way of getting women who couldn't scream for help. She'd seen it too many times between her caged visits to his rooms and the dungeon guards taking advantage of the poor souls sent with blankets during the winter months. Some way to treat holiness.

Arya walked down the hall, taking a pitcher of water from the wall and walking to the side of the hall with her eyes down. There were many times Arya had been dragged through these halls, sometimes silent as she was now, other times throwing curses out like they were feed for chickens.

Getting to the dungeons, Arya carefully walked down the steps like she'd seen the mute do before. Looking in both directions, Arya walked over to where they typically kept the used girls. They sat in their revealing clothing, impatiently waiting for their time to be of service like a bird in a cage. While beautiful, a mix of human and fae within, none were Winslet.

A girl looked up at Arya, no older than fifteen, yet dressed in a skirt that barely covered her and chains for a shirt. Her red hair was shorn at her shoulders, but the blue of her eyes told Arya all she needed to know. She was a Selkie.

Arya motioned for the girl to come closer, filling a cup of water for her. The other women noticed, but said nothing. "They have your skin?" The girl nodded. She took the cup sipping slowly from it. Arya pulled down her mask, showing her full face. "Was another woman here with you? One with long blonde hair and blue eyes. Small in height."

"She was not here long," another woman said, "they took'er after a few minutes. Guards said they felt bad fer her."

Arya looked at the woman, finding she was another Selkie, most likely from the north of Asita from the accent. These were her people, trapped behind bars, forced into a similar position as she was.

"I'll get you out," Arya promised. "I won't forget you."

The woman from before smirked. "Miss Arya, you get yerself out first, otherwise, we're all dead."

They knew her? That was not a good sign.

Instead of pondering on it, Arya lifted her mask, leaving the pitcher by the cell. Hopefully, they hadn't been without their skins long enough where they couldn't wield water.

Taking to the stairs, Arya walked to the one place she knew Roderick would take Winslet. A room that she had been saved by Emeric not to long ago.

Fury built inside of Arya as she climbed the stairs. Water gathered behind her, sliding along the creases of tile and between the bricks of the wall. Arya had come so far, seen so much, and was ready to kill the person responsible for all her misery. Not only that, but finally avenge the death of her sister.

Arya kicked the door to the ballroom open. The air hung thick with the smell of blood and iron. Winslet hung with her hands above her head, gripping the metal cuffs that burned into her skin. Her blonde hair had been shorn off in a choppy fashion, partly soaked in a rusty hue. Blood. Her clothes had been discarded below her, torn in shreds.

She barely lifted her head as Arya marched in, blue eyes missing the recognition that used to be there. A glassiness coating the orbs while the skin around them were marked with spiderweb like burns.

Anger fueled Arya as she moved forward, the bonds of her mates flowing into her with an energizing glory. Arya would not allow these filthy creatures hurt her friend. The only one who had always done what she could to protect her. They had killed Leif. Injured and kidnapped Winslet. Murdered Meriah. Tortured her. Enough was enough and Arya was ready for him to pay.

"Miss me?" She growled.

Emeric refused to look at her, as if he was some beaten dog. His head bowed, but it wasn't in submission to her. No, he was like that before Arya had entered the room. Pathetic and weak, Estelle clutching tightly onto his pant leg as if he was her father and not Mies—or a former incarnation of Mies.

Surprisingly, Roderick laid on the floor beside the throne that faced away from Arya. His body was curled, red and bloody from what looked like lashings. He was completely nude, eyes staring vacantly though life still echoed through his skin. It was not what she expected.

Someone more powerful than Roderick or Emeric was present upon that throne. The energy in the room changed, electrifying into excitement and domination.

"Hello, Arya."

The voice sent a chill through her. She knew that voice and the owner of it. Her throat closed at the idea of the impossible. Arya took a step back, the horror of what that voice meant refusing to be seen as real. No, this had to be some sort of play on her worst fear. The reason Idoh and Mies told her she wouldn't be able to defeat Evelyn. She had seen it happen, hadn't she? The mutilation of the corpse. Arya thought back to everything she knew, her mind going fuzzy from the confusion and rush of memories that were real, yet some weren't. Was that memory real? The pike that hosted her head while the crows ate the flesh.

A delicate hand was placed on the armrest of the throne, two heeled shoes clicking as her legs uncrossed. A dark red dress dropped around her feet as she stood. Arya took a step back, knowing the color had left her. Light brown hair hung down to her waist in intricate braids, tied with ribbons and rubies. Tan skin, cheeks tinted with just the lightest hue of blush. But it was the eyes, so full of life, that got her. The same eyes that Kai had. The same eyes as their mother.

"Meriah," Arya squeaked.

The woman smiled. No—Meriah smiled. "Hello, sister."